A Political Marriage
Colony World 1.5.3E

A. A. Cheshire

Mantler Publishing

Copyright © 2013 Sarah Dahlmann

ISBN:1927507006
ISBN-13:9781927507001

Library and Archives Canada Cataloguing in Publication

Cheshire, A. A., 1982-

A political marriage : colony world 1.5.3E / A.A. Cheshire.

ISBN 978-1-927507-00-1

I. Title.

PS8605.H467P64 2013   C813'.6   C2012-906401-7

For Rachelle
I hope you enjoy this one

Other Works by A. A. Cheshire

Hunting the Dephlendar
Experiment Redemption Part One
Experiment Redemption Part Two

Beneath The Waves

A NOTE ON DATES

All dates given read as:
Day-month-year-century-millennium since migration

MONARCH'S TOWN, NORSECOUNT
30-09-48-06-04SM

Life at court definitely isn't all it's reported to be. And we haven't been formally introduced yet. Not to say we're sitting around bored though. All our wardrobes have been gone over... some twice... and our various hairstyles, piercings, and tattoos have been criticized, disapproved or approved of. Mostly criticized.

There're ten of us, all with very different, strong, personalities. Physically about all we have in common is long hair... and that only because I've always insisted on it. Oh, and Natalia Burren claims we're all descended from the remnants of the nobility of Estorika. Not that any of us have concrete proof to back that up. Something to do with the collapse of infrastructure that accompanied five hundred years of civil war.

"My lady?"

Everyone in the room turns to see a maid servant standing in the doorway. I get to my feet and go over to her.

"Yes?"

"Natalia Burren wishes to speak with you, my lady." The maid looks slightly uncomfortable.

I nod. "Where?"

"This way, my lady." The maid tilts her head down the corridor.

Before following, I turn back to the young women lounging around the room. Almost immediately I catch Laine's eyes and she nods. To actually give her a verbal order would be redundant.

Laine is my closest friend, foster sister, and second-in-command. Has been since my aunt brought her home thirteen years ago. In terms of appearance, she's a couple centimetres shorter than I am. Thinner than I am too, with dark grey eyes, straight blue-black hair, and pale skin. Most people would say she's seventeen; we think she's closer to twenty-six. But without knowing her birth date or place or her parents names, we can't say much for sure.

I do have to give one order before leaving the room though. "Sefu! Stay with Laine."

I'm all too aware of his indignant, tawny eyes on my back as I follow the maid. Sefu is a half grown, orange and white striped, winter tiger I took on last June after his mother was killed. He's generally pretty good about listening to me, but he's definitely not a pet. Fortunately he's nearly as strongly attached to Laine as he is to me.

Natalia Burren is waiting in a receiving room near the entrance of this wing of the palace. She's blonde, green eyed, well tanned, and passes for twenty-five really well. I know she has to be significantly older than that though, because I know she served as Pleasure Society Chancellor for about twenty years some fifteen hundred years ago. I don't know how human she is, but I do know she's extremely powerful by any standard.

The maid doesn't stick around and Natalia gets straight to business.

"All of you are all set for this evening?"

I nod. "At least as far as I know."

"Good. Will Sefu be with you?"

"Probably," I sigh, "The servants won't go near him and I don't want to leave him alone."

"Actually," Natalia's brief smile is wry, "It's probably best if he's with you at all times. Now, about the engagements I've been working on..." She hesitates, "I've got eight candidates, but we're uncertain who to pair with whom..."

"Are the guys themselves here?" I query when she trails off.

"Either here or arriving shortly. But the families are requesting a meeting to discuss it."

"How about if Laine and I met with them?"

Natalia considers that for a moment before nodding. "That would probably be best. They've requested this morning..."

"That's fine," I respond quickly, "Just give us a chance to change."

"Thank you," Natalia smiles appreciatively, "A servant will be waiting when you're ready."

She leaves and I return to where the others are still lounging around. Laine looks over as soon as I enter the room.

"What's up?"

"You and Sefu 're coming with me."

Laine looks somewhat surprised, but she and Sefu accompany me to the suite we share.

"We're meeting with the families of the engagement candidates," I explain as we change from jeans and shirts to dresses, "To iron out the last details... like who marries who."

Laine rolls her eyes. "Wasn't Natalia s'posed to look after all that?"

"Only so much she can do. Just back me up, okay?"

"Nerita," Laine shakes her head slowly, "You should know I've always got your back. Now hold still so I can finish this."

Laine and I invariably end up doing each other's hair, even if it's just the standard east continent style braid.

While she does that, I study my reflection in the vanity mirror. I'm the tallest of the ten of us and usually taller than any women I encounter... taller than a few guys I've met too. Other than that, I'm slim with barely any curves and thick brown-blonde hair. I've heard my eyes described as silver or white, but they're actually a very pale grey-blue. And, unlike Laine, my skin tans with sun exposure.

"There," Laine ties off my braid, "Anythin' you'll need?"

"Just these," I pick up an old, worn satchel from a table as we leave our suite.

The maid is waiting outside our door and escorts us to one of the larger conference rooms on the main floor of the palace. Natalia is already there, along with quite a few others of all ages and descriptions. The conference table is a round one and the only two empty chairs are right beside Natalia. Laine and I sit as the various conversations cease. Sefu stretches out on the floor behind my chair.

Natalia clears her throat, attracting everyone's attention, before speaking, "I'd like to introduce Nerita Chassaven, who is effectively head of family for the young women I told you about."

She's being diplomatic. Black Oak Court, which I'm the leader of, is considered a street gang for lack of a more accurate term.

A stout, overdressed woman immediately frowns. "You said there would be no demands..."

I cut her off, "I'm not here to make demands." My voice is cold, but I don't much care.

Natalia adds, "Nerita is simply here to give you an idea of what the young women in question are like and perhaps answer a few questions."

The overdressed woman continues to frown.

Natalia turns to me, "What do you have there?"

In response, I remove the papers from the satchel and pass them to her. Natalia studies each one with growing surprise. Finally, she hands them back.

"Who's this John Simeon?"

"De facto magistrate in the absence of any formal government officials," I explain, "He signed as witness to all births, marriages, deaths, and legal transactions in our neighbourhood. Occasionally acted as a judge as well."

Natalia nods to herself.

"How far back would such unofficial records go?" A dignified middle aged gentleman enquires.

"A hundred years... maybe a hundred and fifty," My tone is considerably warmer, "You have to remember that people living in Arawn don't want to be able to prove they're descended from the Estorika nobility. Official confirmation is a death sentence."

"And entirely too many have died already," Natalia puts in grimly, "But I've already explained living conditions there, so if we could please move on."

"Any particular order?" I ask her.

Natalia shakes her head. "Just start with full name and age, please."

That means descending order by age, since that's the order the papers are in. I set them on the table in front of me.

"Rowena Trinette Halth," I read from the top paper, "Currently twenty-four."

"Birthday?" A tiny elderly woman queries.

"November eighteenth."

She nods to herself. "And what does she look like?"

I glance at Laine. She's always been better at describing people than I am.

"Black hair," Laine begins, "Green eyes, average height..."

"Long hair?" The overdressed woman demands.

"We all have long hair." Once again my voice is cold.

"What about unusual piercings or tattoos?" A stern faced young man enquires.

Laine has to think about that. I don't.

"The only one likely to see Rowena's tattoo is whomever she marries." I inform him. I have seen it... it's a beautiful piece... but it's also on her ass.

"But what is she like?" The elderly woman recalls our attention.

Laine replies, "Usually pretty easy going. Maybe a bit blunt at times..."

I have to shake my head. "More like very blunt... especially if she doesn't like something."

"Low tolerance for bullshit seems to be a common trait in the graduates of Experiment Redemption," Natalia observes, "Who's next?"

"Ilaria Bethany Nevett, twenty-four," I move on to the next paper, "Born May twelfth."

"Not quite as tall as I am," Laine continues, "Blue-green eyes, golden brown hair. Fairly quiet... more or less..."

"No tattoos," I add, "Just lots of earrings."

"And rings and bracelets." Laine rolls her eyes.

When no one else has any questions, I flip to the next paper. "Amalia Nicolette Varlok..."

"Descended from Lord Varlok of South Plain?" A nondescript middle age man asks.

Natalia shakes her head. "The Varloks of South Plain retreated to Star Stone Seat."

"Amalia is twenty-two," I continue, "Born October seventh."

"Again not quite my height, brown eyes, dark brown hair..." Laine breaks off, seeming uncertain what else to say. Hard to blame her because there isn't much we could say that would so much as reassure this crowd... forget impressing them.

When she realizes we're stuck, Natalia raises an eyebrow. "Amalia struck me as rather quiet and ladylike..."

I sigh raggedly. "Only when it suits her."

"Who else is there?" The dignified gentleman enquires.

"Andrina Camille," I can't quite suppress a brief scowl, "Her family used the name Guerra, which she was required to drop, and she's been using Sumatiku."

Before anyone can ask, Natalia adds, "There are only a very few descendants of the original Guerra family; Andrina isn't one of them."

"Andrina is twenty-two; born December second."

Laine picks up the description, "Average height, grey eyes, auburn hair, fair skin..."

I immediately add, "She seems quiet, but that's about the only way she impresses anyone."

Several people look surprised at the admission. Finally the elderly woman speaks up.

"You would avoid saying anything negative of one and yet..."

I take a deep breath. "Amalia has her rough edges... and a few interesting piercings, some of which are more obvious than others. Andrina is all rough edges and anyone who would marry her deserves some warning."

Laine grimaces. "Andrina has a few tattoos too. Some easier to hide than others."

The overdressed woman turns on Natalia, "You expect one of our sons to marry this girl?"

"Doesn't have to be yours," Natalia replies coolly, "There are seven others. Nerita, if you would."

I nod and move to the next paper. "Danya Lesli Sumatiku, twenty-two, born July fourth."

"A little over average height, blue eyes, blonde hair, well tanned, reasonably ladylike... as a general rule..."

"Tough though," Before anyone can say anything I explain, "When we were learning to ride horseback, her mount stepped on a sharp object and threw her. Danya was right back on her feet and trying to calm the horse so we could figure out what happened."

Laine shivers. "That was a nasty piece of business. Danya sure impressed the stable master though."

"The stable master liked all of us." I remind Laine.

Natalia shakes her head. "That's impressive of and by itself. Forrest Kontyrn doesn't particularly care for people in general."

Obviously the others at the table have heard of Forrest. Almost all of them appear surprised.

"All of you ride?" The nondescript man queries.

I nod. "We were taught to skate and swim as well."

"Does this Danya have piercings or tattoos?" The stern faced man demands.

Laine and I glance at each other, then I shake my head.

"Not that I know of."

No one else seems to have any questions, so I read from the next paper. "Haylie Cynthia Nevett. She's twenty-one, born February twenty-sixth."

Laine continues, "Not quite as tall as I am, grey-green eyes, really long blonde hair, pretty good tan..."

"Just don't toss anything in her direction and expect her to catch it," I allow a brief grimace to show, "Haylie always means well, but it's hard to watch her do anything with her hands... she tries so hard and gets so frustrated with herself."

Laine sighs. "She's been getting better... slowly."

"Is she related to that other girl... Ilaria, I believe?" The dignified gentleman enquires.

"Second cousins, I think."

"Tattoos or piercings?" The overdressed woman demands.

"Not really..." Laine glances at me.

"A couple tattoos," I correct, "Although not anywhere just anyone would see them."

A tall, thin, dignified looking older woman frowns. "Why would anyone allow such places to be seen, much less pierced or tattooed?"

I shrug. "I've never figured out why anyone would even get a tattoo..."

Laine shakes her head. "Depends on the person mostly... sometimes what they were high on..."

The overdressed woman opens her mouth, but is cut off by the tiny elderly woman.

"Some of you have used drugs?"

"Experimentation," I explain quickly, "Not addiction."

"Moving on, please." Natalia passes a stern look around the table.

"Lillian Blanche Castlivon, twenty-one, born June seventeenth."

Natalia frowns. "Why does that sound familiar?"

"Probably because she shares a birthday with Angelita," I respond, "Which would be why very few knew Lillian's birthday 'til recently."

Natalia nods to herself and indicates for Laine to continue.

"A little taller than average, blue eyes and blonde, but looks almost like someone tried to wash away her colour. For the most part, she's pretty ladylike."

"Nothing in the way of tattoos or extra piercings," I quickly add, "And finally, Nadine Lacey Halth, nineteen, born August twenty-third."

"Average height, hazel eyes, brunette..." Laine trails off and glances at me.

"Related to Rowena Halth at all?" The tall thin woman asks quietly.

"They claim they're not..." I set Rowena's birth record beside Nadine's and compare parents' names.

"That's to avoid admitting to being related to Teodor Halth," Laine's voice is quiet, "Who, I believe, was their father."

I nod in confirmation. "The man was a cad. No two of his children had the same mother... and none of them ever cared to admit being related to him."

"Tattoos or piercings?" The nondescript man queries.

"No tattoos... a couple extra piercings though."

Silence falls over the room as the various people consider what has been said. Natalia, Laine, and I sit quietly and wait. Then the stout, overdressed woman turns to study Laine critically.

"Who are you?"

"My mother called me Laine Rose," Her voice is cool, "Beyond that I know nothing of who I am or where I'm from."

"I have a few theories." Natalia observes quietly.

Laine scowls openly. "So does Tory, but 'til she turns up with something more..."

The overdressed woman frowns disapprovingly. "And you expect to find a match..."

Laine cuts her off coldly, "No. I have no intention of ever marrying."

I suppress a groan.

Natalia intervenes before the situation can worsen, "Now that you know something of the young women in question, we need to settle engagements. If each family representative would please present their suite."

Immediately the overdressed woman gets to her feet. Natalia doesn't look at all impressed, but I'll be just as happy to be done with this bitch.

"I am Lady Agatha Pondurst..." She goes on about the family and their holding until Natalia scowls outright. The only thing I really care to know is they're middle nobility.

Finally Natalia interrupts her, "If you would please get to the point."

Lady Pondurst frowns in irritation, but complies, "Zale is my third son... recently turned twenty-six. Both his brothers are long married, yet without heirs. Still, it is difficult to find brides for third sons," Distaste enters her expression, "Though I would prefer a ladylike young woman without unsightly body ornamentation."

If I look at Laine I'm going to burst out laughing. Lady Pondurst is just too much.

"Do you have any specific preferences based on what you just heard?" Natalia enquires.

Lady Pondurst purses her lips while she considers that. Then she shakes her head.

Natalia turns to me, "Any thoughts, Nerita?"

"Danya." Not only because she more or less fits Lady Pondurst's requirements, but because she's about the only one who could deal with Lady Pondurst as a mother-in-law.

"That will be fine." Lady Pondurst sits.

"Zale Pondurst and Danya Sumatiku," Natalia makes a note on the pad of paper in front of her, "Next suite, please."

The dignified middle aged gentleman straightens in his chair. "I am Lord Alexandre Rossa, speaking on behalf of my second son, Lysander. He's twenty-one and would prefer a bride younger than himself, so I think perhaps Nadine."

"It would have to be," I nod to myself, "All the rest of us are at least twenty-one."

This gets raised eyebrows and surprised looks all around the table. I'm twenty-two, whether I look it or not. Laine is older, even if we don't know exactly how much.

"Lysander Rossa and Nadine Halth." Natalia notes that down.

Next, the tiny elderly woman eases herself to her feet. "I am Lady Frances Tremauld and I seek a bride for my grandson, Raymond, who is twenty-two. I think Haylie would be most suitable."

Judging from the relieved looks on several faces, I would guess no one else particularly wanted Haylie joining their family.

"Raymond Tremauld and Haylie Nevett." Natalia nods approvingly.

As Lady Tremauld seats herself, the stern faced young man stands.

"I am Leonard Skystar. On behalf of my father, Lord Skystar, I seek a bride for my youngest brother, Nathan. A question, if I may?"

I nod.

"Are any of those still unattached noted fighters? Nathan has been allowed to run wild and our father and I believe only a strong young woman would survive marriage to him."

"Ilaria... maybe..." I glance at Laine, who shakes her head.

"Better be Amalia."

Leonard considers briefly. "Amalia, then."

"Nathan Skystar and Amalia Varlok." A hint of an amused smile flickers over Natalia's face.

The nondescript late middle aged man straightens in his chair. "I am Lord George Pelmont. Marcellus is my youngest child, but only son. He is thirty-two and has been married once already..."

Which explains why Lord Pelmont is here. Families here in Norsecount don't seem to like marrying their daughters to young widowers.

Lord Pelmont takes a deep breath. "Rowena Halth is the oldest of the young women, is she not?"

I nod.

"I would not have Marcellus marry a woman too many years his junior... however limited the options."

"So Marcellus Pelmont and Rowena Halth?" Natalia waits for Lord Pelmont to nod before recording that.

The tall, thin, dignified woman stands. "I am Lady Lily Bowerstone. Edmund is my second son and youngest child. He is perhaps a little over-serious for twenty-one. I would see him marry this Lillian Castlivon."

An elderly gentleman who has remained silent throughout the proceedings frowns, but doesn't speak.

"Edmund Bowerstone and Lillian Castlivon." Natalia notes that on her paper.

Now the elderly gentlemen rises to his feet. "I am Lord Cyril Xelloverd. 'Tis harder to find a bride for a fourth son; however, neither Killian's three older brothers nor his sister seem inclined to produce an heir. Of the two remaining young women I would prefer Ilaria."

"Kilian Xelloverd and Ilaria Nevett." Natalia nods to herself.

"Leaving Andrina to my Nikolai." The woman who stands is fairly young and tiny with light colouring. I hadn't really noticed her until now. She has a serene, approving smile that I have to wonder about.

"I am Lady Jane Gris, youngest daughter of High Lord and Lady Gris."

Most wouldn't announce that where others can hear. It means she's a junior line of the upper nobility and her son was probably born out of wedlock. It's a little surprising their head of family would allow him to marry at all. Or there's a whole lot more to the story.

"Nikolai Gris and Andrina Sumatiku," Natalia's small amused smile suggests there's more to the story," Will all the young men be present this evening?"

There are nods all around the table as Lady Jane seats herself.

"Does anyone object to these engagements being announced this evening?" Natalia glances around, "As it is my understanding that all of you wish these marriages arranged quickly and quietly."

Natalia gives them a couple minutes to respond, during which no one speaks. Then she addresses me and Laine, "I believe that's all for this morning. Thank you."

Both of us nod politely and I'm careful to ensure all the papers are back in the satchel before we leave the room. Sefu yawns and stretches as he gets to his feet to accompany us.

The three of us are about halfway to our quarters when a woman's voice comes from behind us.

"Lady Nerita!"

We turn to see Lady Jane Gris round a corner behind us. It doesn't take long for her to catch up with us.

"Do you have a few minutes?" She enquires slightly breathlessly.

"If you don't mind coming with us." I wait for her to shake her head before beginning to walk again.

"I know you're wondering about my situation and my choice of Andrina for my son over the others..."

Laine raises a sceptical eyebrow. "You make it sound like you had a choice."

Lady Jane's smile carries a touch of amusement. "I suspected that if I waited to last, she would be left. Few are inclined to misguided charity when it comes to their children's marriages."

"Your son may or may not thank you for that." I can't help chuckling. Lady Jane Gris obviously isn't typical nobility and I like what I've seen so far.

"Call it a gut feeling," Lady Jane responds, "I have little enough to offer... though it would be a great deal less without his majesty's support," She abruptly changes the subject, "Lady Natalia tells me you know a little of the Sedyr."

"A little." Laine confirms without giving me a chance to speak.

Lady Jane nods. "Nikolai's father was one of their hunters... it was a Sedyr marriage, which my parents still refuse to acknowledge. His majesty, however, has been understanding enough to grant me autonomy... the title of lady and a small holding in the mountains."

That explains a whole lot, even though I know less about the Sedyr than Laine.

Laine frowns. "Your son is less than a quarter Sedyr?"

Lady Jane nods. "I have little, if any, of that blood myself and his father was only a little over a quarter. Lady Natalia would not have approached me on the matter were it otherwise."

"What does your holding entail, if you don't mind my asking?" Mostly I'm just curious.

"Mountain forest, my home, the Sedyr watcher post, and lodgings for visiting hunters," Lady Jane admits, "Almost all we have comes from the land or the Sedyr."

"Sounds pretty isolated." Laine observes.

Lady Jane chuckles. "It isn't as bad as it sounds. Nearly all those who would pass through the mountains spend a night as it's a very long trip and no inns. And then there are poachers and runaways..."

I nod to myself. "Not a bad set up."

"But not one that allows us a great deal of time to travel or visit. I'm seldom at court and this is Nikolai's first time."

"I can't see Andrina objecting to that."

Laine nods in agreement.

"I must admit I'm glad to hear that," Lady Jane looks relieved, "Thank you. If you will excuse me, I will see you tonight." She slips away down a side corridor while Laine and I enter the wing of the palace containing our living quarters.

"You know," Laine slowly shakes her head, "If Andrina likes this guy even a little..."

I nod. "I know. I just wish I knew the others would have it as good."

"There is one weird thing though," Laine frowns thoughtfully, "Why would middle nobility be looking to third and fourth sons for heirs?"

"Not entirely sure," I admit, "But I bet we find out before too long."

We find all eight of the others still lounging around where we had left them.

"What's up now?" Rowena asks as Laine and I claim seats.

"Just helping Natalia sort out some details." Which's all the information I'm prepared to volunteer. They already know there're arranged engagements in the works. Besides, they'll meet the guys this evening."

Andrina scowls. "Fuck that shit!"

"Give it a chance." I respond coldly.

"Her specifically or all of us?" Nadine hasn't exactly been happy about the whole thing either.

"Both."

None of us are lacking for formal clothing, shoes or jewelry. But even with the help of servants to fasten things up and style hair, getting ready for this evening is a long, frustrating process. Laine, who has the least on the line, is ready first and spends the rest of the time doing what she can to soothe frayed tempers. Including mine.

Part of my problem is I know Natalia is working on an arranged engagement for me as well. But that's all I know. We're guessing it's something seriously political. I just wish someone would tell me something, official or otherwise.

Finally all ten of us are as ready as we're going to be. Everyone is nervous, although having Sefu with me helps a little. Then Natalia herself comes for us.

"Two things before we go," Natalia glances over each of us and nods her approval, "Not everyone will be present when we arrive. You'll be announced anyhow..."

"What about these engagements?" Danya wants to know.

"Those will be announced around mid-evening. And no, you won't be formally introduced before that. This way, please."

As we walk through the corridors, Natalia falls into step with me. "Nerita, we had word from High Lord Chassaven this afternoon..."

"They don't want anything to do with me?"

Natalia nods and sighs. "Essentially. However, that has little effect on the engagement I'm working on. Just please be careful to avoid compromising what little reputation you have here."

"I'll do my best." I promise her. Fortunately my reputation from the streets of South City in Arawn hasn't preceded me.

We arrive in a room near the ballroom to find Natalia's husband, Dolan, waiting. He's pretty nondescript. In fact, from what I've seen, he's primarily Natalia's shadow. That said, there has to be more to both him and their relationship... I just don't know what. Especially considering they've been married since she was nineteen.

Fortunately we only have to wait a minute or two before a page appears.

"My lady," He looks nervous at addressing Natalia, "It's time."

"Thank you." Natalia and Dolan lead the way to the ballroom doors.

"Pleasure Society member Natalia Burren and escort." The page announces as Dolan and Natalia enter. They immediately move aside.

I pass the page the embossed card I had been given earlier, all too aware that everyone in the crowded ballroom is focused on the doors.

"Miss Nerita Chassaven."

We had been instructed to curtsy and move aside on being announced. I manage the curtsy somehow, then guide Sefu to the side.

"Miss Laine Rose."

Laine looks as cool and collected as if she's done this hundreds of times. But as I said before, she really has nothing on the line right now.

"Miss Rowena Halth."

I glance over the assembly and spot Lord Pelmont nodding his approval.

"Miss Lillian Castlivon."

Lady Bowerstone isn't immediately visible, but several others look impressed.

"Miss Ilaria Nevett."

Ilaria is wearing a little less jewelry than most times. Lord Xelloverd is frowning though.

"Miss Danya Sumatiku."

There're several stout, overdressed women visible so I can't pick out Lady Pondurst. Probably just as well.

"Miss Amalia Varlok."

I don't see Leonard Skystar, but an older, similar looking gentleman near the front nods to himself. Likely Lord Skystar.

"Miss Andrina Sumatiku."

Andrina is pissed off, but hiding it well. Which's typical. She hates formal events. I'm pretty sure she'll like Lady Jane Gris though.

"Miss Haylie Nevett."

Which means she managed not to fumble her card. She curtsies as neatly as anyone I've ever seen. Lady Tremauld is front and center and smiles her approval.

"Miss Nadine Halth."

Lord Rossa is nowhere to be seen. Probably just as well. Nadine is the most visibly nervous. She's also the last of us to enter. Natalia catches my eye and nods her approval.

The light background music changes to a traditional ballroom dance; however, Natalia indicates for all of us to gather around her.

"I should've mentioned this before, but do yourselves a favour and stay in the ballroom, whether you dance or not." Then she turns to me, "Nerita and Laine, there are some people I'd like you to meet."

The other eight remain with Dolan as Laine, Sefu, and I follow Natalia around the edge of the room.

There's a small dais set up in one corner with three throne-like chairs set on it. Two of those are occupied. As the four of us approach, those seated straighten themselves quickly.

"Good evening, Natalia." The regal, elderly man's expression doesn't change, but I suspect he doesn't really like her.

"Good evening," Natalia replies, then addresses me and Laine, "I'd like to introduce Monarch Reginald and the Princess Carina."

There's still no change in the man's expression. Princess Carina, however, smiles cheerfully. She's bright eyed, blonde, and wearing a fluffy, pink confection of a dress with pearls. She looks like a small girl's idea of a faerie tale princess and I have a disgusted feeling she has the sweet, bubbly personality to match.

Before anything can be said, Natalia continues, "May I present Nerita Chassaven, Laine Rose, and Sefu."

At this Monarch Reginald raises an eyebrow slightly. "Related to the former Princess Angelita's tiger companion?"

"From the same litter, your majesty."

Princess Carina studies first Sefu, then me, curiously. "You know Princess Angelita?"

"Yes, your highness." I glance quickly at Natalia. I never did like the former princess of Estorika, which makes it a dangerous subject. Natalia evidently understands that.

However, Monarch Reginald speaks first, addressing Natalia, "Where has Angelita been? It was my understanding she was coming to Monarch's Town from Camp Streton."

"She went with Tory, Ford, and Nikki to see Sedya," Natalia replies quietly, "The earliest they could be back is the sixth. When you will see her next depends more on Tory than anything else."

Somehow I don't think the Monarch likes that too much. Not that he's any too happy with Angelita right now. Something about her recent marriage.

He turns to me next, "The engagements for your friends are now settled?"

"Eight of them, your majesty."

"And for yourself?"

"I haven't heard, your majesty." Out of the corner of my eye I can see Natalia scowling at him.

Monarch Reginald moves on to Laine, "And what do you intend to do?"

"I'm not sure yet, your majesty. Tory Genstang promised me some personal information and until I get that..."

The Monarch nods to himself. "Arrangements have been made for you to remain here as long as necessary."

"Thank you, your majesty."

"Carina," He addresses the Princess, "Will you please introduce our guests to your sisters."

"Yes, your majesty." Princess Carina slips from her seat and we have little choice but to follow her.

We end up in a courtyard off the ballroom which is equally crowded, but not nearly as noisy. We find the rest of the princesses of Norsecount off in one corner. They get to their feet and form a line at our approach. There are five of them, all blonde and bright eyed; all wearing similar dresses in various pastel colours.

"His majesty asked me to introduce you to Nerita Chassaven and Laine Rose... and Sefu." Princess Carina informs her sisters. To us, she adds, "I'd like you to meet Letitia, Delia, Elana, Kamilla, and Nerissa."

Sefu growls low in his throat. I rest a hand on his head. I'm no more impressed than he is, but he has to learn to be polite.

"Is that a winter tiger?" Princess Elana shivers.

"He is," I nod, "But he's not a pet."

Princess Carina swallows hard. "He's not dangerous..."

"He's housebroken," I reply, "But he's still a cub and he'll try to protect me if he thinks I'm in any danger."

Princess Nerissa, who can't be more than twelve or thirteen, studies Sefu carefully. "How old is he?"

"We're not sure exactly. He was half this size and still nursing when I found him last June."

"Would he bite?" Princess Nerissa keeps her hands at her sides.

"Leave him alone." Princess Letitia orders sharply.

Sefu turns cool tawny eyes on her, then steps closer to Princess Nerissa. Lowering his head, he gently butts it against her hand. He obviously likes her because he usually reserves that kind of behaviour for me, Laine or Angelita.

Princess Nerissa gently strokes his head. "He understands what we say?"

I nod. "After a fashion."

The other five princesses look sceptical and return to their corner. That's fine by me.

"His name 's Sefu, right?" Princess Nerissa glances at me, "Does he have brothers or sisters?"

"One brother, two sisters," I nod, "Their mother died and they were all adopted."

"I thought winter tigers only had two cubs at a time." The girl frowns.

"Every once in a long while they have more. Four is pretty rare though."

She nods to herself. "You're staying in the old east wing, aren't you?"

"For now."

"Until you can get married?"

"Or we move on," Laine grimaces briefly, "We don't know what all's going to happen yet."

Princess Nerissa nods again.

Laine, Sefu, and I remain in the courtyard with the girl until Natalia comes out, looking for us.

"Lady Natalia!" Princess Nerissa spots her first and grins.

"Good evening, your highness," Natalia smiles fondly, "I need to steal your new friends away. Your father wants to see you anyhow."

"Yes, my lady." Princess Nerissa gives Sefu one last pat before slipping away.

"It's time?" I query.

Natalia nods and starts back to the ballroom. "What do you think of Nerissa?"

"She's not like her sisters," Laine observes, "That's for sure."

"The older five are almost exactly like their mother," Natalia explains, "Nerissa takes more after her father and brother."

"Where is her brother?" I enquire.

"His highness avoids Monarch's Town unless explicitly ordered home," Natalia replies, "Undoubtedly you'll hear why sooner or later."

We enter the ballroom and join the other eight near the dais. Everyone else has moved back against the walls, leaving the center of the floor open. Natalia moves to stand beside the dais as Monarch Reginald stands.

"Good evening. We would like to welcome everyone here..."

Sefu growls low in his throat. I know something is bothering him and it's not Monarch Reginald's long winded speech. The problem is I don't dare kneel down to ask him about it. Instead I lightly rest one hand on his head. Sefu immediately turns his head and I look in the same direction in time to see a shadow slip along the far wall behind the crowd.

"Something wrong?" The voice is soft and male. Out of the corner of my eye I can see Dolan behind me.

"Sefu doesn't like something." I respond equally softly, without moving.

Dolan nods and disappears into the crowd. Sefu remains at my side, although tense and hyper alert.

Finally the Monarch winds down and turns things over to Natalia.

"Thank you, Honoured Monarch," Natalia inclines her head politely, "Having nothing to add, let us begin."

That recaptures the attention of everyone present. Sefu relaxes under my hand, then stretches out on the floor at my feet. That could only mean that the problem has been dealt with.

Natalia continues, "I would like to join Lord George Pelmont in announcing the engagement of his son, Marcellus, to Rowena Halth."

Lord Pelmont is still unimpressive to see. His son, however, is noticeably taller and darker. Both step out of the crowd on hearing their names and Rowena moves to meet them when hers is announced. Her expression is hard to read as Marcellus takes her hand and they turn to face the Monarch.

"This union has Our blessing." The phrase sounds well practised, so it's probably a traditional wording.

Marcellus bows and Rowena curtsies. Then they go stand with Lord Pelmont.

"I would like to join Lord Cyril Xelloverd in announcing the engagement of his son, Kilian, to Ilaria Nevett."

Kilian Xelloverd has the dark colouring typical of natives of Ouestlun... probably due to intermarriages between the nobility of Norsecount and Ouestlun. He's also significantly taller than Ilaria. She manages a somewhat nervous smile as he takes her hand.

"This union has Our blessing." There's no change in tone or expression.

Natalia waits until they are standing with Lord Xelloverd. "I would like to join Lord Leon Skystar in announcing the engagement of his son, Nathan, to Amalia Varlok."

Nathan is more or less what I pictured from his brother's brief description: Roguish and scruffy... too long brown hair, at least a days worth of beard, and well tanned. Not bad looking though and well dressed for the occasion. Amalia gives him a brief, speculative once over as she approaches him. He's clearly not impressed... whether with her or the engagement, it's hard to tell.

He's slow to take her hand and I can't help noticing Lord Skystar's frustrated expression. When Amalia and Nathan are finally facing the dais, the Monarch gives them a stern look before speaking.

"This union has Our blessing." There's slightly more emphasis on the first word. Makes me wonder just how infamous Nathan Skystar is.

Amalia curtsies properly, but Nathan's bow is delayed and I suspect he's getting a taste of her iron grip. A few people look relieved as they head over to Lord Skystar. Natalia certainly does.

"I would like to join Lady Jane Gris in announcing the engagement of her son, Nikolai, to Andrina Sumatiku."

Andrina can't quite conceal a surprised look when Nikolai steps forward with his mother.

"They met earlier," Danya explains so only Laine and I can hear, "Been dancing together too."

I nod, feeling very relieved. Andrina and Nikolai look pretty happy as he takes her hand and they face Monarch Reginald.

"This union has Our blessing."

They join Lady Jane quickly. Before Natalia speaks again, I spot Nikolai slip an arm around Andrina's waist and bend his head to whisper something in her ear.

"There better not be any delays on that wedding." Laine murmurs. And we better remember to make sure Andrina returns to our quarters with us tonight.

Natalia moves on, "I would like to join Lord Alain and Lady Agatha Pondurst in announcing the engagement of their son, Zale, to Danya Sumatiku."

In appearance, Zale takes after his tall, well built, fair father. He looks as calm and collected as Danya as they join hands and approach the dais. But I know Danya, at least, is extremely nervous. I also know she hasn't had the greatest luck with guys in the past.

"This union has Our blessing."

Zale guides Danya over to stand on the far side of his father from his mother.

"I would like to join Lady Frances Tremauld in announcing the engagement of her grandson, Raymond, to Haylie Nevett."

Raymond Tremauld has the same kind of light, washed out colouring as Lillian. He's pretty solid though and a head taller than Haylie.

"This union has Our blessing."

Raymond and Haylie go over to Lady Tremauld and all three step back into the crowd.

"I would like to join Lord Edward and Lady Lily Bowerstone in announcing the engagement of their son, Edmund, to Lillian Castlivon."

Lord Bowerstone is tall, thin, and dignified, just like his wife, and their son is the same. Edmund's face looks very serious, which I'm sure isn't making Lillian any less nervous.

"This union has Our blessing."

That leaves only Nadine with me and Laine. She's trying to breathe evenly and not succeeding.

"I would like to join Lord Alexandre Rossa in announcing the engagement of his son, Lysander, to Nadine Halth."

I don't think Lysander is much taller than I am. And he doesn't look much older than Nadine. He's at least as nervous as she is though.

"This union has Our blessing."

Once Lysander and Nadine are standing with his father, Monarch Reginald returns to his seat and the music resumes. This one is intended for the newly engaged couples and they're the first onto the floor. Others soon join them... even Laine manages to find herself a partner.

"I'm doing the best I can on your behalf." Natalia comes to stand beside me.

"And if that doesn't work out?"

"How many people do you think would care to take on me and Angelita and Tory?"

I suppress a groan. "Nice to know I'm popular."

"In the meantime," Natalia looks over the couples on the floor with a grimace, "You'll have enough on your hands keeping your ladies in line until they're married."

"I know," I sigh, "Just how quickly and quietly are these people thinking?"

"That I don't know yet," Natalia admits, "You'll hear once I do."

"Thank you."

Sefu and I remain off to one side for the rest of the evening with Princess Nerissa and occasionally Laine for company. Then, finally, it's over and I make sure all eleven of us return to the old east wing together.

"What do you think?" I ask Laine as I change into old jeans and a sleeveless top.

"So far so good. Except..." Laine scowls, "For Nathan and Amalia."

I nod to myself. "I want to talk to each of them tonight yet. Sefu, stay here."

He looks disappointed but crosses the room to curl up at Laine's feet. I leave them, headed for Andrina's suite.

I find her outer door wide open, but knock anyway before entering. She's only just beginning to prepare for bed.

"You'd already met these guys, hadn't you?" Andrina shoots me an irritated look.

"Not the guys themselves," I cross the room to help her with her hair, "Just a representative of the family. I thought you'd like Lady Jane, anyway."

Andrina shakes her head, her expression wry. "How'd I luck out this time?"

"Just do everyone a favour and behave for now," I request, "You can sleep with him all you want once you're married. Which should actually be fairly soon."

"Yeah... fine." She sets the last hairpin on the dressing table, "Help me undo this thing, please."

I carefully undo all the tiny hooks in the back of her formal gown.

"Thanks."

"Good night." I head next door to Danya's suite.

After I knock, I can hear her muffled, "Come in!"

Letting myself in, I find her soaking in the giant bathtub, which is full of bubbles.

"Nerita," She watches me sit on a nearby stool, "How'd I get stuck dealin' with that Lady Agatha bitch?"

"Because you're the only one who fit her requirements who could deal with her," I allow a scowl to show briefly, "What do you think of Zale?"

"Not sure yet," Danya makes a face, "Give it a couple days. He asked me to go riding with him in the morning... apparently his family keeps horses in the stables here."

"Just the two of you?" I can't help frowning.

"And his father," Danya reassures me, "His mother 's already promised to visit a friend."

"That's fine then," I nod, "Natalia 's pretty sure the actual marriages will take place before too long, but we need you to behave 'til then."

"Did you tell Andrina and Amalia that?" Danya queries dryly.

"Andrina, yes; Amalia, not yet."

Danya nods to herself. "I'm okay for now. Like I said, give me a couple days."

"Fair enough," I stand, "Good night then."

"Night."

Leaving Danya's suite, I step across the corridor to knock on Amalia's door. She opens it almost immediately, still in her ball gown, but with her hair down and no extra jewelry.

"Hey, come on in."

I follow her into the dressing room of her suite, where she returns to preparing for bed.

"When Laine and I met Nathan's brother earlier, he warned us Nathan 's been allowed to run wild..." I begin.

Amalia laughs it off. "He'll get his... after we're married. Don't worry, Nerita, I won't do anything worse than this evening before then."

"I had hoped your first meeting would go better..."

Amalia shrugs. "It could've gone a whole lot worse... and now I know what I'm dealing with. How soon do you think? Realistically."

"Even Natalia isn't sure," I grimace, "The words quickly and quietly were used, but what that means under the circumstances..."

"I'm not gonna hold my breath. I would kinda like to get to bed though."

"That's fine. Good night."

I go next door, to Ilaria's suite, and knock on the half open door.

"Come in." The words are muffled and I find her already in bed, although sitting propped up against the pillows.

"Thought you'd be around," Ilaria sets her book aside, "You do know I'd never intentionally embarrass you... or Natalia... right?"

"I wasn't worried about that," I sit on the edge of the bed, "Are you gonna be able to deal with this guy and his family?"

Ilaria chuckles softly. "I think we'll be okay. We'll see how tomorrow goes though. I've been invited to meet the rest of the family over a late breakfast."

I nod. "Then I'll let you get some sleep. Good night."

"Good night."

The suite across the hall is Rowena's, but I can hear voices through the half open door. Entering, I find Haylie and Nadine sitting with her in the outer room.

"How much say did you an' Laine actually have?" Nadine demands immediately.

"Very little," I sigh, "Some of the families had specific requirements and some chose for themselves based on what Laine and I said."

Rowena nods to herself. "So you wouldn't've really heard much about the guys themselves."

"Some more than others." I seat myself next to Haylie.

Rowena nods again. "What'd Natalia have to say?"

"She expressed some concern about everyone's behaviour between now and the actual weddings."

Nadine rolls her eyes. "Is that really gonna be a problem?"

"For some more than others," I give her a stern look, "But that doesn't mean I'm not concerned about the relationships themselves."

"We'll be fine," Nadine shrugs it off, "If anythin', he's more scared of this whole deal than I was. His father's nice enough though."

"So's Lady Tremauld," Haylie speaks up, "Raymond... well... I guess things'll be okay."

"Give it a few days," I suggest, "Lady Tremauld did request you specifically."

Haylie looks a little reassured.

Rowena glances meaningfully at the clock. "You two should go to bed."

"Good night." I add firmly as Haylie and Nadine reluctantly leave the suite. Rowena gets up to close the door behind them. Then I follow her into the dressing room to help her with her hair and gown.

"Did Natalia give you any idea how long 'til the weddings?" Rowena begins removing her jewelry.

"She hasn't heard."

Rowena nods to herself. "Marcellus actually had quite a bit to say... both about himself and what's going on."

"Laine and I heard a little from his father," I pass her the pins and ornaments I've removed from her hair so far, "Enough to know there has to be more to it."

Rowena chuckles. "That's always a given. Anyway, Marcellus is his father's heir... all his sisters are married to oldest sons... and he's been married once before. From what his father said, I'm guessing her death was pretty awful... and several years ago."

"That's a pretty good set up for you."

"It is and it's not," Rowena grimaces, "There's another woman involved. She thinks she likes Marcellus... never mind that she's married to someone else... but he has no use for her."

"You're sure?" I can't help frowning.

"All he actually said was that she's spoiled, brainless, and entirely too popular. Well, that and she's the one who started the lies about his wife's death. Pretty much no other woman will go near him now... either because of her stories or because they don't want to have to deal with her."

"Oh fuck..."

Rowena smiles nastily. "She won't fuck with me more than once. That's more or less what I told him too."

"You actually like him?" I set to work brushing out her hair, "Or are you just looking for a shot at her?"

"Little of both," Rowena shrugs, "Marcellus would like a few days for us to get to know each other, but he and his father are talking married inside a week."

"Okay..." I have to admit that's sooner than I was thinking.

Catching my expression in the vanity mirror, Rowena chuckles. "I don't mind. 'Sides, the sooner the eight of us are married, the less time there is for trouble. Though I've got a disgusted feeling that Nathan Skystar could find lots in a hurry."

"The more he finds, the worse Amalia's going to work him over once they're married." I set the hairbrush down so I can undo the back of Rowena's dress.

"Couldn't happen to a more deserving guy... least from what I've seen of him," Rowena shakes her head, "I've got enough shit coming up without that."

"Sounds like it," I sigh, "I should check on Lillian yet."

"She's prob'ly already in bed," Rowena informs me, "Said she wasn't feeling well."

"Thanks," I nod, "Good night."

"Night."

I find Lillian's door closed and there is no answer to my soft knock. Letting myself in, I discover that all the lights are off. Lillian is in bed, but definitely not asleep. She's sobbing into a pillow and doesn't move when I sit beside her on the bed.

Now it's not that Lillian never cries... anyone will under the right circumstances... it's just a sign that something is seriously eating at her. In this case I can make a pretty fair guess. But first I need her calm enough to talk to me.

Lillian makes no effort to resist as I shift her so her head is in my lap. She continues to sob for quite a while and I keep silent, stroking her long, loose, pale hair.

Finally the tears slow and she raises her head to look at me. She's still too breathless to speak though.

"How bad?" I keep my voice soft.

Lillian swallows hard and takes a deep gulp of air. "He... wouldn't talk... just... so stiff..." She starts sobbing again. I continue to stroke her hair until she looks up again.

"Even stupid polite stuff... the music... or anything," Lillian swallows again, "He didn't have anything to say about anything..."

"Could've been nerves," I suggest gently, "His mother did describe him as over serious though."

Lillian scowls. "His parents 're pretty stiff too. Well," Her expression softens, "I guess Lady Bowerstone was trying to be friendly..."

"It would help," I brush loose, pale hair from her face, "If we were getting more chances to relax. Do you have plans for tomorrow?"

Lillian shakes her head.

"Go soak for a bit," I suggest, "Or read. I doubt it's going to matter much if you're up a little later tonight."

"Okay," Lillian nods, "Thanks."

"Good night."

Laine and Sefu are curled up together on our bed when I enter our bedroom.

"Things not going so well?" Laine eyes my damp jeans and shirt.

"Apparently over serious means stiff and unresponsive," I strip off the damp clothes, "So Lillian hasn't had the best night ever."

Laine frowns thoughtfully. "Maybe he's just scared."

"I suggested that," I stretch out across the bed, "And that she read or soak for a bit."

Sefu moves over to curl up beside me. For some reason we just can't train him to stay off our bed. He'll stay off any other piece of furniture and anyone else's bed, but not the one Laine and I share. He's going to be in for a shock whenever I finally get married.

"What else?" Laine shifts position to sit, cross legged, beside me.

"Found out why Marcellus Pelmont's been having trouble finding a second wife. Rowena seems to think she can handle it though."

"Do you think Natalia knows about that?"

"Probably. I doubt there's much she could do though. It's very little to do with Marcellus himself and a lot to do with some girl who thinks she likes him."

Laine bursts out laughing. "She'll only fuck with Rowena once. What about Amalia though?"

"She's promised she'll behave... 'til she's married to him..."

"And then she'll work him over?" Laine is still laughing.

"Probably," I shrug, "Not my problem at that point. Everyone else 's fine for now."

Laine nods, turning serious. "Except for you. Is Natalia getting anywhere with that?"

"Not right now," I shift to rest my head on Sefu's side, " I kinda got the impression she's waiting for Tory to back her up."

Laine nods to herself. "The way I understand it is Angelita suggested this one and Tory seconded it. Obviously Natalia approves as well, but until Tory 's ready to make her move..."

"Considering neither Tory nor Angelita 're even on the continent right now," I scowl, "I still don't see what they could do that Natalia can't. She's only supposed to be the most powerful woman in the world..." I break off as Laine shakes her head.

"Sedya's direct blood descendants are far more powerful. The Eltephraph of Eltdar Phimq, Amy Cadney Kress, Tory..." Laine takes a deep breath, "I think we've barely begun to see what Tory can do. She won't be quite the same when she comes back from this trip."

My scowl deepens. "Why does every fucking thing always come back to Tory?"

Laine shrugs. "That you'd have to ask Natalia."

"And since when does Angelita do me favours?"

"I'm not sure this's entirely a favour," Laine responds, "She does still owe you a headache or two. We should get some sleep. I bet anything tomorrow 's gonna be another long day."

01-10-48-06-04SM

Laine and I are just barely finished getting dressed when there's a knock on our door. Going to answer it, I find Natalia standing in the corridor, along with Lord Skystar and Lady Jane.

"Good morning," Natalia begins, "I was hoping you'd have a few minutes before breakfast. Hopefully this won't take long."

"Come in." I hold the door open so they can enter. Reflexively, I kick one of Sefu's balls aside. He immediately bounds across the room to pounce on it. Natalia chuckles at Lord Skystar and Lady Jane's expressions. I guess neither had really noticed Sefu before.

"Sefu, we'll go play after breakfast."

He promptly abandons the ball and comes to stand beside me.

"Sit anywhere you like," I tell my visitors, "He stays off the furniture."

Sefu remains at my side until Natalia, Lord Skystar, and Lady Jane are seated. Then he accompanies me to the chair beside Natalia and lies at my feet. Laine joins us a moment later, taking the chair beside Lady Jane.

"Some concerns have come up after last night," Natalia begins quietly, "Though I imagine you're already aware of that..."

I nod, indicating for her to continue.

Natalia turns to Lady Jane, "If you would."

"Thank you," Lady Jane bows her head briefly, "While I must say I'm pleased to see an arranged engagement turn out so well, I cannot help being concerned that perhaps the couple in question get along too well..."

Laine is trying not to laugh and not entirely succeeding. I shoot her a stern look.

"You'd like to see them married as soon as possible?" I address Lady Jane, who nods.

"How about this afternoon?"

All four of us turn to Natalia in surprise. I recover first, recalling what Rowena said last night.

"That's doable?"

"Only because you have those birth records, however unofficial," Natalia explains, "I brought them to Reg's attention yesterday and he felt they would be acceptable for our purposes. I also mentioned them to President Gayre, since I'm aware that he is looking for any such records. But yes, everything could be ready late this afternoon."

"I would greatly appreciate that, my lady." Lady Jane looks relieved.

Lord Skystar addresses me, "Do you think either young lady involved would object to a double ceremony? I fear any delays in this marriage would only allow one or both parties time to do something foolish."

"I have Amalia's word that she'll behave... which may not seem like much to you, but she knows better than to break it. Still, under the circumstances, I can't see either Amalia or Andrina objecting to a double ceremony."

"Then if you would please let them know," Natalia requests, "And that I wish to see both directly after breakfast. Do you know if anyone else has plans for this afternoon?"

"Not that I know of. I was going to ask over breakfast anyway."

"Thank you. And if I could please get those birth records, that should be all for now."

I retrieve the appropriate papers for Natalia and see all three of them into the corridor. Then I drop into the chair beside Laine's.

"How could you've possibly been expecting that?" Laine demands.

"Last night Rowena told me the plan is for her and Marcellus to be married inside a week."

"Oh."

I absently rub Sefu's head. "I guess I better go tell Amalia and Andrina. And see how Lillian 's doing."

Laine glances at the ornamental clock. "'Specially considering breakfast 's in half an hour."

Still, I make no effort to move. "Sefu has to get some exercise this morning, too. And then a double wedding this afternoon..."

"I told you it was gonna be a long day." Laine grimaces.

Reluctantly, I haul myself to my feet. "Sefu, stay with Laine." Not that I object to his company; it's just easier to talk to some people without him around.

Down at the other end of the corridor, I find Andrina, Danya, Amalia, and Ilaria gathered in the outer room of Amalia's suite.

"What's up?" Ilaria enquires on seeing me.

"I just had a visit from Natalia, Lady Jane Gris, and Lord Leon Skystar."

Andrina suddenly looks more interested. Amalia makes a face.

I continue, "The lord and lady had opposite concerns, but the end result 's the same."

"How soon?" Amalia demands.

"This afternoon... we're hoping you won't mind a double ceremony."

Andrina raises an eyebrow in surprise. "That's pretty short notice..."

"Natalia 's sure it's doable," I respond, "And she wants to see both of you after breakfast."

"Will the rest of us be there?" Danya queries.

"That'd be my guess, since Natalia asked if any of us had plans this afternoon. That shouldn't affect anything the rest of us have planned for this morning."

Danya looks relieved. If for no other reason than she's looking forward to being able to ride.

"Anyway, I'll see you at breakfast." I wait for all four of them to nod before leaving the room.

Lillian's door is wide open, although she's nowhere to be seen. What is immediately visible is a crystal vase full of multicoloured roses. I knock on the door frame and she appears from the dressing room, fully dressed, but with her hair loose and her brush in one hand.

"Hey, Nerita." Lillian manages a wry smile.

"You look better. Who're the roses from?"

"Edmund," Lillian flushes slightly, "They came a few minutes ago, along with a note. Mostly to apologize for last night, but also to invite me to have lunch with the family today."

I nod. "That's not so bad. You won't be able to stay all afternoon though."

"Okay." Lillian disappears back into her dressing room.

Leaving her suite, I head for the room we've all been eating our meals in. Laine and Sefu are already there, which's normal. It's just easier if he eats before the rest of us.

"Lillian 's doin' better?" Laine guesses.

"He sent her roses, along with an apology and a lunch invite.. so we'll see."

"Not bad," Laine nods to herself, "One thing I gotta wonder about though... Natalia can see the future as well as the past, right?"

I shrug. "You probably know more about that than I do."

"It just seems to me these arranged engagements 're working out awfully well..."

"So far," I can't blame Laine for being a little wary, "But how 'bout we just watch and see how things go from here?"

Laine nods and the subject is dropped. Sefu is pretty much finished his breakfast anyhow and the others begin to turn up for theirs.

When we first arrived at the palace, I'd received strict guidelines as to where I could take Sefu for walks. But I don't really walk him so much as throw balls for him to chase. Because he always obeys my voice commands, I don't see any reason to run after him. I have other means of keeping myself in shape.

After breakfast, Laine and I take Sefu outside by way of an old servants entrance in our wing of the palace. From there, it's a short walk through the gardens to a series of multipurpose fields. There's always at least one free where Laine and I can take turns throwing a ball. Since Sefu will always bring it back for more, we don't have to move around much.

Today we end up in the far field, nearest the stables, which means we can see anyone who comes and goes from the main stable door. We haven't been out all that long before we spot Danya, Zale, and Lord Pondurst, all dressed for riding and on their way out. Sometime later, the six princesses can be seen, also heading to the stables. Five of them don't seem to notice us, but Princess Nerissa gives the three of us a longing look. I somehow get the feeling she doesn't much care for her sisters' company.

Less than half an hour later, I'm surprised to see Princess Nerissa emerge alone. She glances around hesitantly, before starting toward me and Laine. As soon as Sefu spots her, he abandons his ball and heads straight for her. I'm just not sure she's quite up to one of his enthusiastic, playful greetings.

"Sefu!" My voice brings him up short, "Get your ball!"

He reluctantly changes direction while Princess Nerissa covers the remaining distance between herself and us.

"My mare threw a shoe," Princess Nerissa explains, "And until the farrier can look at it..."

Sefu joins us, the ball in his jaws, and I accept it from him, but don't throw it immediately.

"My sisters went without me," Nerissa continues, "Even though they're not supposed to and I didn't want to bother the stable master."

"Does he at least know where your highness is?" I keep my voice gentle.

Princess Nerissa nods. "He has to report this to his majesty, but until someone comes for me..." She trails off with a dejected sigh.

"Here," I pass her the ball, "Just don't throw it toward the stable."

Princess Nerissa nods.

Her throwing arm is pretty impressive even if it's nowhere near as good as mine or Laine's. Sefu doesn't much care. And since we're in plain sight of both the palace and the stables, I doubt anyone will say too much.

Still, when I realize the morning is nearly gone and no one has come looking for Princess Nerissa, I can't help wondering what's going on. Normally I wouldn't make it my business, but Laine, Sefu, and I have to head in soon and I don't want to just leave her alone out here.

Then Lord Pondurst, Zale, and Danya step out of the stable and Danya signals for me to join them. I leave Princess Nerissa with Laine and Sefu.

"Is that Princess Nerissa?" Lord Pondurst frowns in the girl's direction.

I nod. "Her highness told me her mare threw a shoe and her sisters went without her. And that the stable master was to report it. She's been out here since."

Lord Pondurst's frown deepens, but he changes the subject, "Danya tells me two of your friends are to be married this afternoon already."

I nod. "Natalia seemed to think everything could be ready in time. Though I suspect she's doing little else today."

"Then Lady Natalia would be the one to speak to if we wished matters arranged for... say... tomorrow?" Lord Pondurst queries.

"She would be the one making the arrangements," I confirm, "But she'll need the birth record in my possession."

Danya grimaces. "How did you get your hands on those anyhow?"

"John Simeon was a good friend of my family's," I remind her pointedly, "He'd've given me a lot more than just the birth records, had I asked."

Danya rolls her eyes.

"I imagine Natalia would come get that," I return to Lord Pondurst, "Once you've spoken with her."

"Thank you," Lord Pondurst bows his head briefly, "If you would send Princess Nerissa over here, we," He indicates Zale and Danya, "Will see her to her rooms."

"Thank you." I tell him appreciatively before returning to where the girl is still throwing the ball for Sefu.

After the midday meal, Laine, Sefu, and I return to our suite to find Natalia waiting. She accompanies us into the first room, where we take seats.

"Just a few things that have come up," Natalia begins, "First: An explanation of this morning."

Laine raises an eyebrow, but doesn't speak.

"On your arrival, I took the liberty of explaining where and how you learned to ride to the stable master. I gather he later spoke to Forrest... the result being that any of you would be hard pressed to do wrong around the stable here."

"So long as Sefu stays outside?" I guess dryly.

"Likely," Natalia chuckles, "Suffice it to say the stable master didn't see any harm in leaving Nerissa in your care... especially as you remained in his sight. He did, however, report the incident just as he told Nerissa he would," Natalia smiles fondly, "Her highness has as many allies among the palace staff as her sisters do enemies. And the staff are as quick to respond to her likes and dislikes as Reg's... or Derian's."

"That'll make Sefu a lot more popular round here." Laine figures.

I frown. "Princess Nerissa strikes me as being very lonely... neglected even."

Natalia nods. "She is. Paternity of the princesses is suspect... at best, and Reg prefers to avoid open scandal, so he distances himself from all of them. Their mother died shortly after Nerissa's birth and her sisters don't even pretend to understand or care for her. Derian, I think, would, were he at court more. And it doesn't help that Reg gave orders that keep the princesses somewhat isolated from noble children their own age... partly because he has no intention of allowing any of them to marry."

Laine frowns. "Shouldn't the younger ones be at school?"

Natalia shakes her head. "The children of monarchs seldom attend school. Most are taught by tutors and governesses."

"So we won't see all that much of her?" I query.

"We'll see how things go," Natalia replies, "In the meantime, Reg has given orders for the two of you to attend court sessions, audiences, and certain other events and you're being assigned two more staff. A page to let you know where you're wanted and when and a permanent ladies maid."

"Okay." I'm more than a little surprised. Laine is just plain unimpressed.

"And it's understood that Sefu goes where you do," Natalia adds, "Now, I understand Lord Alain Pondurst spoke to you earlier..."

I nod. "You need Danya's birth record then?"

"Please. Lord Pondurst would prefer early afternoon and since no one else has approached me yet..."

I get up to retrieve the paper for her.

"Why 's he in such a rush?" Laine frowns.

"Lord Pondurst wished to see Zale married a number of years ago, but Agatha keeps derailing his plans. Even now that she's forced to admit the necessity, she'd try to postpone the wedding indefinitely... if not force a break-up."

"Who's the head of the family?" I query as I search through the old satchel.

"Lord Pondurst," Natalia replies, "And he's maintained his authority quite well, despite his wife. But he wants to see Danya and Zale married while Agatha is preoccupied with other matters ... or he's trying to trigger the heart attack or stroke the physician claims she's such a high risk for."

"Does anyone actually like that woman?" Laine wants to know.

"She has a small circle of friends," Natalia doesn't look impressed, "Almost all of them as pompous, officious, and ill-mannered as herself."

Laine rolls her eyes. "Their parents arranged their marriage, right?"

"Nobility seldom marry any other way," Natalia observes dryly, "Although most arranged marriages turn out well enough."

I give her the paper before reclaiming my seat. "How late this afternoon is the ceremony?"

"Four o'clock. It will be formal though. So if you want a chance to speak with either of them and still have time to get ready, you'd best get started."

I nod. "Thank you."

Natalia gets to her feet. "Do either of you know where Danya is currently?"

Laine and I both shake our heads. Danya hadn't joined us for lunch, but I know she intends to be present at the ceremony.

"Thank you." Natalia leaves the room.

I turn to Laine, "You coming with me?"

She frowns briefly in confusion, then her expression clears. "No, I'll talk to them later."

I nod. "Sefu, stay here." Not that he really needs to be told right now; he's pretty much asleep. Leaving him and Laine, I head for Andrina's suite.

I knock on the closed door and immediately hear her muffled voice, "Come in!" Entering, I find her getting out of the shower.

I study her critically, just for a moment. "For a girl who once vowed no guy could tempt her to marry..."

Andrina laughs. "I was what, fifteen, when I said that?"

"Something like that," I shrug it off, "Not that I think Lady Jane and her son'll be easier to live with than you've ever been."

"Like you're any prize," Andrina retorts, "We'll get used to each other. 'Sides, Nikolai and I'll be staying here at least 'til the eight of us 're married. Lady Jane has to go back, but Nikolai 's never been here before and she thinks he should stay a while."

"You'll be moving to their quarters, won't you?"

"Yeah," Andrina shrugs it off, "Newly married or not, spending all day every day with anyone 'd be too much. You guys 'll see me around."

I nod to myself. "Speaking of which, they're planning Danya's wedding for tomorrow afternoon."

"I heard," Andrina responds dryly, "She's getting the mother-in-law from hell."

"I have every confidence in Danya's ability to handle Lady Pondurst."

"How 'bout Amalia's ability to handle Nathan?" Andrina queries, her voice still dry.

I just laugh. "Something for you to keep in mind though: If you ever need anything... any help... call me first."

Andrina nods. "Every time. And, Nerita..." She takes a deep breath, "Thanks."

I nod. "You better get ready."

Leaving her to do that, I head for Amalia's suite. Her door is open and I can hear other voices, which I quickly identify as Ilaria and Rowena. All three look over at me when I enter the dressing room.

"Something up?" Amalia enquires curiously.

"I'd just like to talk to you."

Rowena and Ilaria don't wait around for a second hint. Amalia closes the door behind them as I study the items set out on the vanity. One in particular catches my eye.

"After five years you're not getting that back through."

Amalia shrugs. "I can hope. Though if I can't, there's no point hanging onto it any longer."

I just shake my head. Five years ago, when Amalia wanted to join Black Oak Court, I told her she had to take the metal barbell out of her tongue. I've never heard her complain, except once, but I should've know she'd hang onto the thing. I'm just glad that as of this afternoon, she and her piercings are someone else's problem. Although I'll admit a certain amount of curiosity as to Nathan's reaction.

"What'd you want to talk to me about?" Amalia seats herself at the vanity.

I study her briefly. "I can't see you having trouble handling Nathan... but still... you'll be having to deal with his family as well..."

"I'll be okay."

"And there's something else," I continue, "Something Laine noticed when we first met the families: There has to be something odd going on when middle nobility starts looking to third and fourth sons for heirs."

Amalia nods to herself. "Danya 's been kinda wondering about that too. And yeah, she told me she's getting married tomorrow afternoon."

"Just keep alert," I remind her, "And if you ever need anything..."

"Call you," Amalia finishes, "That's one thing you've always been good about. And don't worry, I will."

"Good. I'll leave you to get ready."

Amalia laughs. "Even if I do somehow get it through, I promise you won't see it."

Returning to my own suite, I find Sefu still asleep, but no sign of Laine anywhere. Knowing she'll be back sooner or later, I hit the shower before getting dressed.

Those of us not getting married are ready and waiting by three-thirty. We're gathered in what's more or less become our recreation area. Someone taps on the open door and I look over to see one of the palace pages. Getting up, I go over to see what he wants.

"Miss Nerita Chassaven?" He can't quite conceal his nervousness.

I nod, well aware that my eyes are cool. I know it doesn't help him feel any better; I just don't care.

"My name is Carl Huntistre. I've been assigned as your page..." He swallows hard, "Umm... Lady Natalia said to escort you and your friends to the chapel."

I nod, turning to the group, "It's time to go."

Carl doesn't even try to speak again. He just guides us through the palace corridors to the chapel used for the weddings and funerals of middle and lower nobility at court. Still, it's quite large and beautifully decorated.

Natalia, Dolan, and Lady Jane are already present and Monarch Reginald arrives once the eight of us are seated. His presence surprises me. I would've thought the Monarch would be too busy for anything like this. Lord Skystar and Leonard arrive next, followed closely by the other young men and their family members. I should've known; all the guys are close in age as well as middle nobility so they would each other fairly well. Then, as the court official in charge of marriages takes his place, I notice Princess Nerissa slip in and take a seat in the very back. Somehow I don't think she was invited, but I remember what Natalia said about her having allies among the staff.

At exactly four o'clock, Nathan and Nikolai enter through a small side door and take their places. Nikolai just looks nervous; Nathan is about ready to bolt. It's all too obvious he doesn't want to be here.

Then the doors at the back open and everyone stands. Neither Andrina nor Amalia had asked anyone to be their bridesmaid; in fact there're no attendants at all. Not that either looks much like a bride. Both are in the dresses they wore to Angelita's wedding. That means Andrina is wearing a rich green and Amalia is wearing burgundy. But then, as I recall, Angelita was married in pale blue... with good reason.

Andrina and Amalia enter together and make their way to their places at the front. Everything proceeds smoothly from there and it's a relief to a few people when the final benediction is pronounced. Most notably Nathan's father and brother.

The newly married couples head up the aisle and out the door. The rest of us are slower to get to our feet and file out. There's no receiving line in the corridor and no sign of either couple until we're seated in the reception hall next door. Then they enter and take their seats at the head table.

The reception is extremely simple: Dinner and time to visit... and gifts from Natalia and Dolan and the parents of the grooms.

Nathan joins the other young men present as soon as he can and Amalia joins me at a table with Natalia, Lord Skystar, Lady Jane, and Laine.

"I had hoped Nathan would behave himself better today." Lord Skystar gives Amalia an apologetic look.

"He'll learn." Her slight difficulty with the words and the way she's barely opening her mouth tell me she somehow got that barbell back into her tongue. Nathan is in for something of a surprise later.

Lady Jane frowns slightly. "Neither of you own something white?"

Amalia grimaces. "Married in white 's overrated... or whatever it was Angelita said."

Natalia winces. "Actually, I believe what Angelita said was that her in white would be a sick joke."

"Angelita?" Lord Skystar frowns.

"Formerly Princess Angelita Regina of Estorika," I explain, "Now Angelita Mendus Straisen. And she prefers it that way."

Lady Jane raises an eyebrow. "You know her?"

"About as well as I care to." My voice takes on a cool edge. Amalia and Laine are trying desperately not to laugh."

Lord Skystar frowns sternly. "You would speak so of your former princess?"

I sigh. "When I first encountered her several years ago, she was working street corners in South City under the name Erica. More recently, she's been a member of a mercenary crew out of Central City and known as Angel. The idea was to keep anyone from so much as suspecting who she really was."

"Mild Peyt Syndrome doesn't help matters," Natalia adds grimly, "Nor do the strong anti-monarchy sentiments left over from the civil war."

"Still..." Lord Skystar remains stern.

Natalia changes the subject, "The newlyweds will be remaining at court a while, will they not?"

Lady Jane simply nods.

"Until their friends are married, at the very least." Lord Skystar confirms.

02-10-48-06-04SM

Danya's wedding is set for one thirty this afternoon. That means an early lunch so we can prepare. Apparently Lady Pondurst attempted to delay things, claiming she couldn't possibly attend. To which her husband responded that she didn't have to be present. I think he's had enough of her bullshit.

I'd planned to take Sefu out immediately after breakfast; however, I return to my suite after the meal to find Carl waiting.

"Lady Natalia wishes to see you," The page informs me, "And she said to bring the birth records."

I'm not dressed for any kind of meeting, but this morning I don't care. I just hope I have time to take Sefu out after. He'll sit through the wedding better if he's had some exercise.

"Just let me get them."

This time I only bring the five papers Natalia may need. I also grab one of Sefu's balls. Then he and I follow Carl through the palace. Laine is busy with something this morning; she doesn't always tell me what.

The meeting turns out to involve Natalia and representatives of the remaining five families. I take the empty chair beside Natalia and set the papers on the table. When Sefu remains standing behind me, I roll his ball toward an empty corner.

"He needs to get out?" Natalia queries softly.

I nod.

"Then we'll try to keep this short," Natalia glances at the papers, "Those are all the birth records?"

"All except my own." I pass them to her.

"Thank you," Natalia looks over her notepad, "There are five more weddings to set dates and times for... preferably soon. Were any of you considering tomorrow?"

Lady Lily Bowerstone nods. "Late in the afternoon, if that's possible."

"It is," Natalia makes a note on her paper, "That's Edmund and Lillian, correct?"

Lady Bowerstone nods. I make a mental note to talk to Lillian.

"What about the fourth?" When no one responds, Natalia continues, "The fifth?"

"Kilian and Ilaria," Lord Cyril Xelloverd speaks up, "Around three o'clock was the suggestion."

"That's fine," Natalia writes quickly, "Anyone for the sixth?"

After nearly a minute, Lord George Pelmont says, "Marcellus and Rowena would like the evening of the seventh."

"Thank you," Natalia notes that, "Nerita, have either Haylie or Nadine spoken to you?"

"Not directly. Rowena mentioned they were discussing a possible double ceremony."

Natalia nods to herself, then addresses Lady Frances Tremauld and Lord Alexandre Rossa, "Would either of you object to a double wedding?"

Both shake their heads.

"Which leaves the question of when." Natalia writes more notes.

"I was thinking the eighth." Lord Rossa begins slowly.

"The eighth is fine," Lady Tremauld responds, "Say early afternoon?"

Lord Rossa nods.

"Anything else?" Natalia queries, "Since I believe that's everyone." When no one speaks, she turns to me, "You'd best take Sefu out for some exercise."

"Thank you." I bow my head politely. Then I get to my feet. "Sefu, bring your ball."

He obeys, following me from the room. We find Carl standing at attention in the corridor.

"Which is the nearest door to the stables?" I ask him.

"This way." The page leads us to a door from which I can see the fields and stable. He disappears as Sefu and I head for the nearest empty field.

Sefu has way too much energy this morning and I'm too busy watching him to notice Princess Nerissa approaching. In fact Sefu spots her first and promptly abandons his ball.

"Sefu! Come here!"

He obeys reluctantly.

Princess Nerissa frowns as she gets close enough to speak normally, "I thought he wouldn't hurt me."

"Not intentionally," I reply, "But it wouldn't take much for him to knock you off your feet."

"Oh." She swallows hard, "Where's your friend?"

"Laine 's busy this morning. Your sisters went riding without you again?"

Princess Nerissa shakes her head. "They're not allowed to leave our rooms after yesterday. I'm supposed to check on my mare, but she still doesn't have her new shoe. The stable master will come for me when the farrier 's done."

I nod. Sefu goes bounding off to retrieve his ball.

"Does your highness sneak into weddings often?"

The girl's face falls. "You saw me?"

"When you came in," I pick up the ball Sefu drops at my feet and throw it, "I doubt anyone else did."

Princess Nerissa nods dejectedly. "It's just I like to see the ladies... they're always so pretty... I know his majesty won't ever let me marry..."

"How old are you?"

"Thirteen... fourteen in February."

I have to conceal my surprise. I'd thought she was only twelve.

"A lot can change in two years," I tell her, "Two years ago I wouldn't've believed anyone who had tried to tell me I'd end up here."

"I guess," Princess Nerissa looks uncertain, "People say you and your friends come from Estorika. What's it like there?"

"The former princess Angelita would tell you Estorika was long gone before her birth," I throw the ball for Sefu again, "And I hope your highness never has to see anything as bad as Arawn."

"It's really that bad?"

"Worse. Nothing grows in Arawn... not even grass... and there're no birds anywhere. Very, very few animals of any kind either. Even most of the sewer rats have two legs."

Princess Nerissa shivers. "I heard President Gayre declared all animals endangered."

I nod. "He did that after military men killed Sefu's mother."

"So where do the people live?"

"In the cities and military camps. All the old cities got bombed out early in the war, but they just put in support pillars and built on top of them."

"What about the villages and farms and all that?"

"All gone. Arawn has lots of ruins though."

"So where did you live?"

"South City... in the Old Quarter, which's one of the few parts nobody built on top of."

Before Princess Nerissa can ask another question, a male voice calls, "Your highness!"

"That's the stable master." The girl heads for the stable.

I just hope she doesn't have too vivid an imagination. And I didn't tell her the worst of living in Arawn. I wouldn't... I don't even like to remember the things that happened.

I continue to throw the ball for Sefu to chase until he starts to tire and Rowena comes looking for us.

"You okay, Nerita?" Rowena looks concerned on seeing me.

"I will be," I accompany her towards the old east wing, "Just every once in a while something reminds me just how little I miss Arawn."

"You an' everyone else who 's managed to get out." Rowena shudders briefly.

At the end of lunch, I accompany Danya to her suite and into the dressing room since she has a very limited time to prepare. She immediately begins digging out anything she intends to wear.

"How're you and Zale getting along?" I watch her move around the room.

"We'll be fine."

"What about his family?"

Danya sighs. "We'll see. He seems to think the worst of it'll be his mother."

"Just remember you can call me any time... no matter what."

"Always and forever," Danya chuckles, "You've always been good for that."

"Just take care of yourself."

"Thanks, Nerita."

This time only Laine, Sefu, and I are waiting when Carl turns up just after one to escort us to the chapel. All the others are going with their fiancés or husbands. We arrive to find we're the last except for Lord and Lady Pondurst, who arrive as Laine and I take our seats. Apparently Lady Pondurst was able to rearrange her schedule... not that I believe for a second there was a real conflict.

The official arrives at the same time as Princess Nerissa slips in. She definitely has the help of someone around here. Then, right at one thirty, Zale takes his place. He's obviously nervous, though I have to wonder if it isn't because of his mother.

Danya, when she enters, is wearing the light blue dress she'd gotten for our graduation from Experiment Redemption. Probably because she wore her dress from Angelita's wedding for the ball the other night.

The ceremony proceeds uninterrupted, despite Lady Pondurst's presence. I notice that Zale looks a lot less nervous as he and Danya start up the aisle. Lord Pondurst really must have some means of persuading his wife to behave.

The reception is the first I've really seen of Andrina or Amalia since yesterday evening. Andrina is happier than I've ever seen her and she and Nikolai stick close together. I just have to wonder if she'll ever willingly admit she's seriously fallen for him.

Laine and I manage to get seats at the same table as Nathan and Amalia, although we don't get much chance to talk to them until near the end. They certainly seem to be getting along better.

"Was it still morning when you got up?" Laine asks Amalia.

"That's none of your business." Amalia replies coolly.

I laugh. "Long as you're happy."

Amalia laughs as well. "We reached an understanding."

"We nothing," Nathan's arm is resting comfortably on the back of his wife's chair, "I poke so much as a toe out of line and I'm fucked."

"You don't exactly look like you're hurting any." Laine observes.

Nathan shrugs it off.

Zale and Danya, who have been making their way around to each occupied table, join us. Zale studies Nathan with an amused expression.

"Why not go sit with them?" Zale indicates the table the other young men are gathered around.

"I don't want to listen to them." Nathan responds easily.

"Give them about a week." I suggest.

Laine raises an eyebrow. "Who's planning what now?"

"I had to sit in on another meeting with Natalia this morning. Found out the last of these weddings is the eighth."

"Of this month?" Zale is the first to recover enough to speak.

"That's how I understand it." I nod.

"So who's next?" Danya queries.

"Lillian. Then we get a day's break."

Laine frowns, but doesn't say anything until we get back to our suite for the night. Even then, she waits until the three of us are sprawled out across the bed.

"Lillian 's getting married tomorrow?"

"Late afternoon," I confirm, "Though I fully intend to talk to her before then."

Laine nods to herself. "What's been bothering you all afternoon?"

"I saw Princess Nerissa again this morning... she was waiting for the farrier... and asking more questions."

"About?" Laine prompts.

"Arawn. Someone told her that's where we're from. I prob'ly said more than I should've... just about the land itself. I didn't go into the people or the political military bullshit."

Laine sighs tiredly, suddenly looking far older than usual. "How old do you think she is?"

"I asked, actually. She said four months short of fourteen."

Laine slowly shakes her head. "Seems a lot younger. Maybe 'cause kids her age in Arawn have to be pretty much grown up."

"Even by local standards she seems young for her age. Though I can't begin to say why. As if I don't have enough problems right now."

"Well," Laine yawns widely, "Problems 're usually easier to deal with on a full night's sleep."

03-10-48-06-04SM

"Laine," I wait until she looks at me, "Would you please take Sefu out this morning? I don't know how long this talk with Lillian will take."

Whether she believes that or not, Laine nods. "No problem."

The truth is, while I do need to talk to Lillian, I need some downtime first. Dealing with too many people too many days in a row, especially irritating people, seems to trigger some of my less endearing personality traits. While I don't test out a true psychopath, I have, in the past, demonstrated some dangerous psychotic traits. Hence my 'homicidal psycho bitch' reputation in the neighbourhood where I grew up.

Then Laine chuckles. "Nice to know you're learning to identify your triggers," She scoops up one of Sefu's balls from the floor, "How 'bout if you lock the door after us."

I nod. "Thanks."

"C'mon, Sefu." Laine waits for him to follow before leaving the suite. I close and lock the outer door behind them, then head for the bathroom to soak for a while.

I'd had an episode that really scared me just before FTK pulled us out of South City for Experiment Redemption. Even after two years of treatment, I had another episode during their so called 'stress test' just before we finished the program. Seems like all treatment did was help me identify what will trigger an episode. On the upside, knowing my triggers helps a little toward prevention. It won't save anyone if I actually have one though.

It's lunchtime before I feel ready to face anyone. I get dressed in the first jeans and shirt that come to hand and ignore my hair. Leaving the suite, I find Natalia waiting in the hall.

"Feeling better?" She studies me with a touch of concern.

"Back to my normal anyway. Is something up?"

"Nothing serious. I just got confirmation that Tory and Angelita are on their way back."

"Already?"

"I would guess that their interview with Sedya went as per her normal," Natalia sighs, "I don't know what it is about Sedya and her direct blood descendants, but they can be fucking frustrating!"

I'd never really heard Natalia swear before. I do recognize long pent up frustration when I hear it. I suspect, however, that the primary target of that frustration is actually her sister-in-law.

"You mean there're worse things than dealing with Tory by herself?"

"Tory 's a child, comparatively... or has been up until now. Sedya 's been around for tens of thousands of years; Amy 's seven years older than I am. But we'll see what Tory 's like now before too long."

I shrug it off. "Right now Tory 's the least of my problems. My main one at the moment being Lillian and her wedding."

"Are you planning anything for tomorrow?"

"Not yet."

Natalia nods to herself. "I'll let you get some lunch."

"Thanks." I head for our dining room to find everyone else already there. Sefu immediately comes bounding across the room and I have to brace myself to keep from being knocked off my feet.

"Easy, Sefu." But I ruffle the fur of his head and neck. Then I join the others at the table.

"What'd Natalia want?" Laine enquires once we're eating.

"Mostly to check on me. She also said Tory 's on her way back."

"Will she have that information now?" Rowena queries.

Laine shakes her head. "She told me more than just what you guys heard. Tory and Ford have another trip to make and she'll have answers for me after that."

I frown. "Didn't she say you'd know before this next winter?"

Laine shrugs. "She's got time yet."

"Maybe a month," Nadine reminds us," We're in Norsecount now, remember?"

Which means we'll actually get to see real winter for the first time in our lives. However, because Monarch's Town is right on the coast, it won't be as bad as it would be... say in the mountains farther inland.

Little else is said during the meal and after, Sefu and I accompany Lillian to her suite. I wait until we're seated before speaking.

"Things are going better?"

"Not exactly," Lillian grimaces, "More like I've got a better idea what's goin on."

"How bad?"

"Edmund really wants this to work, but he's scared... well, more like terrified. I've met both his sisters... they could be clones of Lady Bowerstone."

"She doesn't seem all that bad."

Lillian smiles wryly. "They can all be pretty stiff. But it sounds like Edmund's brother's wife 's a real ice bitch."

"You haven't met her yet?"

"This afternoon. They'll only just be in time for the wedding."

I can't help frowning. "You're sure you'll be okay?"

Lillian laughs. "Edmund and his parents 're really counting on this working. And if you think I can't handle the sister-in-law..."

I nod, relaxing in my chair. "I doubt she'd fuck with you more than once."

"It helps though... knowing you'd never just abandon any of us."

"Not on my worst day," I confirm, "No matter what else happens."

"Thanks." Lillian glances at the clock and takes a deep breath, "His sisters offered to help me get ready... they're the ones who've been doing the real planning..."

"They want you in white?" I raise an eyebrow.

"Fuck no," Lillian shudders, "Nerita, you're the only one of us who could get away with that. This's just going to be a little more traditional."

"Well, you better go then. I think Haylie and Nadine are waiting anyway."

The ceremony today is set for four thirty. That means Carl turns up for me, Sefu, and Laine just after four. The chapel is still mostly empty when we enter.

"Nerita, is it not?"

I turn to see Lady Bowerstone rise from a chair in the back row. I nod politely.

"Lillian speaks highly of you. She also mentioned briefly that you're related, although not how."

"Our mothers were sisters. Very few even know that because I was raised by a paternal aunt while she grew up in a kind of unofficial foster care."

Lady Bowerstone nods to herself. "Do you know why she seems so reluctant to admit her age or birth date? I'm aware she has both in common with the former princess Angelita."

"Ingrained habit. All too many girls in Arawn have been killed because some anti-monarchy fanatic thought they might be Angelita. Which's an extremely sore point with Angelita herself."

A touch of scepticism flickers over Lady Bowerstone's face. However, she leaves the subject alone. "Thank you. I think we'd best take our seats."

Almost everyone else is already seated and the official appears shortly. And, once again, I spot Princess Nerissa sneaking in.

At four thirty, Edmund enters accompanied by Lysander Rossa as his best man and Raymond Tremauld as groomsman. All three are well dressed, even if no two of their suits match.

Then Nadine enters from the back, wearing a short, rose coloured dress I don't recognize. When she reaches her place at the front, Haylie appears wearing a green dress in a similar style. Once Haylie is in place, everyone stands for Lillian's entrance. Her long, formal gown is the colour of antique lace; more yellow than white. It fits well enough, but I suspect it originally belonged to Lady Lily. Lillian is also wearing a veil; again more yellow than white. With the lilies in her hands, she looks more like a bride than the previous three.

Edmund is pale and sweating visibly, but other than that, the ceremony goes smoothly. He really does seem scared... I just never considered Lillian all that intimidating. But then, I'm not the second son in a stiff, formal, noble family.

As Edmund and Lillian start up the aisle, Haylie accepts Lysander's arm and they follow. Neither appears comfortable with the arrangement. Nor do Raymond and Nadine. I can't help noticing that when the wedding party enters the reception hall, Nadine and Haylie have switched escorts.

Lady Bowerstone had insisted that Laine and I join her family at their table for the reception. I would've preferred to sit with the recently married couples so I can see how Danya and Zale are doing. Her ladyship had also immediately introduced us around.

Edmund's sisters, Violet and Rosa, are nearly identical to their mother, both in appearance and personality. Their older brother, Emile, also bears a strong resemblance to their mother. His wife, Opal, however, looks like a marble statue... in colouring as well as figure. The problem is she's about as friendly as a marble statue. By the end of the dinner and speeches, Laine and I are both ready to kill her. Without her having said a word to either of us.

"Can that girl touch anything without dropping it?"

I think Haylie has been doing really well today. Obviously Opal doesn't share my assessment of the situation.

"Can you open your mouth without complaining?" Laine's voice is cold and hard. I suppress a groan. Then I notice Violet and Rosa's silent applause. Lord and Lady Bowerstone don't appear to have noticed the exchange.

"You will speak respectfully." Opal turns on Laine. I know what Laine's standard response to that kind of thing is and give her a stern warning glance. Laine looks a little mutinous, but settles for giving Opal a look of ice cold distain. In response, Opal shoves her chair back and stalks from the reception hall.

Violet slowly shakes her head. "When will she learn to act like a proper lady?"

"I hope you don't expect me to answer that," Emile grimaces disgustedly, "I'm merely her husband."

"A proper lady is equal to any situation," Laine murmurs, mostly to herself, "Yet always humble before her husband."

Lady Bowerstone frowns sharply. "Might I ask where you heard that?"

"It's one of the few things I remember my mother saying... before she died," Laine shrugs, "I don't know where she'd heard or read it."

"I believe," Lady Bowerstone continues to frown, "It's a line from a play that was very popular just before the beginning of the civil war."

Laine shrugs again. "I remember a few of the things my mother said. I don't remember even knowing who she was or where she was from."

"Is that common in Arawn?" Violet enquires with a touch of curiosity.

"It is and it's not," I reply, "Orphans certainly are, but so are separated families. The end of the war was accompanied by an absolute chaos that all but wiped out any semblance of order that had survived to that point. Even basic family."

There are noticeable shudders around the table. I doubt they can truly imagine what I mean though. Family is the most important social structure in the monarchies.

Violet slowly shakes her head. "How does anyone survive there?"

"You don't want the answer to that," Laine informs her, "There're reasons we don't miss living there."

Lady Bowerstone studies Laine quietly for a long moment. "You said you have no intention of marrying although you're the only one of your group. Might I enquire as to why?"

"It's a combination of things," Laine replies, "There's what I don't know about myself and my family, the things I do know without knowing how I know them, several inexplicably bizarre incidents..."

"Innumerable one night stands don't help." I add disapprovingly.

Laine shrugs that off. "And I just can't see myself making any man a good wife."

Lady Bowerstone nods to herself and leaves the subject alone.

Shortly after that I get a chance to slip away. I immediately cross the room to where Andrina, Amalia, Danya, and Lillian are sitting together.

"Where'd the guys go?" I claim an empty chair.

All four shrug in response.

"How're you doing?" I'm mainly addressing Danya and Lillian.

"Well," Danya grimaces, "We established last night that Zale will take my side over his mother's."

Amalia chuckles. "You mean he realizes there're more benefits to a wife who'll sleep with him than that bitch's good will?"

Danya rolls her eyes. "Something like that. Though I got the impression his brothers prefer their wives to their mother... benefits or not."

"This wouldn't happen to have anything to do with the lack of heirs I've heard about, would it?" I query.

Amalia and Danya scowl.

"I don't know how this started," Amalia begins, "But it's completely fucking ridiculous..."

Danya shakes her head. "It's real simple though. The entrenched belief among guys here is all women are completely and totally frigid... well, maybe not entrenched..."

"Pretty fucking widespread," Amalia's scowl deepens, "The other side being that women here believe all guys are lousy in bed and will just take without consent. And this bullshit's obviously been around for years now."

I groan. "Fuck."

"That doesn't completely explain Opal." Lillian grimaces.

"I think Opal would still be an ice bitch," I respond, "Though I'm guessing your husbands don't entirely believe that."

"Not now anyway." Amalia grins impishly.

"Somehow I don't think Nikolai ever did." Andrina puts in.

"I think," Danya observes, "We got paired with some of the few guys around who don't completely believe. What Zale actually said was he'd been hoping since we're from Arawn."

Lillian sighs. "From what I've seen, Opal seems to be the only one in the family. But we'll see how tonight goes."

The other three may have advice for her, but I don't stick around to hear it. Although, as I look around for Laine, I spot Zale, Nathan, and Nikolai huddled around Edmund at a corner table. Somehow I don't think Lillian needs to worry.

05-10-48-06-04SM

Ilaria tends to be more quiet than the others, so it's no surprise I've heard little from her regarding her rapidly approaching marriage. However, Laine brought the amount of time Ilaria has been spending alone lately to my attention last night. That bothers me. Rowena, Haylie, and Nadine also have yet to marry, but they've been spending time with their future husbands... or at least their future in-laws. It doesn't help that Ilaria usually prefers Amalia or Danya's company. But with the four already married all happy with their husbands... at the very least... Ilaria has been left on her own.

It's with all this in mind that I knock on the outer door of her suite immediately after lunch. There's no response; however, I know Ilaria is inside somewhere.

"It's Nerita." I call through the door. There's still no response, so I try the door. It's unlocked and I let myself in. No lights are on anywhere. I find Ilaria sprawled face down across the bed. Going around to the far side, I sit near her head and gently brush her hair from her face.

I've never actually seen Ilaria cry. Even now it's just silent tears streaming down her face. Ordinarily I'd let her cry herself out, but we've only got a little over two hours until the ceremony.

"What went wrong?" I keep my voice soft, "Feels like I've barely seen you since the ball."

Ilaria neither moves nor speaks, nor do the tears slow. I don't press; I just stroke her loose, tangled hair. Finally, several minutes later, she blinks and swallows hard.

"After the ball..." Her voice is rough, "I honestly thought things would be okay. Even the next morning, when I met his family..."

"But...?"

"I can't seem to get close to him... can't even really talk to him," She props herself up on one elbow and attempts to wipe the tears from her face, "I won't back out of the deal now... it's just seeing the others..."

I nod. "Remember the hassle Amalia had with Nathan to begin with?"

"I know," Ilaria grimaces, "I just can't seem to convince myself things could still turn out okay."

"Have you showered today?" I brush a stray damp hair from her face.

"Not yet."

A knock can be heard on the suite door.

"Go shower. I'll deal with that."

"Thanks." Ilaria manages a watery smile.

I wait until the bathroom door closes behind her before answering the door.

The unfamiliar woman standing in the corridor is about thirty, with the same dark colouring as Kilian and a small trunk under one arm. She looks a little surprised, but I doubt she was expecting to see me.

"Nerita, is it not?" She waits for me to nod before continuing, "I'm Elizabeth Xelloverd Reiner. Is Ilaria okay?"

"She isn't exactly having her best day ever."

Elizabeth nods to herself.

I add, "She's in the shower right now."

"Mind if I come in? I'd like to talk to her and this thing 's heavy."

I hold the door open for her. "Go ahead and sit."

While she does that, I go into the bathroom where Ilaria is washing her hair.

"Who's here?" She calls over the running water.

"Looks like Kilian's sister." I lean against the counter.

"Elizabeth?" Ilaria sounds surprised.

"Yeah."

Ilaria frowns. "She say what she wants?"

"To talk to you. She's got some kind of box with her too."

"Yeah, fine. I'll be out when I'm done."

I leave Ilaria to do that and return to the outer room.

"You would interrupt her in the shower?" Elizabeth looks extremely surprised.

"My family's house in South City had four bedrooms," I respond, "One of the bathrooms had a leaky tub and the other had a makeshift shower. Even after my aunt died there were always at least ten of us... plus transients."

Elizabeth frowns. "What about with Experiment Redemption?"

"Camp Streton was a military camp, then a prison before Experiment Redemption took it over. Each of the barracks buildings was converted to living quarters for one group. Eight bedrooms, four bathrooms, kitchen, and recreation area."

"That's still pretty close quarters."

I shrug. "You don't miss what you never had."

Elizabeth nods thoughtfully. Neither of us says anything more until Ilaria appears, wrapped in a dressing gown.

"You wanted to see me?"

Elizabeth nods. "I thought talking to you might do more good than lecturing my boneheaded baby brother... again."

"You mean the one who's barely spoken to me in four days?" Ilaria comes over to sit beside me.

"Grandmother Xelloverd says bone-headedness is typical of Xelloverd males," Elizabeth informs us, "She's still our head of family; she's just too old to travel anymore. So I'm supposed to keep the family men from doing anything too foolish."

"That's possible?" Ilaria sounds slightly amused.

"Extremely difficult," Elizabeth concedes, "And so far all my sisters-in-law haven't been much help. Anyway, Grandmother asked me to do what I can to help you through today."

"Okay..." Ilaria looks sceptical.

"When Mother died, I inherited all her personal effects: Jewelry and clothes and that," Elizabeth indicates the chest, "I know you've got your own things, but I thought maybe you'd like to look at least. I prefer what I've gotten as gifts from my husband."

"Most of what I wear was my grandmother's," Ilaria responds, "At least for jewelry. Let's see though."

"Just keep an eye on the time," I remind them, "And Ilaria, if you need anything... ever... just call me."

She nods. "Thanks, Nerita."

Leaving them to sort through the chest, I head to my own suite where I find Laine just getting out of the shower.

"Ilaria 's okay?"

"I think, between his sister and his grandmother, Ilaria 'll be just fine. Whether Kilian comes around or not."

"Oh?"

"Something about a 'boneheaded baby brother' and an offer of the late Lady Xelloverd's jewelry and clothes for today."

Laine just bursts out laughing.

Elizabeth is nowhere to be seen when Laine and I take our seats in the chapel. Almost everyone else is already present, but she slips in just ahead of the usual young, uninvited guest as the official takes his place at the front.

Kilian appears promptly at three o'clock, looking stiff and uncomfortable. Then everyone stands for Ilaria's entrance.

She's wearing the gold gown she'd gotten for Angelita's wedding, the most earrings and bracelets I've seen yet, and some flower shaped hair ornaments I haven't seen before. She isn't wearing any rings though, which's highly unusual.

Kilian looks increasingly uncomfortable as Ilaria approaches. In fact, all through the ceremony, he seems very agitated; stuttering when he has to speak and nearly trips when they start up the aisle at the end.

Beside me, Laine groans softly and mutters, "What the fuck 's his problem?"

I don't have an answer to that, so I keep silent.

I don't know where the bride and groom go between the ceremony and the reception. Obviously Ilaria had a few words with Kilian somewhere though. When they appear in the reception hall, he's noticeably calmer and I spot a trace of her lipstick on his jaw.

This time Laine and I are sharing a table with Elizabeth and her husband and the recently married couples. Giles Reiner looks like the village farmer he was prior to his marriage. Apparently Grandmother Xelloverd likes occasionally adding new blood to the family.

The reception is the usual speeches, gifts, and dinner, followed by time to visit.

"Amalia," Elizabeth is frowning, "If you don't mind my asking: What is that on your tongue?"

I look away as Amalia shows off her tongue piercing.

"What would prompt you to put a piece of metal through your tongue?" Elizabeth shudders.

Nathan flushes bright pink as Amalia laughs.

"It has it's uses."

"That's already too much information." Andrina observes dryly.

"Don't start," Laine gives both of them stern looks, "The less said about piercings... and tattoos... the better."

"Kilian 's your brother, right?" Danya turns to Elizabeth, "Any idea what his problem was earlier?"

"Likely the earful he got from Grandmother Xelloverd this morning," Elizabeth chuckles, "Not that he didn't deserve every word of it."

"So long as they got the portrait done before Ilaria gave him another earful," Danya comments wryly, "Although... where'd she get even more jewelry?"

"I gave her some of my mother's," Elizabeth replies, "A few more rings too."

Amalia shakes her head. "She doesn't have enough fingers for the ones she already has."

"It's interesting though," Elizabeth continues, "She has some pieces that must pre-date the Estorika Civil War."

"You mean the pieces of the Nevett Family heirloom set? She's had all of them longer than I've known her."

Everyone at the table looks at me in surprise and shock. Elizabeth recovers first.

"Including the locket?"

I shake my head. "The locket was never part of the set. Even if it had been, it would've been destroyed centuries ago."

"No wonder she's always been so careful," Danya shakes her head slowly, "It'd've been her death warrant in the wrong hands."

"First you'd have to be able to pick the pieces of the set out of all the other jewelry she owns," I point out, "She's got expensive taste and a sharp eye."

Elizabeth chuckles. "I noticed."

07-10-48-06-04SM

Having a days break on both sides of Ilaria's wedding was really nice. Especially since no one demanded I go anywhere or do anything either of those days. But now there're two more weddings to get through. Starting with Rowena's.

Originally Lord Pelmont said evening, but the ceremony was finally set for four o'clock. The only other thing I know for sure is Rowena asked Nadine to be her bridesmaid.

Carl Huntistre has become something of a fixture, but there's been no sign of the ladies maid Natalia mentioned. Unless they're waiting for all the others to be married off first. Laine and I don't mind. We're too used to looking after each other.

All five of us still living in the old east wing had taken Sefu out this morning. He isn't too fussy about who throws his ball. We'd gotten the field nearest our quarters and no one had disturbed us. I think Rowena, Nadine, and Haylie just needed the distraction. Despite everything they're all getting nervous.

Ilaria, on the other hand, is doing just fine. Her relationship with Kilian is slowly improving and she and Elizabeth are great friends. Sounds like Grandmother Xelloverd approves, which definitely helps.

After lunch, Laine, Rowena, Nadine, Haylie, Sefu, and I are lounging around when Carl appears.

"What now?" Laine studies his slightly flustered expression.

"Security says there're a lady and a winter tiger at the gate," Carl swallows hard, "The lady has asked to see Sefu..."

Five of us burst out laughing. Sefu raises his head and looks around.

"Bring them here." I instruct. While I'm not sure 'lady' is the word I'd use, as far as I know there's only one other domesticated winter tiger in the country.

Carl bows his head briefly, then vanishes.

"Asking to see Sefu?" Rowena can barely speak for laughing.

"Since it has to be Angelita and she sure as hell isn't here to see me." I point out.

Laine shakes her head. "I didn't know she was back yet."

I shrug. "Ask her 'bout that."

It doesn't take long for Angelita and her tiger, Xylia, to join us. Would've taken less time if she'd announced herself properly, which she obviously didn't.

Like Sefu, Xylia has orange and white stripes and tawny eyes, but, because she's female, she'll always be smaller. The two of them greet each other enthusiastically before curling up together.

Angelita Mendus Straisen hasn't changed since I've seen her last. She is not quite my height with long, loose, strawberry blonde curls; icy green eyes, and a well developed figure. Today she's dressed in old sandals, even older blue jeans, and one of her husband's t-shirts. She doesn't look like she was ever a princess, although I have a disgusted feeling I know how she got the guards to pass along her message. Angelita has two powerful extrasensory abilities: Empathic projection and animal communication. Both of which I've seen her use.

"Hey," Laine greets her, "When'd you get back? Natalia said you'd gone with Tory."

"Docked early yesterday mornin'," Angelita claims the chair between Laine and Rowena, "Natalia 's arranged for us to stay at the Old Imperial Hotel for now. But Tory 's off again today an' not sure when she'll be back."

"Where now?" Rowena queries.

"Back into Arawn, of all places," Angelita makes a face, "Her, Ford, Nikki, and Fae, so I'm guessin' they're goin' underground."

"So the rest of you are kicking around the hotel?" Laine guesses.

"We don't exactly have much else to do. 'Specially since Tory 's the one who knows what we're doin' next," She shrugs it off, "What's been happenin' with you guys?"

"For starters, anyone you don't see 's already married," Rowena informs her, "And it's my turn late this afternoon."

"Then us tomorrow." Nadine adds, indicating herself and Haylie.

"That fast?" Angelita looks surprised.

"Little point waiting," Rowena points out, "Not when it's all arranged engagements. All middle nobility too."

"All younger sons?"

"With two exceptions," Rowena smiles wryly, "Marcellus Pelmont 's the only son, but he's had an awful time finding a second wife."

"He's your fiancé?" Angelita guesses.

Rowena flushes and nods.

"Then there's Andrina's husband, Nikolai Gris," Laine puts in, "Only son of Lady Jane Gris and one of the Sedyr hunters. But that one's a special case."

Angelita nods to herself, then addresses me, "Has Natalia told you what's up with your engagement?"

"I think she's waiting on Tory to back her up."

"Figures," Angelita scowls, "Stubborn ass."

"Considering that's all I know about it." I can't help frowning.

Angelita shakes her head. "Tory 's the one really set on this. Ask her when you get a chance."

"Speaking of Tory," Laine begins warily, "How much did she change this time?"

"She looks the same," Angelita replies, "But, while she doesn't have all the same abilities as Sedya, she's Sedya's equal in power. Tory an' Nikki both have full control over all their abilities now."

"Nikki too?" Haylie frowns.

"Nikki's a healer... same abilities as Channa actually, only far stronger. Speakin' of Channa," Angelita is mostly talking to Laine, "All of the Second Shield are married now."

"To whom?" Laine looks surprised.

"Stephen Verdas."

"What?!" I'm not sure who said it first, but all of us are pretty stunned.

Nadine swallows hard. "Channa 's the blue haired merc from the west continent?"

Angelita nods. "My understanding is it wasn't either's first choice."

I can well imagine. I haven't seen much of Channa, but I got the impression she's like Laine when it comes to relationships. General Stephen Verdas, aside from being a leader of Arawn's military, is well known to be a confirmed bachelor.

"They were both just looking to get laid?" I guess.

"Prob'ly," Angelita shakes her head ruefully, "It's the same kind of bond as Natalia an' Dolan, Rylle an' Devlin, an' Stacie an' Jake. Far as I know the other two 're Sedyr marriages."

Laine nods.

After that the conversation turns to less interesting things until Angelita has to go and we have to get ready for Rowena's wedding. Xylia may've come to see Sefu, but Angelita has been known to hang out with Laine, Rowena, and Nadine. Lillian is going to be irked to have missed her. Haylie and Nadine tried to talk Angelita into coming to their wedding tomorrow... unsuccessfully. I suspect our former princess is avoiding Monarch Reginald, who's her de facto head of family and none too happy with her at the moment. Something to do with her turning down his son in favour of her boyfriend. Although I can understand why she did.

When all of us leave our recreation area, I accompany Rowena to her suite and into her dressing room. She immediately drops onto the stool at the vanity and stares at her reflection in the mirror.

"How can she still be...?" Rowena sighs tiredly.

"If you mean Angelita, near as I can tell she and Devin 've been practically married since UnderGround Club signed on with Experiment Redemption," I pull a chair over so I can sit beside the vanity, "But that's not what's bugging you."

Rowena grimaces. "It's mostly nerves, I think. Just seems almost like everything 's going too well."

"Andrina said something to that effect too, but maybe it's just time something went your way."

"Thanks, Nerita," Rowena's grimace turns wry, "The rest of us can't wait 'til it's your turn, you know."

"Then you could be waiting a while."

"We'll see," Rowena shrugs it off, "Guess I better get my shit together..."

"Be an idea. Just one thing though: If you ever need anything..."

Rowena laughs. "I know, believe me. Good thing Laine 's around to look after you."

It's my turn to grimace. "I can look after myself, you know. Anyway, Nadine 's probably looking for you."

"Thanks," This time Rowena is serious, "For everything, Nerita."

As Laine and I take our seats in the chapel, I glance over the other guests. Of the eight young men, Marcellus is the only one I don't see. But I know the bride and groom each have an attendant today. Evidently the best man is someone I haven't met.

When the official takes his place, I watch for Princess Nerissa, but for once there's no sign of her. Something to ask about next time I speak with her. Not that I've even seen her since Ilaria's wedding.

Marcellus appears promptly at four o'clock, accompanied by an unfamiliar man of at least thirty. The stranger is a little taller than Marcellus, light eyed and light haired. There's something vaguely familiar about his features, but I can't place the resemblance. He's easily the best looking guy I've seen since being at court and his lack of rings on either hand suggests he's unmarried. Makes me wonder who he is.

Suddenly the stranger's eyes meet mine and I flush, realizing I've been staring. No one else seems to notice.

Part of the reason for the delay in Rowena's marriage was so she and Nadine could get new dresses for the occasion. So when Nadine enters, I know her short wine coloured dress isn't one she's worn anywhere else. I can't help noticing that she looks unusually nervous as she moves to her place at the front.

Rowena, on the other hand, doesn't seem at all nervous as she starts down the aisle. Her gown is nearly the same style as Angelita's dress had been, but in the same deep, rich green as her eyes. Rowena's veil is a rich cream colour that complements the dress. She also has a bouquet of white and deep pink roses.

The ceremony proceeds beautifully. Maybe it's because Marcellus and Rowena both look so happy. I really hope they'll stay that way.

After, when Nadine has to take the best man's arm, she looks more nervous than ever. He barely seems to notice. But as they pass, my eyes meet his again and I have to wonder just who he is.

In the reception hall, Laine and I end up seated with Lord George Pelmont, his daughters, and their husbands.

"Who's the best man?" Laine asks first opportunity she gets.

Georgiana, Marcellus's oldest sister, frowns in surprise. "You don't know?"

"We're new here." Laine reminds her.

"And he's seldom enough at court." Lord Pelmont adds sternly. To me and Laine, he explains, "That is the Monarch's son, Crown Prince Derian Regan. He and Marcellus are long-time friends and occasionally get together to commiserate similar unfortunate circumstances."

No wonder Nadine is so nervous. Not that he appears to be a particularly attentive escort. As the reception progresses, I repeatedly catch him watching me. If our eyes meet, he redirects his attention elsewhere, but only until I look away from him. Quite a few people are noticing too, even the bride and groom. I can feel Laine's eyes on me nearly as often as Prince Derian's. It's a little odd though. Very few people, especially guys, give me so much as a second glance.

After dinner comes the best man's speech, during which Prince Derian keeps his attention on Marcellus and Rowena. That's followed by the presentation of gifts from Natalia and Dolan, Lord Pelmont, and each of Marcellus's brothers-in-law. I suspect, from what I've seen, the Pelmont family is both prominent and powerful within the middle nobility.

Then, finally, the speeches are over and there's time for visiting. Nadine escapes the head table in favour of the one occupied by Haylie, Raymond, Lysander, and the recently married couples. Laine also slips away to join them, but I continue talking with Marcellus's sisters.

From the corner of my eye, I can see Prince Derian talking to Marcellus and Rowena. There's no reason why he shouldn't, so I don't pay it a lot of attention. However, when he accompanies the newlyweds in our direction, I start to get nervous.

"Good evening, Lord Pelmont." Prince Derian inclines his head politely, first to the man he's addressing, then to each of Marcellus's sisters and their husbands.

Rowena moves to stand behind me. "Where'd Laine go?"

"Over there." I tilt my head in Laine's direction.

"Derian," Marcellus ignores the looks he gets from his brothers-in-law at the familiar address, "If I may introduce Nerita... Chassaven?" Marcellus glances at me for confirmation and I nod.

"And Sefu." Rowena reminds her new husband as my tiger gets to his feet, studying the Prince with a quizzical expression. Prince Derian glances over Sefu with a raised eyebrow, but it's hard to tell what he's thinking.

"Nerita," Marcellus continues, "This is Crown Prince Derian of Norsecount."

I should properly curtsy, but that's hard to do when I'm sitting and Sefu and Rowena are right behind my chair.

"Marcellus," Lord Pelmont shakes his head reprovingly, "You've gone and put your lady's friend in an awkward position."

"Then perhaps I should make it up to her by inviting her to come sit with us."

There're times when I wish I could trade places with my tiger. Although it's obvious I'm not the only one who thinks it's a rather shameless ploy. Georgiana gives her brother a stern look, but Lord Pelmont just shakes his head.

"First Sefu would have to move." Which he does almost before I've finished speaking. I turn to Lord Pelmont, "If your lordship will excuse me."

"Yes, of course."

Sefu and I accompany Marcellus, Rowena, and Prince Derian not to the head table, but a recently vacated one just below it.

Once we're seated, Prince Derian addresses me, "The guards say a lady with a tiger arrived early this afternoon... surely there can't be that many domesticated winter tigers around."

"That was Sefu's sister, Xylia. And as far as I know, there're only two in Norsecount."

"And the lady?" The Prince queries.

"Angelita Mendus Straisen." Rowena replies when I don't.

Prince Derian frowns. "Why didn't she come to court when she first arrived in Monarch's Town?"

"You would have to ask her," I can't help shaking my head, "Although my guess would be she's avoiding his majesty."

The Prince chuckles. "Wise of her. What with one thing and another Father hasn't been the easiest person to deal with recently."

"Recent court rumour suggests that's understating the case," Marcellus observes dryly, "Although it has been suggested the former princess of Estorika is one of the sorer points."

"That'd be because he's focused on who and what she was born," Rowena suggests, "To those of us who know her personally and or by reputation..."

"I saw the report Becky Riverson sent up when they first realized Angelita was with Experiment Redemption," Prince Derian grimaces, "I recall Father mumbling something about slander and impossibilities."

I shake my head. "Then he doesn't understand what she went through after Star Stone Seat fell. She was one of several children sold to slavers. She doesn't remember how many times she was bought and sold before she managed to escape."

"And the kind of people who buy and sell children like that aren't looking for labour," Rowena adds, "Or at least not in Arawn. And then there's the anti-monarchy bullshit. She didn't want anyone to even suspect she could be Princess Angelita."

She managed that pretty well," I grimace, "I don't know how many different names she went by, but she was working street corners when we first met her and went on to play bait for a mercenary crew."

"And someone married her?" Marcellus raises an eyebrow.

"He has his own issues," Rowena responds, "But they seem happy with the arrangement."

"Father does tend to be very set in his ways," Prince Derian sighs, "He claims it's a privilege of age, but I think it'll come back to bite him yet."

Marcellus shrugs. "Maybe it will, maybe it won't. I'd rather not get into that tonight."

Prince Derian chuckles. "It's still a bit early for you to leave, you know."

Marcellus glowers at him. Rowena and I exchange glances.

"Just how long have you two known each other?" Rowena is mostly addressing her husband.

"As long as either of us can remember," Marcellus shifts his chair closer to hers, "I probably spent more of my childhood at court than my family's home."

"And yet some members of your family still wince when you drop titles." Prince Derian doesn't look entirely amused.

"I didn't have any say in my sisters' marriages," Marcellus scowls briefly, "I'm no favourite of their husbands at the best of times."

The Prince sighs. "Someone needs to shake some sense into the nobility in this country... Father won't and it seems no one else can."

I can't help frowning. "How did things get this bad?"

"According to High Lady Irina of Ouestlun, who was a cousin and close friend of Mother's, it's the lack of a strong, positive female influence," Prince Derian grimaces, "Of course she claims there hasn't been one since Mother's death."

"You think she's wrong?" Marcellus shakes his head, "It's said many places your mother was the last to be both liked and respected."

"You mean liked or respected," The Prince scowls outright, "Victoria did her utmost to tear the court apart, Gabrielle would go with whoever had the last word..."

"And the princesses are barely more than ornaments," Marcellus finishes, cutting off any comments on the Prince's second wife, "But what are the odds on anything changing before it's too late?"

Rowena glances at me, "Do you think Tory 'll stay in Norsecount after this trip?"

"I think it's more a question of whether or not she takes any interest in the current situation."

Prince Derian and Marcellus both frown in confusion.

"There was a merc crew that went through Experiment Redemption with us," Rowena explains before either can ask, "That was either the cause or the target of some really bizarre stuff. They call themselves UnderGround Club and from their leaders on down, if a person dug deep enough, they're all unusual."

"How so?" Prince Derian queries.

Rowena glances at me again, "Top or bottom?"

"Maybe if you start with Shawnda Tory won't seem so incredible," I turn to the guys, "Keeping in mind neither of us knows the whole story on any of them."

"Still..." Marcellus looks curious.

"Shawnda Silver," Rowena grimaces, "Only joined UnderGround Club a little over a year ago and she's barely sixteen. But they don't know how she survived before Experiment Redemption took her on. There's something about her... I don't know..."

I shrug. "All I know 's she's not as shy or submissive as she was. And she's still a mouse."

"I guess Rylan Tobin would be next," Rowena moves on, "Since he also joined the group while they were with Experiment Redemption. It's said though that when his original group first came he was addicted to every kind of drug out there."

"I don't think it was quite that bad," I observe, "Whether it was or not, he's beaten all of them. The real weird one's listening to him just talk 'cause if his memory 's at all accurate he has to be at least thirty-five, if not forty."

"He doesn't look that old."

I shrug. "I don't know enough to explain."

"Kyle Hysan 's probably the least unusual of the group," Rowena leaves off speculating on Rylan, "Near as I can tell he's just another guy out of lower Central City. Except apparently what he doesn't know about knives isn't worth knowing. Logan Hysan 's more interesting."

"He looks pretty average," I observe, "But I seem to remember someone saying he's pure human."

Prince Derian looks surprised. "That shouldn't be possible."

Rowena shrugs. "Neither's the number of crude words he can cram into a simple sentence. They kept him around because he can drive and fix anything on wheels. Then there's Fae..."

I shake my head. "It's properly Pharessya Norst and she's not from Arawn."

"Sounds Sedyr." Prince Derian observes.

"She is... well, with a little human blood as well. We met her mother when we came underground from Camp Streton."

"Fae 's a apt nickname," Rowena grimaces, "But I guess Nikki Genstang 's next..."

"Skip her then," I suggest, "Try Devin."

Rowena nods. "Devin Straisen, now married to our ex-princess. I don't know how long his family's history is with the military, but he ran away from one of their experimental programs. He's a genius with math, electronics, and computers."

"Hacker?" Prince Derian queries dryly.

I nod. "Code breaker too."

"Anyway," Rowena continues, "His father, Devlin Straisen, 's also ex-military. He's now a martial arts instructor with Experiment Redemption and married to Rylle Staldak."

The Prince frowns. "She's Second Shield. How long ago?"

"Over a year," I guess I shouldn't be surprised he's heard of the Second Shield, "They have a baby daughter... and Sefu's other sister."

Marcellus changes the subject, "Angelita is part of this group?"

Rowena and I both nod, then I add, "I got the impression she's been with them for years and isn't planning to just leave."

"Which leaves us with the founding members," Rowena grimaces, "The sisters, Tory and Nikki Genstang, and Ford Straisen."

"Related to Devin?" Marcellus queries.

I shake my head. "Devlin and Devin took Ford's name when the law forced them to drop the name they had been using. Kyle shares Logan's name for the same reason."

"It's hard to know what to make of Ford," Rowena returns to the subject, "There was one guy bigger at Camp Streton, but not by much. And then Ford's eyes are really light sensitive so he always wears dark glasses."

"And yet he's the closest thing to a real people person in the group," I shake my head, "Animals don't seem too fond of him though."

"According to Angelita he's also an unrepentant prankster."

Prince Derian glances at Marcellus, "Sounds like an interesting man."

Marcellus shrugs. "Now what about these sisters?"

"First off," Rowena takes a deep breath, "They're not sisters in the traditional sense. They're the survivors of an illegal genetics project and... I don't know... it's hard to explain."

"Are they human at all?" Prince Derian enquires.

"Nikki more than Tory, I think," I grimace, "They also have Sedyr blood, plus whatever race Rylle and Channa are, and something else. Nikki passes for human, Tory doesn't."

"What kind of training do they have?"

"Nikki 's mainly into all kinds of sports," Rowena thinks back, "Tory on the other hand..."

"Martial arts prodigy and master of multiple disciplines, master of all kinds of weapons, also locks and code breaking," I have the Prince's undivided attention, "And that doesn't even get into her 'other' abilities."

"She isn't like Natalia, is she?"

"More abilities and more powerful."

"And her sister?"

"Channa's abilities, but again more powerful."

"And with the group you described backing them," Prince Derian frowns thoughtfully, "Do you think they would take an interest in the situation here?"

I shrug. "I'm not about to guess what Tory 's into. I've got enough to deal with."

Rowena nods fervently. "If you ever meet Tory you'll see what we mean."

Marcellus glances around the room, then turns to his bride, "We should go and speak with others before they start to leave."

He and Rowena get up to do that, leaving me with Prince Derian. All of a sudden I'm feeling very self-conscious.

"Nerita Chassaven, correct? Descended from the middle nobility of Estorika?"

"My family believed so... Natalia as well, but there's no concrete proof."

The Prince nods to himself. "What do you think of Norsecount so far?"

"It's so different from Arawn it's like being in another world."

"There are only two more of your friends yet to be married?"

"Of the ones with confirmed engagements. It'll be a double ceremony tomorrow afternoon."

"What will you do after?"

"Hang out with Laine and Sefu until something better comes up," I shrug, "Everything up 'til now 's been focused on these marriages."

"What would you do if you could do anything you wanted?"

"See if there's a way to find out what's happening with the people I knew in South City."

Prince Derian looks surprised at that. "Did you have to leave family behind?"

"No, my only living blood relation came with me. It's just other people I knew... some I grew up with, some I worked with," I sigh, "I don't miss living there... Arawn 's a harsh place to live, but still..."

The Prince studies me thoughtfully. "Your parents are dead?"

"Since I was six."

"Do you remember them at all?"

"Bits and pieces."

He nods to himself. "I hear you've gotten to know Nerissa a bit. At the very least she's decided she likes you and your tiger."

"My tiger anyway."

Prince Derian chuckles. "Nerissa 's pretty much my shadow when I'm here... and I got in early this morning. I'm just surprised she didn't sneak into the ceremony..." He breaks off to study me with undisguised interest, "She snuck into your other friends' weddings, didn't she?"

I nod. "I was going to ask about it next time I see her."

"You don't mind her, I take it."

"She's interesting to listen to. And she reminds me of... some things."

The Prince looks curious, but it's a subject I'd rather not talk about.

I quickly change the subject, "I've heard a few people say you're not here much."

"I'm not," Old pain flickers over Prince Derian's face, "Some of it's work I do for Father, but more of it's just bad memories and no real reason to stay."

"Not even for Nerissa?"

He sighs. "I find she's too much in large doses."

I nod knowingly.

08-10-48-06-04SM

I wake slowly, too comfortable to want to move or even open my eyes. My feet feel a little odd though, as if Sefu isn't lying on them. He usually sleeps across the foot of the bed, but not always. Then my memory starts to return: Talking to Prince Derian until the reception hall was nearly empty... wandering through the palace gardens with him until very late evening... kissing him... more than kissing him...

My eyes fly open. I'm not in my bed or my bedroom and it's not Laine asleep next to me. Sefu is stretched out on the floor beside the bed. He'd been with us the whole time, but evidently not too worried about anything that happened. Laine is gonna kill me... once she's finished laughing. I roll over and bury my face in the pillows.

Gentle fingers brush through my loose hair. Then an arm slides around me, pulling me against a warm, naked body. There's pressure against my back like Derian is pressing his face in my hair. After a moment, it's gone.

"Nerita... I..." He sounds uncertain, almost scared.

I lift my head and turn my face to look at him. He's closer than I'd thought. So close it doesn't seem like either of us moved, but somehow we're kissing. Suddenly I have a whole lot better idea how I ended up in this predicament.

"We're both gonna be in trouble, aren't we?" Derian absently toys with a strand of my hair.

I lift my head from his chest so I can look at him, "I don't know about you, but I can think of a whole list of people who're gonna be pissed off at me... starting with Laine, Natalia, and Tory."

Derian sighs. "Father won't be too happy either. He's still looking to set me up with some 'suitable' girl. Although, why would Natalia or this Tory care what you do?"

"Because Natalia 's trying to arrange an engagement for me as well. Apparently Angelita suggested it to them and Tory 's really set on it."

Derian frowns. "I didn't think you and Angelita were especial friends."

"We're not. We have a long history of ugly fights and I know she doesn't owe me any favours. She isn't above passing off a headache or two though."

"Do you not know who they wish you to marry?"

I shake my head. "I tried asking Angelita when I saw her yesterday, but she just said to ask Tory, who's headed back into Arawn."

"Why would she do that?" Derian's frown deepens.

"Hopefully to get the information she promised Laine. Beyond that, I don't know."

Derian is silent for several minutes, clearly considering what I've just told him. I lay my head on his chest again. I wish I could stay like this and not have to face anyone else. The only way I could possibly get out of this one without serious repercussions is if it's Derian they're trying to set me up with. I just can't see that being the case. But then I'd've never guessed Angelita was a princess either. And Laine has, in the past, gotten after me for not seeing what's right in front of my nose."

"Could you be pregnant?"

Looking up at Derian, I can see that his expression is serious. I hadn't even thought of that, but it's the one thing that could make this situation worse.

"Maybe... at least, there's nothing to stop it."

The arm around me tightens as he sighs. "Even if you weren't, would you want to marry me?"

The question doesn't completely catch me off guard, but I'm surprised he'd consider asking it.

"I hope that's not just guilty conscience."

"Only partly," Derian's eyes meet and hold mine, "Some of it's a ploy to keep you in my bed. But also... I think maybe you're what this court... this whole country... needs."

"His majesty won't just approve."

Derian scowls. "You've only begun to see the mess Father's 'approval' has created. Norsecount 's stagnating while the whole rest of the world 's changing. Maybe it's time to shake things up here too."

"Could you marry without his majesty's approval?"

Derian sighs. "No. But it may be possible to force his hand. Nerita, will you marry me?"

I know he's serious, but I also know how easily things could go sideways... especially considering the discrepancy between his position and mine. Still, I'll admit I like the idea of being crown princess, even under the current circumstances.

"And if I say yes?"

"Nerita..." Old pain flickers through his eyes.

"Hey, I'm not trying to mess with you. It's just it's one thing to talk about this and another to get it past other people."

Derian nods. "True. Still, you'd get a ring and if the announcement were made properly, Father would have a lot less say. I can go over his head that far."

"And not entirely without support," I observe, "Yes, I'll marry you."

Our lips meet, but before things can go any further we're interrupted by Sefu setting his front paws on the edge of the bed and sticking his nose in my hair. Derian grimaces, propping himself up on one elbow so he can look Sefu in the eye.

"You are going to learn to stay off the bed."

"I haven't been able to teach him that yet. Most nights he sleeps on my feet."

"Not if you're sleeping with me."

I laugh. "He thinks we should go so he can have breakfast."

"Oh, well, in that case maybe we should get up," Derian brushes my hair from my face, "But there's one thing I want to do before you go."

"That's fine. His breakfast won't be ready just yet."

We both get out of bed, somewhat reluctantly. I don't have much choice but to pull on my dress from last night. Derian rummages through a battered duffel and comes up with a pair of faded jeans.

"A lot of my work for Father is 'diplomatic'," He explains as he pulls the jeans on, "I pretty much live out of this thing and my valet, when he's around, isn't allowed to touch it. Anyway, in here."

Sefu and I follow Derian through three rooms, to what appears to be his study. He goes around behind the desk and opens a wall safe, from which he removes a strongbox. Then he comes back around the desk and retrieves a key from the top desk drawer. Inside the strongbox are several jewelry cases.

The first case he looks into, Derian tosses aside with a scowl. "Eleanor's rings," He explains, "Early on in our marriage I hinted that, as husband and wife, we should share a bed occasionally. She pulled off her rings and threw them in my face. I should've gotten rid of them then."

"So you never slept with her?"

"She wasn't interested... neither was I, to be honest. After she died, the coroner's report said she'd never slept with any man." He checks another case, "This was Mother's engagement ring. Father gave it to me with a less than subtle hint that I should give it to Gabrielle. I never did. Her rings," Derian closes the strongbox and returns it to the safe, "Were buried with her. Anyway," He passes me the case containing his mother's ring, "If you like that one, I'll get it cleaned and re-sized if need be."

The ring is gold, I'd guess high carat, set with three stones of indeterminate colour. It really does need cleaning.

"I believe it's diamond and sapphire."

I'm hesitant to try it on, but Derian take it out of the case and slips it onto my hand.

"What do you think?" His lips brush the edge of my ear.

"It's fine... it fits fine."

"Then I'll get it cleaned," Derian slides the ring off my finger, "And back to you as soon as possible. When's the ceremony today?"

"One thirty, I think."

He nods to himself. "I'm going to see about an announcement for either this evening or first thing tomorrow. In the meantime," He retrieves a small object from the top desk drawer, "I'll ask you to hang onto this."

It's his signet ring, which he needs to seal letters and official documents. I can't help swallowing, even as I nod.

"You should go," Derian wraps my hand around the heavy ring, "One thing though: If you see Nerissa, don't say anything to her just yet."

"I won't."

"Thank you. You're staying in the old east wing, right?"

I nod.

"I'll show you a short cut the guards don't know, since I don't think you want to be seen."

"Thanks."

Derian goes back to the bedroom for a shirt before guiding me and Sefu through the palace. There's no sign of anyone.

"I'll see you later." Derian kisses me once more. Then he heads back to his suite while Sefu and I continue to ours.

Laine is seated in the outer room, wrapped in a dressing gown and looking like she didn't sleep well. Hardly surprising since she never sleeps alone, one way or the other.

She studies me critically and scowls. "Nerita! Where the fuck 've you been?"

I shrug evasively as I start for the dressing room.

"Oh no you don't." Laine is on her feet fast, but not fast enough to intercept me. Her scowl deepens and she leans against the door frame. "What the fuck do you think you're pulling? Better yet, where's half your fucking shit?"

"I'll get it back." I set Derian's signet ring on the vanity and hunt up jeans and a sweatshirt to change into.

"What else d' you misplace last night?" Laine crosses her arms over her chest.

"Why're you bothering to ask?"

"After everything you've said in the years I've known you... everything you've done... now you go and fuck it all up? Nerita, if Natalia doesn't kill you, Tory will."

"Maybe, maybe not."

Laine opens her mouth to say something more, but there's a knock on the outer door. She goes to answer it while I finish changing and brush out my hair. I can hear Natalia's voice in the next room, so I take the signet ring when I go out there.

Natalia immediately turns a stern look on me, "Where were you, Nerita? Of all of you, I thought you at least would know enough to stay out of trouble."

"You can't see what happened?"

Natalia shakes her head. "I'm able to see less and less these days. With Tory come into her power, the Second Shield wanes. Still, I do hope you can give a reasonable account of yourself."

I hold out my hand, the Prince's ring on my palm. Natalia looks at it carefully, then lets out a breath of relief, although she doesn't completely relax.

"How did you come by that?"

"He said to hold onto it for now. I imagine he'll trade it for the ring he intends to give me fairly quickly."

"Good," Natalia nods to herself, "Still, be careful, Nerita. You're not entirely out of trouble yet."

"I know."

"Then I'll see you this afternoon." Natalia leaves, closing the door behind her.

Laine turns a disgusted scowl on me. "What the fuck was that?"

"I think I've figured out who they want me to marry."

"You're fucking lucky then... unless you're gotten yourself pregnant."

"We're not ruling that out."

Laine frowns. "How long've you been awake?"

"An hour... closer to an hour and a half."

She shakes her head, then a thought occurs to her. "He's giving you a ring after one night? Just because you could be pregnant?"

It's my turn to shake my head. "After the reception we went out to the gardens. Must've been at least midnight when we came inside. And we were just talking. Not even personal stuff."

Laine sighs and slumps into a chair. "Sometimes I just don't understand you."

I have to laugh at that. "I could say the same. Anyway, I think Sefu 's looking for breakfast."

Haylie, Nadine, and I are already eating by the time Laine joins us. I suspect she still isn't happy with me and I don't invite her to come outside with me and Sefu. I have Derian's ring in my pocket for safekeeping. If I lose that I'll really be in deep trouble.

Almost all the fields are empty this morning. Sefu and I claim the nearest one to the old east wing and I begin throwing his ball. At least he's acting like his usual self.

After about half an hour, I spot Princess Nerissa and an elderly woman approaching. Sefu has just returned the ball to me and I keep him at my side. The woman stops at the edge of the field while Princess Nerissa joins me and Sefu.

"Good morning." The girl greets us politely. Sefu immediately goes to her and she kneels down to pet him.

"I didn't see your highness yesterday." I pass her the ball.

"I didn't dare sneak in," Princess Nerissa explains, "Derian would've seen me for sure. But it doesn't matter; I got to see the bride when he was introduced to her and the bridesmaid before the ceremony. I just wish Derian was here more," She throws the ball and Sefu goes bounding after it, "I think that's mostly because his wives used to say things about him that aren't true and people believed them. And it's been even worse since the second one died."

It's interesting information, especially combined with what I've learned from Marcellus and Derian. I don't dare comment on it, so I keep silent.

"Anyway," Princess Nerissa keeps talking, "The guards said a lady and a winter tiger came to see Sefu yesterday."

I laugh. "That was Sefu's sister, Xylia."

"Oh. So who's the lady?"

"Your highness," I study her carefully, "You know how you don't always want people noticing you?"

The girl nods.

"Well, she doesn't either."

"But who is she?" Princess Nerissa accepts the ball from Sefu and throws it again.

"Someone my friends and I've known a long time. You'll find out more when you meet her."

Princess Nerissa looks disappointed.

I change the subject, "Will I see you this afternoon?"

"Maybe. They said it's a double ceremony, but they also said Derian 's still here. Even though he said he was leaving after the reception yesterday. I really wish he'd just stay here."

If we keep talking about her brother, I'm scared I'll give myself away, so I change the subject again, "Where is your highness supposed to be this morning?"

"Studying history," She makes a face, "I convinced my governess to bring me out because she's always complaining I'm too far ahead of where I should be. All the tutors say I'm just like Derian that way..."

Since her brother seems to be her favourite topic this morning, I let her talk uninterrupted while she continues to throw the ball for Sefu. Then, abruptly, she looks up at me, "I think you'd like Derian. You should meet him while he's here."

"You think so?" It's all I can do to maintain a conversational tone.

Princess Nerissa studies me carefully. "You already met him."

I laugh. "At the reception yesterday."

"Oh." The girl turns bright pink.

"Sefu and I need to go in, your highness, if we're to have time to eat and get ready for this afternoon."

Princess Nerissa nods as she hands me the ball Sefu has just returned to her. "Maybe I'll see you later." She goes over to her governess while Sefu and I head into the old east wing.

Laine is nowhere to be seen when we reach our suite, but there's still twenty minutes before lunch. I want a chance to talk to Haylie and Nadine after we eat, so I head for the shower now.

Once the water is turned off, I can hear voices in the outer room. I can't tell who's out there so I get dressed properly and braid my hair. Then I make sure I have the signet ring before going out to see what's going on.

It's just Laine and Natalia, seated and talking. Both look up when I enter.

"Has something come up?" I'm mainly addressing Natalia.

She sighs. "Reg has accused me of setting up last night."

"It was Marcellus who introduced us... in full view of everyone at the reception."

"And that only at Derian's own request," Natalia adds, "Although I gather Derian's been busy this morning."

"I'm guessing his majesty's upset..."

"Try livid," Natalia corrects, "And far from viewing the matter rationally. I have one more thing to take care of here, after today, and then I intend to find somewhere else to be. You'd best watch your step."

"Would Tory know?"

"She does," Natalia nods, "I was able to reach her. If anything, she's amused. However, she says she can't possibly be back before the tenth, but she may have something for you as well as for Laine."

I frown. "Something that would help me?"

"I don't know," Natalia sighs, "Tory's as far above me as Sedya herself and they answer to no power other than the

Creator. That said, even Tory's support will do little to endear you to Reg."

Laine looks thoughtful, but doesn't say anything. I have to wonder if she doesn't somehow know something more about the situation. Before I can ask, there's a knock on the door. Laine gets up to answer it and lets Prince Derian and Princess Nerissa into the room.

The Princess looks a little bewildered, so I'm guessing she doesn't know yet. Derian glances at Natalia as he takes a ring case from his pocket. Then he crosses the room to get down on one knee in front of me. He opens the case and now I can see a brilliant diamond flanked by two bright sapphires.

"Nerita Chassaven, will you marry me?"

There's no real need for him to ask again, except as a show for the others present.

"Yes, I will."

Derian slides the ring onto my finger before getting to his feet. He kisses me and I take the opportunity to slip him the signet ring, which he pockets.

"Congratulations," Natalia is the first to speak, "Is the formal announcement set yet?"

"For early this evening," Derian replies, "Although word may have gone a certain distance by then."

"Are you going to attend the wedding this afternoon?" Natalia enquires.

"I was thinking I'd escort my lady," Derian's arm tightens around me, "And yes," He turns to his sister, "I think you can come with us."

Princess Nerissa is too excited to speak. Just seeing her brother propose to me had her grinning from ear to ear. I'm sure whichever tutor or governess was supposed to be teaching her this afternoon will be just as happy not to have to deal with her.

Derian turns back to me, "We'll be back in time for that."

I nod and accept another kiss.

Natalia leaves with Derian and his sister.

Once they're gone, Laine studies me with a bemused expression. "That sounded rehearsed."

"Considering that was the third time he'd asked this morning."

She nods to herself. "Let's see the ring."

I hold out my hand so she can examine it. "He said it was his mother's."

Laine frowns. "Shouldn't he've given it to his first wife?"

I shrug. "Apparently he didn't. Anyway, we better go eat."

Haylie and Nadine are too nervous to eat much and too preoccupied to notice my new ring. Neither Laine nor I mention it and after the meal, I accompany Haylie to her suite. She doesn't have a lot of time to prepare so we head straight to her dressing room.

"Are you and Raymond getting along any better?" I watch her pull things from a wardrobe.

Haylie shrugs. "I still think we'll be okay. His family 's been pretty nice so far... especially Lady Tremauld."

I nod. "Don't forget you can call my at any time... no matter what."

"I won't," Haylie smiles appreciatively, "Thanks, Nerita... for everything."

"Any time."

As I let myself out of her suite, I encounter Lady Tremauld and a young woman, who I believe is Raymond's sister.

"Good afternoon, Nerita," Lady Tremauld smiles warmly, "How is Haylie?"

"Fine. Just getting changed."

"Thank you."

They go in while I head for Nadine's suite. I find her seated at the vanity, staring at the contents of a large jewelry case. She blinks and looks up on realizing I'm in the doorway.

"You okay?"

"Yeah," Nadine sighs, "Just wishing I had flowers instead of jewelry."

Glancing around, I spot a vase holding a large mixed bouquet. "Are those from Lysander?"

She brightens immediately. "Thanks, Nerita."

"Any time. Don't forget that."

Nadine nods. "You've always said that. But what're you gonna do with everyone but Laine married?"

"Don't you worry about that. A wedding is supposed to be the bride's day."

Nadine studies me curiously, absently closing the jewelry case. "Nerita, what's going on?"

"All in good time. I want to know the rest of you are taken care of first."

"I guess," Nadine goes to the wardrobe for her dress, "Why would Princess Nerissa sneak into every wedding except Rowena's?"

I have to laugh. "She didn't want her brother to catch her."

"Oh," Nadine nods to herself, "Have you gotten her to admit why she does that?"

"She said she likes to see the brides."

Nadine shakes her head. "Most of us haven't looked much like brides," She sighs, "Not that I ever imagined wanting to get married. I'll be fine though."

"Good. You'd better get ready. You don't have a lot of time."

Laine, Sefu, and I have just finished getting ready when Prince Derian and Princess Nerissa turn up. Derian offers me his arm, which I accept.

As we walk to the chapel, Princess Nerissa asks, "Shouldn't Sefu at least have a bow or something?"

Sefu gives her a disgusted look.

I just laugh. "None of the winter tigers I've met will tolerate being dressed up."

Derian raises an eyebrow. "Oh?"

"It was suggested for Angelita's wedding. And all four from the litter were there."

Princess Nerissa frowns thoughtfully. "Then if you go to the Harvest Masquerade, he'll give you away."

"We'll see what happens between now and then." Derian responds.

In the confusion of finding seats in the chapel very few of the other guests take much notice of the five of us. The Monarch shoots a disapproving look our way, but that's the worst he'll do in public. Especially with the official taking his place at the front.

Raymond and Lysander enter together at one thirty and everyone stands for the brides' entrance. Haylie and Nadine walk down the aisle together, both wearing their dresses from our graduation from Experiment Redemption. Haylie has left her hair loose and it falls to her knees. She is wearing minimal jewelry and her hands are empty. Nadine, on the other hand, has flowers in her hands and hair and no visible jewelry. Both look calm rather than nervous, which's a pleasant surprise.

Aside from Haylie fumbling a little in placing the ring on Raymond's hand, the ceremony goes well. Then the last two are married. It's weird to think that, for the moment, Laine, Sefu, and I now have a whole wing of the palace to ourselves. The girls of Black Oak Court have been a huge part of my life for a long time. Most I've known far longer than that. Not seeing them everyday is going to take a lot of getting used to.

"Is something wrong?" Derian's question is for my ears only.

I take a deep breath. "Not wrong exactly. I'll explain later."

He nods and gently squeezes my hand.

The reception is the usual food, gifts, and speeches. The four of us are sharing a table with Natalia and Dolan and Sefu is stretched out behind my chair.

As we eat, Natalia turns to me, "Nerita, are you okay?"

"I will be."

She studies me curiously. "If you don't mind answering a question or two, there are a couple things I've been curious about for a while."

"It would depend what you're asking about."

Natalia nods to herself. "What is Black Oak Court? Of all the groups through Experiment Redemption I never heard of anything quite like it."

"That's no surprise." Laine chuckles.

"The girls of Black Oak Court," I pause long enough to sip my drink, "Are any of the teens and young women who've lived in my family's house over the past thirteen years."

"So not just those who accompanied you to Camp Streton?"

I nod.

Natalia considers that silently for a time. "FTK's people in South City were never able to learn much about the Old Quarter. Beyond the existence of you and your group. I would guess they assumed it to be like the lower city, but is that really the case?"

Laine and I glance at each other and laugh.

"The Old Quarter of South City," I turn back to Natalia, "Has been a thorn in the military's side for most of the war. They probably fed FTK the information in hopes that, by getting rid of me, they could gain a foothold."

"This sounds like an interesting story." Derian observes.

"And a very long one." I respond.

Natalia's eyes are closed and a faint white light appears in front of her chest. Then the light fades and she opens her eyes to study me carefully.

"A long and interesting tale indeed, but one I can only follow to your sixth birthday."

I grimace. "That figures."

"It would seem the rest is for Tory to see," Natalia suddenly looks very old and tired, "Still, I can't help wondering about these men, John Simeon and those before him... Do you know anything about them?"

I shake my head. "Each comes, serves as magistrate for a time, and vanishes to be replaced by the next. I worked with John Simeon for most of the years after my parents' deaths and I had free access to all his files, so I doubt anyone knows more than I do."

Derian frowns curiously. "Worked with him doing what?"

"You held the same position as your father and his mother?" Natalia queries.

I nod. "I find it hard to explain though."

Natalia turns to Derian, "If one were to take the duties of a lord or lady to their holding, divide them into administration and everything else, and translate them to the streets of a city, these men have been handling the administration and a representative of the Chassaven family has been doing the rest."

"Except without the privileges of the nobility," I grimace, "I was able to leave because there was someone I trusted to take my place."

"And John Simeon insisted." Laine reminds dryly.

Derian's frown deepens. "I know this isn't considered a polite question, but how old are you?"

"Twenty-two... twenty-three in January. Keeping in mind that in Arawn those who can't survive on their own by seven or eight generally don't."

Princess Nerissa swallows hard.

Shortly after that come speeches and gifts. Once those are done, Danya and Rowena come over to our table.

"Derian," Rowena appears slightly amused, "Would you mind if we borrow Nerita for a while?"

"I think that would be up to her." He replies.

"Depends what you're up to." I add.

"We just want you and Laine to come join us." Danya responds.

Laine, Sefu, and I accompany them to a table across the room where the other six girls of Black Oak Court are waiting. As I sit, I spot the eight guys gathered around a table nearby.

"What's up?" Laine wants to know.

"Most of us leave Monarch's Town either tonight or early tomorrow morning," Danya explains, "And I mean before you two'll be awake."

"And it could be a long time before any of us come back." Andrina adds.

"Maybe, maybe not," Rowena still looks amused, "Depends on if there's anything Nerita would like to tell us."

I glower at her. "How would you know?"

Rowena laughs. "Listening to Marcellus and Derian talk 's interesting."

I bury my head in my arms to hide my crimson face.

"Did they know you were listening?" Laine queries.

"Marcellus did."

"This wouldn't have anything to do with Nerita's escort, would it?" Danya sounds amused.

I extend my left hand towards the center of the table without looking up. Somehow I have a feeling I may never hear the end of this.

"Laine," Ilaria sounds both surprised and bemused, "What's going on?"

"Nerita 's just managed to get herself in a little bit of trouble." The note of sarcasm beneath Laine's amusement suggests she hasn't completely forgiven me yet.

"Considering all the shit she's given the rest of us over the years..." Andrina, at least, doesn't seem to think the situation is funny. But then she's never had much of a sense of humour.

I look up, catching her eye, "You think I'm not well aware of that?" Andrina quickly looks away and I address the whole group, "Could we please find something else to talk about?"

No one speaks for a minute or two, but after that we get into a session of do-you-remembers: How people joined or left the group, life in South City, life at Camp Streton. Somehow so many things seem funnier now than when they happened.

Very few others are left in the reception hall when Marcellus comes over to stand behind Rowena.

"I hate to interrupt a good time, but we have to be ready to leave by seven."

Rowena sighs. "I know."

Marcellus turns to me, "We'll be back by the nineteenth at the latest. Father has court duties starting the twentieth and he wants my help."

I nod.

Rowena leaves with Marcellus as the other young men come looking for their wives. Derian appears behind my chair.

"The announcement should be in just a few minutes."

"Okay."

Laine and Sefu accompany us into what appears to be a recent addition to the palace. At the end of an especially long corridor we find a man waiting for us.

He bows deeply. "We're almost ready, your highness. You're certain you wish to go with Lady Natalia's wording of the announcement?"

"Yes, I'm certain." A hint of impatience enters Derian's voice.

"This way, please." The man holds a door open for us. Once we're inside, he turns to Laine, "Unless my lady wishes to appear on camera, you should stay off to the side."

Laine nods.

"Sefu, stay with Laine." I add. For once he obeys without complaint. Maybe because he's overawed by the room we're in. I certainly never suspected the palace contained anything like it. It's huge for starters, very bright, and full of electronics equipment. At one end is a railing overlooking another, lower room full of row on row of computers.

"Our communications centre," Derian explains over the noise, "Father won't announce our engagement properly at court, but from here we can go multiple media to most of the world."

"The whole world, your highness," The man corrects, "Via radio, television, and internet."

"This," Derian continues, "Is Rupert Ranger, our media relations coordinator, who will be sure to blame me if Father gets upset about this."

"Oh he is, your highness... and I did," Rupert grimaces, "But if you would come stand over here." He directs us to stand in the middle of the room. Once we're in place, Derian slips an arm around me. Rupert disappears into the chaos across the room as a harried young woman approaches us.

"Everything looks good, your highness, my lady. The live broadcast will only be a few seconds and I'll give you five seconds warning."

Derian nods. "Thank you."

She moves to a tall stool nearby.

A male voice echoes through the room, "Are we ready?"

Responses come from below.

"Norsecount is standing by."

"Midkingsen is standing by."

"Ouestlun is standing by."

"The patch worked. Arawn is standing by."

"Chancellor Hall is standing by and ready to relay to the west continent."

"Rupert, you're live in three... two... one."

Derian and I can't hear the actual announcement, but we're watching the young woman.

"And live in five... four... three... two... one."

Which means Derian and I are on camera for the whole world to see. I wonder if anyone in the Old Quarter of South City can hear or see this.

"And off."

Rupert reappears, "Would your highness like to see the recording?"

Derian glances at me, "Are you interested?"

I shake my head.

"I'm sure it's fine," Derian tells Rupert, "Just keep a lid on the speculation for now."

"As your highness wishes." Rupert bows.

Laine and Sefu join us as we head into the corridor.

"That's it for now?" Laine queries.

"Until Father can be manoeuvred into letting us marry," Derian sighs, "Although I don't know what that'll take."

We head for the old east wing, to the suite Laine and I share. She goes inside immediately, but Derian and I hesitate in the doorway.

He brushes a hand over my hair. "You look tired."

"I'm okay, actually."

Derian bends his head to kiss me and I slide my arms around his neck.

"Oh for fuck's sake!" Laine sounds exasperated, "This isn't the place for that."

Derian breaks off the kiss to brush his lips against my ear, "She has a point."

"Sefu," I glance around until I spot my tiger, "Stay and keep Laine company."

09-10-48-06-04SM

The sound of pounding on a door is followed by an angry voice, "Derian!"

There's a groan beside me, then muffled cursing. I bury my face in the pillows.

"Nerita," Derian brushes his fingers through my hair, "You'd better wait here."

I look up at him, "I'm not going anywhere."

His lips brush mine before he gets up. I close my eyes and pull the blankets tight around me. I can hear Derian moving around in the next room, probably getting dressed, then a door opening.

"Yes, Father?"

"Did you not promise to look into the complaint Hrad made a few days ago?"

"You woke me up at six in the morning to ask about that?" It's hard to blame Derian for being upset, "Yes, I will look into it... when I head out that way next."

"I want it dealt with as soon as possible."

"As you wish, your majesty. Is that all?"

I can't quite hear what else is said, but the door slams shortly, followed by muffled cursing. Derian returns to bed not long after that.

"Is this his version of petty revenge?"

Derian sighs. "More or less. He's forcing me to leave court and he'll do his damnedest to keep me away. And there isn't much I can do."

"How long would just this errand take?"

"Two or three days... most of that travel. I originally meant to do it after Marcellus's wedding," Derian pulls me close against him, "Be very careful while I'm gone... please, Nerita. And don't trust Father."

I nod. "How long before you leave?"

"I'm not going anywhere until breakfast."

"Nerita?" Laine studies me in concern when I enter our suite, "Is something wrong?"

"Just his majesty being a fucking ass," I set my armload of stuff on a table before slumping in a chair, "He's sending Derian off on some errand."

"Oh fuck!" Laine scowls, "That leaves you wide open 'til Tory gets back here."

"I don't think his majesty knows about that yet," I straighten a little, "She should be here tomorrow, so if I can survive today..."

"True," Laine's scowl softens, "I guess that leaves you stuck with me tonight."

"If that's such a bad thing there's nothing stopping you from finding someone else to sleep with."

Laine abruptly changes the subject, "You missed meeting our ladies maid, Mattie Conors."

"No loss there."

"And Carl turned up to say we're expected to attend court this afternoon and tomorrow."

"Fuck."

"Anyway, you might want to change before breakfast."

Laine and I are just finishing breakfast when Andrina turns up. She studies each of us with a raised eyebrow.

"What's with you two?"

"The never ending shit around here," Laine responds sourly, "What's your excuse?"

"Actually, I was hoping you could come shopping with me this morning. Lady Jane gave me a list... mostly clothes... and some money."

"She thinks you need more clothes?" I can't help being somewhat sceptical.

"She said something about winter in the mountains," Andrina grimaces, "Nikolai 's s'posed to come along, but still..."

Laine chuckles dryly. "Just you and him on a clothes shopping trip couldn't possibly go well."

"Speaking of clothes shopping..."

All three of us turn to see Natalia in the doorway.

"You think we need more shit?" Laine demands.

"Welcome to life at court," Natalia sighs, "You've got the Harvest Masquerade, Princess Letitia's birthday ball, and a reception for the new ambassador from Arawn coming up... and you two would have to be dying to avoid that last... plus I seriously doubt either of you have enough dresses appropriate for court... and then there's winter gear, since this is Norsecount and even the coast gets quite cold and snowy."

Laine groans. I manage not to.

Natalia continues, "Angelita and Shawnda also need a few things, so I've arranged a vehicle for all of you. And for Devin to tiger-sit."

"Okay..." This's sounding progressively worse.

"Nerita," Natalia enters the room to hand me a paper and a hard plastic card, "These are the lists of necessities for the four of you and my charge card. You'll need to sign all the receipts and get copies for me."

"Spending limit?" Laine queries.

"Even the four of you'd be hard pressed to drain that account in one morning," Natalia replies, "I don't mind you picking up a few extra things, if you want. Your driver will know where to go..." She turns to Andrina, "For your things as well."

"Thank you."

"I'll leave you to that," Natalia tells us, "And I'll see you at noon." She leaves the room.

Andrina studies first me, then Laine and chuckles. "She's worse than Becky."

Laine rolls her eyes. "They are good friends. I guess we better go though."

Andrina goes to get her husband while Laine and I change and braid our hair. Then the four of us and Sefu meet up at the vehicle and are taken to the Old Imperial Hotel, where we leave Sefu with Xylia and Devin and pick up Angelita and Shawnda.

As soon as they're seated, the driver starts for the first store, which turns out to be an outfitters. By the time we're finished there, Andrina is almost finished her list, although surprisingly nowhere near broke, and the rest of us are set for coats, cloaks, boots, and cold weather accessories.

Next is a women's clothing store where we finish off the lists for Angelita, Shawnda, and Andrina. Pick up quite a bit for me and Laine too.

And lastly a dress shop so Laine and I can order what we'll need for the upcoming formal events Natalia mentioned. Plus our masquerade costumes.

I'm careful to obtain a receipt for every purchase and keep them with the charge card. I notice it's Natalia's personal card; the kind only Pleasure Society members use. I'm also careful to ensure the four of us get everything on our lists. As far as I'm concerned anything extra is between Natalia and whichever of us wants it.

Somehow it's only eleven thirty when we leave Angelita and Shawnda at the hotel and pick up Sefu. Continuing on to the palace, we find Natalia waiting for us.

"That wasn't so painful, was it?"

"You tell me," I hand her the wad of receipts and her charge card, "Since you paid for most of it."

Natalia laughs. "I seriously doubt all these'll add up to what I budgeted for this. But you should go eat and prepare for a very long afternoon."

Laine makes a face. "How long does it take to build up an immunity to boredom?"

"I'm beginning to think that's impossible," Natalia sighs, "Although you'll build up a certain tolerance quickly... or you'll snap."

"Not comforting," I respond, "You of all people should know what can happen when I have an episode."

Natalia nods grimly. "You'd best get going."

Nikolai, who has been frowning, waits until we get inside to query, "An episode?"

"Long story," Andrina replies quickly, "I'll see if I can explain over lunch."

Her husband nods.

"Nerita," Andrina turns to me, "You don't know when your wedding will be, do you?"

"Probably sometime after his majesty acknowledges the engagement," I grimace, "Whenever that will be."

"It's just we have to leave this afternoon," Andrina sighs, "Something 's come up and Lady Jane needs us there quickly."

I nod. "You two take care then."

10-10-48-06-04SM

Court yesterday afternoon was as tedious as we feared, but the rest of the day was uneventful. Or at least Laine and I really didn't see or hear from anyone. But Tory is supposed to arrive today, so things should get a whole lot more entertaining.

The first sign of things to come is when Derian turns up just before one instead of Carl.

"That was fast." There's no concealing my surprise on seeing him.

"Tory sent Ford and Nikki to get me," Derian looks bemused, "I am finished that job though. But we should go."

The Prince guides us through the palace by way of little used corridors and hidden doors. We enter the throne room from an unguarded side door, which Derian has to unlock.

"Go to your places," He instructs quietly, "Father doesn't know I'm home yet."

Yesterday Laine, Sefu, and I had been up at the front and no one contests our right to the same spot today. Meanwhile Derian seems to have disappeared and there's no sign of anything else unusual.

The first three quarters of an hour are pretty much the same as yesterday. I kinda envy Sefu; nobody cares if he naps through this bullshit.

Then one of the main doors opens just enough for a guard to slip inside.

Monarch Reginald frowns sternly at the interruption, "What is the meaning of this?"

It takes a moment for the guard to manage any words. He's terrified of something and I don't think it's the Monarch.

"A... a woman... two women... y-your majesty," The guard stammers, "And a man... a-and a winter tiger."

"And what do these people want?" Monarch Reginald demands.

"They... she... the woman said to... to announce them..." He swallows hard," She... she's not human... and the tiger..."

The Monarch scowls, just for a second. "Show them in."

At my feet, Sefu lifts his head and looks around.

The guard slips back through the open door. A moment later, both doors are thrown open and the aforementioned group enters.

The guard was right: Tory Genstang isn't strictly human and it shows. Physically she isn't actually all that big; well below average height and slender. She's got long hair like spun gold, absolutely white skin, and mismatched cat eyes... one green, the other blue. Her extrasensory abilities include extreme telekinesis, which's probably what's causing her loose hair to fly out around her. And, as usual, she's dressed in jeans and a t-shirt with her feet bare. But then, she's always barefoot. And right now she's as pissed off as I've ever seen her.

Slightly behind and to Tory's left are Angelita and Xylia. At least Angelita is properly dressed for a court appearance, with her hair braided back.

However, on Tory's right, walking even with Angelita, is Ford Straisen and he looks almost exactly like I saw him last. Ford may not be the biggest guy I've ever met... just a close second. He's tall and solid and the dark glasses necessary to protect his light sensitive eyes don't make him any less imposing.

His long curly hair is streaked black and white and tied back in a ponytail. Jeans, t-shirts, and old runners... usually in black... are nothing new on him. It's the bejewelled sword strapped across his back that I haven't seen before. It's also really odd for two reasons: Ford never, ever fights with anything beyond his bare fists and this sword looks vaguely familiar somehow.

The four of them stop a respectful distance from the throne, but Angelita's curtsy is the only other sign of respect from any of them.

Monarch Reginald looks irritated, which doesn't usually bode well for the target of said irritation. "And what is the meaning of this?"

Tory doesn't respond. Instead Ford approaches the throne. Drawing the sword, which I now recognize as the Sword of the First, he holds it horizontally across his body, the blade between him and the Monarch. Monarch Reginald swallows nervously as he rests one hand on the naked blade. Then his eyes close.

When his eyes open several minutes later, the Monarch looks thoroughly shaken. Still, he recovers quickly and straightens in his seat.

"As Terantal's Canon binds all those of Imperial descent, We acknowledge you the chosen wielder of the Sword of the First," His voice carries all through the throne room, "And We submit to its judgement."

Ford nods and steps to one side, but the sword remains in his hand.

Tory takes a small item from her pocket and walks right over to me, Laine, and Sefu.

"Terantal's Canon requires that this be returned to you." Tory holds out a very old locket on a broken chain to me. I accept it and immediately recognize the coat of arms of the Chassaven family of Estorika.

I take a deep breath that does nothing to help calm my nerves. "I thank you."

"Might We see that?" The Monarch's face is impossible to read.

I'm far from trusting Monarch Reginald right now, but I doubt he'd try anything in the presence of the sword and its wielder. Sefu accompanies me as I approach the throne and hold out the locket. The Monarch carefully examines it, looking first at the coat of arms, then the authenticating mark. Then he opens it to check the ancient pictures inside. Finally he returns it to me.

"We recognize your noble heritage and confirm on you the title of lady."

I curtsy. "Thank you, your majesty."

As Sefu and I return to our places, Tory takes a cloth wrapped package from her pocket and turns to Laine.

"Your father asked me to deliver this." Tory holds the package out. Laine accepts it warily. Her father has always been one of the biggest unknowns in her life.

Every eye is on her as Laine unfolds the cloth to reveal two very old lockets. I suck in a sudden sharp breath. They're birthright lockets and, if I'm right, both from the upper nobility.

"May we see?" Monarch Reginald requests.

Tory returns to her place in front of Angelita as Laine approaches the throne. She holds out the lockets and the Monarch takes them to examine them. Surprise and amazement war in his face as he looks from the old jewelry to Laine and back. Then he goes to open one of them. Blinding light fills the whole throne room and when it clears, a man is standing beside Laine.

The stranger is perhaps fifty, with iron grey hair and extremely outdated clothes. In the stunned silence following his appearance, he blinks in confusion as he looks around. Then he recovers himself and bows properly to Monarch Reginald.

"Your majesty. Lige Malin, Duke of Estorika, at your service."

Now this isn't entertaining; it's just plain bizarre. Not that the bizarre is anything unusual when dealing with Tory.

The Monarch is the next to recover. His head bows in acknowledgement of Duke Malin's rank.

"Your grace is a man out of his time. We are Reginald, Monarch of Norsecount. We would presume you have an explanation of yourself."

Duke Malin's eyes go to the lockets. "I requested that Tory deliver those to my daughter," He turns to study Laine, "The rest is a long story indeed."

"Humour Us, if you please."

I think everyone wants to hear this one. Duke Lige Malin, most noted for stealing the Sword of the First from the Imperial Mount, was presumed dead long before Natalia was born. Poor Laine is completely bewildered though... not that anyone could blame her.

Duke Malin takes a deep breath and sets down the bag he is carrying. "The theft of the Sword of the First was the rash action of an impatient young man. An action I have regretted a thousand times over. The sword has powers far beyond my comprehension and immediately took possession of me and my home in an effort to protect itself. To the best of my understanding, it created a time anomaly around the manor and grounds. However, I have not been completely unaware of events beyond my walls. The first time the sword allowed a connection to the normal flow of time was to admit a young noble woman inside. It was she who told me Monarch Stephano of Estorika had been killed and the nobility were fleeing to the protection of Star Stone Seat. However, once inside my walls, she was as much a prisoner as myself."

"And she was?" Monarch Reginald enquires when Duke Malin pauses.

"High Lady Rose Nowellyr."

The Monarch nods to himself.

Duke Malin continues, "How long it was before we sought each other's company as an alternative to solitude, I don't know. Nor do I know exactly when in the normal flow of time our daughter was born. I only know she was named Laine Rose Malin and she was perhaps as a three year old when the sword allowed her and her mother to leave. I have been alone from that time until the arrival of Tory and her companions. My home is now yet another ruin in a war blasted country and I am on your majesty's mercy."

"Tory?" Laine looks and sounds so completely like the lost child that it's painful to watch. It's hard to say how much of the Duke's story she really grasps.

"You were born April tenth in the two hundred and eighth year of the civil war," Tory speaks slowly, "You an' your mother left about a hundred years later an' she died within two years of leavin'. But the power you absorbed from the Sword of the First in the time you were exposed to it has been pullin' you in an' out of time since then. In terms of years spent in normal time you were about thirteen when Nerita's aunt took you in."

Making Laine twenty-six now. At least for any practical intents and purposes.

Duke Malin nods to himself. "Do you remember your mother at all?"

"Only a little." Laine replies softly.

"You look as she did." Then he turns to the Monarch, "What of those who reached Star Stone Seat?"

"We had best refer you to a more knowledgeable source." Monarch Reginald indicates Angelita.

Duke Malin turns to look at her, "And you are?"

"Angelita Mendus Straisen. Formerly Princess Angelita Regina of Estorika, daughter of Princess Dorina Regina and High Lord Alick Mendus. I'm also now the sole survivor of Star Stone Seat."

Duke Malin is silent for a moment. "Estorika is no more?"

"It's now the Republic of Arawn under President Gayre," Angelita confirms, "As for Star Stone Seat, we were betrayed from within when I was a child. However, that matter has been taken care of."

"You're certain no others survived?" Monarch Reginald enquires.

"I spent nearly three years searchin'," Pain flickers over Angelita's face, "Changin' my name constantly an' nearly bein' caught a dozen times over. I tracked down everyone the slavers had taken only to find them all killed."

A low murmur ripples across the room at this news. I swallow hard. I know now that I've never given her enough credit.

"I see I am a relic," Duke Malin turns to face the Monarch, "And more on your majesty's mercy than I thought."

"Your crimes have been more than adequately punished," Monarch Reginald announces for the whole court to hear, "Your grace will have a home in Our country for as long as you care to stay. As for your daughter," He holds the lockets out to Laine, "We recognize your noble heritage and confirm on you your mother's title of high lady."

"Thank you, your majesty." Laine curtsies before taking the jewelry.

"Your majesty has my gratitude as well." Duke Malin bows. He picks up his bag before following Laine over to stand with me and Sefu.

Monarch Reginald addresses Tory, "What else would you have of me?"

Tory doesn't respond. Instead Angelita steps forward. The Monarch's expression turns stern, but she doesn't give him a chance to speak.

"There may be neither throne nor Estorika, but I am still Imperial Bloodline, your majesty," Angelita's voice carries clearly, "Bound by Terantal's Canon as surely as you."

"We are aware of that," There's just a touch of frustration in the Monarch's voice," But for the moment We can only confirm on you the title held by your father, the late High Lord Alick Mendus. Anything more must wait until a later date."

Angelita curtsies. "Thank you, your majesty." Then she steps back behind Tory.

Now Tory steps forward. Her hair is really blowing and I'm not entirely sure her bare feet are touching the floor. I'm just glad I'm not the target of her current mood.

"I need to speak with you. But first you've got an announcement to make."

Monarch Reginald obviously doesn't like this. Just for a moment I'm afraid he might try to have her thrown out. He evidently thinks better of it though.

"What you ask of Us would require the presence of all those concerned."

"All concerned are present." Derian's voice comes from directly behind me. I hadn't even sensed him there. Now he steps up beside me and takes my hand.

Natalia wasn't kidding when she described the Monarch as being livid. It's now plain for the whole court to see. But he's caught between Tory and the Sword of the First with no graceful escape.

After several slow, deep breaths to compose himself, Monarch Reginald stands. "We confirm, before this court, the engagement of Our son, Crown Prince Derian, to Lady Nerita Chassaven."

There's a collective sigh of relief as Ford finally sheaths the sword.

"We declare this audience adjourned for today." The Monarch finishes. He starts for a small door in the corner. Tory and Ford accompany him, leaving Angelita and Xylia standing in the middle of the throne room.

It takes a minute or two for everyone to recover enough to grasp that the court is dismissed. Then a few drift over to congratulate me and Derian, but most just leave in small murmuring groups. It doesn't take long before only five of us and two tigers remain in the throne room.

"What more could they possibly want from him?" Laine absently toys with the lockets in her hands.

"Nothing less than his abdication," Derian replies grimly, "It's simply a matter of how and when."

Angelita grimaces. "He'd have more room to negotiate if he didn't keep tryin' to do things the hard way."

"I seem to have missed a great deal." Duke Malin looks understandably bewildered.

"Today's date, your grace, is ten, ten, forty-eight, oh six, oh four, since migration," Derian chuckles gently, "It will take some time to catch you up."

"Thank you, your highness." The Duke bows his head appreciatively.

Laine frowns thoughtfully. "Mother should've been able to tell you some things."

"Up to the beginning of the war," Duke Malin confirms, "But how long was the war and how long has it been since?"

"You're missing more or less five hundred years," Angelita replies, "Although I wouldn't say you missed out on much."

Derian raises a sceptical eyebrow in her direction and she scowls.

"At this point I think I'm entitled to a certain degree of cynicism."

"Only when it's not what you've brought on yourself." I respond.

Now Laine scowls. "Don't you two fucking start!"

Duke Malin looks shocked at her language, but before anyone can comment, Tory and Ford enter the room.

They come over to join us and Tory turns to me, "All your girls are married now?"

I nod. "Eight anyway."

Tory chuckles. "Nine, dependin' how you count it. We were at John Simeon's when the live broadcast came through."

"Mellie and Ross?" I query.

Tory nods. "You'll hear more of that before the end of this month. Anyway, it may take him some time to sort out the shit I just hit him with."

"How long are you giving him?" Derian enquires.

"A few days."

"Derian."

We all look over to see Monarch Reginald in the small doorway.

"I believe you owe me a report?"

Derian grimaces. "Yes, I do." Turning to me, he says, "I'll be by to see you later."

I nod and he kisses my forehead before leaving.

Tory addresses me again, "How've you been doin'?"

"I've been okay... mostly."

She nods. "Then we're gonna head back to the hotel. I'd like some rest while he's thinkin'."

Not having heard otherwise, Laine and I take Duke Malin to our suite in the old east wing. Sefu comes along quietly, not seeming to mind the older man's presence.

In our sitting room, Duke Malin drops into the nearest chair and sets his bag at his feet. "You must forgive me," He sighs, "I've grown unaccustomed to life at court and I'm no longer so young as I once was."

"We haven't been living at court all that long ourselves," Laine shrugs it off, "Only since the end of last month, actually."

"Laine," I wait for her to look at me, "I'm gonna take Sefu out."

She nods. I scoop up a ball on my way out of the room and Sefu follows me.

Laine and I'd taken Sefu out this morning, so he doesn't really need the exercise. Bringing a ball along has become a habit. I want a walk and I know there are a few trails I'm allowed to take Sefu on. Not that I'm counting on anything really helping to clear my head right now. I've just been hit with way more than I can process all at once.

We wander through the gardens, which, thankfully, are mostly empty of people. I'd originally thought to find a trail, but now I realize I've never seen the palace gardens by daylight. Even though it's well into October, there're still quite a few flowers... mostly reds and golds... and the bushes are brightly coloured as well. It all looks pretty amazing, but then I grew up in a place without any vegetation. I can't even begin to imagine what the gardens here will look like in the spring and summer.

Then Sefu butts his head against my hand. As I rub his head I become aware of a familiar voice.

"Lady Nerita!"

I turn to see Princess Nerissa seated on a nearby bench. Close to her is an older man kneeling down to work in one of the flowerbeds. While I had been hoping not to encounter anyone who might want me to stop and talk, especially Princess Nerissa, I would prefer not to offend her.

"I'm sorry, your highness." I change directions to join the girl. Sefu immediately goes on ahead of me and rests his chin on her knee. He's really taken to Princess Nerissa for some reason.

"That's a mighty big pussycat my lady has," The man rocks back on his heels, "Though I've never seen an animal companion so well trained."

Princess Nerissa laughs. "Sefu 's just like a big, furry person."

I chuckle. "More of a child. He's only half grown."

The man nods and returns to his task.

Princess Nerissa looks up at me. "They're saying there was another tiger at court today... and that some really strange things happened..."

"That was Xylia." I sit on the large rock beside the bench.

"Sefu's sister, right?" Princess Nerissa continues to rub his head and neck, "You never told me who the lady with her was. The lady must've been at court too."

I nod. "She's Angelita Mendus Straisen. And today his majesty confirmed her title of high lady."

"That's nothing strange," Princess Nerissa frowns abruptly, "You were there?"

"Laine and I've been ordered to attend certain events," I explain, "That was arranged nearly a week ago, though I'm not entirely sure why."

"You don't really have titles or anything, do you?"

"Actually," I hold up my locket by the broken chain, "This was returned to me today."

Princess Nerissa studies the coat of arms quizzically. "I'm supposed to know heraldry, but..."

"The Chassaven family of Estorika was a junior line of the Chassaven family here. Has your highness been taught to read the symbols or simply to recognize full coats of arms?"

The girl squirms uncomfortably. "It means you're middle nobility, right?"

"So his majesty has confirmed." I make a mental note of the evasion.

The girl nods to herself. "What about Lady Laine?"

"Her father showed up today and she was given the birthright lockets for his family and her mother's... that's where things got downright bizarre."

"So who is Laine then?" Princess Nerissa frowns curiously, "Only nobility have birthright lockets."

"High Lady Laine Rose Malin." Saying it out loud sounds weird. Not only is she upper nobility, I believe both the Malin and Nowellyr families were Imperial Bloodline. Considering what I know of Laine and what she's done, that's harder to wrap my head around than Angelita being a princess.

"Malin?" The man rocks back on his heels again, "I thought that family ended with that crazy thieving duke."

"Apparently not." I respond wryly.

Princess Nerissa continues to frown. "Who were her parents? I know Lady Laine said some of her life's a bit weird."

"I used the word bizarre for a reason. Laine's parents are Lige Malin and Rose Nowellyr."

The man shakes his head in disbelief and returns to work. Can't say I blame him.

Princess Nerissa also looks sceptical. "What else happened?"

"The Sword of the First 's found a new wielder," I reply, "His majesty confirmed that as well. Other than the guy calls himself Ford, I don't really know much about it though."

"Oh," Princess Nerissa looks a little disappointed, "They're also saying there was someone else... another lady."

"Tory 's no lady. And she doesn't care to be. She's barely even human. She is extremely powerful though... even more so than Natalia Burren."

Princess Nerissa shivers. "Lady Natalia 's nice enough... except when she's mad. Then she's really scary."

I sigh. "Tory 's always scary, whether she's trying to be nice or not. Today she was downright pissed off."

"Do you know why?"

"Not well enough to explain properly. I just know there's a lot going on behind the scenes right now."

"That's hardly anything new," Princess Nerissa makes a face, "But only Derian and some of the servants really talk to me." Just for a second she looks as though she might cry. Then the girl composes herself. "Did his majesty actually announce your engagement properly?"

"Under duress, but yes, he did."

"There you are."

All four of us look over to see Derian approaching.

"When did you get back?" Princess Nerissa demands, looking put out.

"Just in time for court this afternoon," Derian replies sternly, "Now I know you're skipping out on lessons yet again. Back to the schoolroom with you and you don't want me to catch you where you're not supposed to be again."

Princess Nerissa gets up, clearly not happy, and disappears in the direction of the palace. Derian sighs tiredly, then extends a hand, which I accept. Once I'm on my feet, the two of us begin walking. Sefu follows somewhat dejectedly.

"I wish Father would just admit Nerissa could actually be his daughter," Derian laces his fingers through mine, "Although he ought to deal decisively with all six of them."

"Is there anyone he would take advice from?"

"Not unasked. And he would only ask if they become a problem too big to overlook."

"And if you had your way?"

"None of them would live at court like they do. Nerissa would go to Ouestlun to foster with Lady Irina, at least until she's sixteen. The other five I know less of."

I nod to myself. "What does his majesty think of Tory?"

Derian laughs. "I think he just gained a new appreciation of Natalia. He didn't say much about it though."

"Lady Nerita."

Derian and I turn to see Carl approaching.

"Yes?"

"Lady Laine wishes to see you."

"Thank you."

Carl bows and turns away.

"Mind if I accompany you?" Derian queries.

"If you want."

Inside the old east wing we find Laine and Duke Malin seated more or less where I'd left them. I'm not sure Laine is entirely happy to see Derian, but neither of them objects to his presence.

I cross the room to sit beside Laine. "What's up?"

"It's not the five hundred years of war that's hard to explain," Laine grimaces, "It's the chaos since. Anyway, Father has some questions for you."

Obviously she and Duke Malin are getting along pretty well. It's definitely gonna take getting used to.

I address the man sitting calmly opposite us, "I don't promise answers."

Derian raises a surprised eyebrow as he seats himself, but Duke Malin chuckles.

"So Laine told me. Nerita Chassaven, is it not?" The Duke waits for me to nod, "'Tis curious. As a boy I knew a Nerita Chassaven and you look very much as she did. However... You were raised by an aunt, correct?"

I nod. "Father's sister. She'd lived with us as long as I can remember, even before my parents' deaths."

"So you remember your parents?"

"Bits and pieces. I was six when they died."

"Do you remember how they died?" Duke Malin frowns.

I shake my head. "I only know it wasn't what my aunt always claimed."

Laine frowns warily. "She told me it was an intruder..."

"And you know better than to believe anything she said," I can't keep the edge from my voice, "I'd've heard something from one of the neighbours sooner or later if that'd been true, but no one ever seemed to know anything more than I do."

Duke Malin's frown deepens at that. "What do you remember?"

A. A. Cheshire

"Mostly just neighbours helping to patch the house back together after," I absently rub Sefu's head, "My aunt hadn't even been home, only me and my parents."

"No one could piece together what happened?" Derian looks and sounds concerned.

"I don't think anyone tried."

"So your aunt raised you after that," Duke Malin nods to himself, "Did she lie often?"

"Compulsively and everyone around knew."

"Had you no family on your mother's side?"

"Mother's sister, who died even before my parents, and her daughter."

"You have a cousin?" Laine looks both surprised and annoyed. Probably because she didn't know.

"Yeah. Lillian."

Laine considers that for a minute. Then she slowly shakes her head. "That explains a few things."

"She's here in Norsecount?" Derian queries.

I nod. "Recently married to Edmund Bowerstone."

"Is your paternal aunt alive?" Duke Malin enquires.

"She was killed just before I turned sixteen."

"But it was she who found Laine and took her in?"

I nod. "I was nine at the time."

The Duke turns to Derian, "Your highness, is there not still a Chassaven family in Norsecount?"

Derian sighs. "There is, although there are problems..."

"Their problems don't much matter to me," I shrug it off, "High Lord Chassaven refused to acknowledge me when we first came, so, as I understand it, for the moment I'm my own head of family."

Duke Malin sighs and shakes his head. "Perhaps I date myself in saying such, but I hardly find that acceptable."

"Foster family's still family," Laine ignores the look I shoot her, "That hasn't changed... even in Arawn."

"'Tis good to know." Duke Malin smiles.

"Laine, will you get over it already?" I can't help scowling.

"No."

I look for a way to change the subject. Duke Malin's untouched bag catches my eye.

"If you don't mind me asking," I address him, "What did you bring that's so heavy?"

He looks a little surprised for a moment, then chuckles. "'Tis a bit of a story, that. You see I met Tory, Ford, and another friend of theirs very early this morning. Yet even after the sword was claimed and its power over my home broken, I could not leave the manor grounds of my own volition. Still, before they left, Tory told me to prepare for my own departure. She gave me no idea of when or how I would be able to leave nor where or when I would be going..."

"Sounds like Tory." Laine rolls her eyes.

"And recalling how Lady Rose ridiculed my wardrobe as being old fashioned," Duke Malin continues, "I thought perhaps items of precious metal and gemstones would serve better than clothing. I have here as many such items as I could carry, though I thought you," He addresses Laine, "Might like some of them for yourself. Especially seeing as Lady Rose left such of her jewelry as she had with her in my care."

"I think I'd have to see it." Laine responds.

He nods. "As you wish."

What he has isn't really a proper bag. It's actually a large sheet tied together at the corners to form a bundle. Once Duke Malin gets the knots undone, we spread the whole thing out on the floor. Sefu, who has been napping at my feet, opens one tawny eye long enough to establish there's nothing edible and goes back to sleep.

"Shit..." Laine stares disbelievingly at the pile of items in the middle of the sheet. I'm too amazed to speak and even Derian is pretty stunned.

It's no wonder the bundle was so heavy. Duke Malin must've stripped his home of small, valuable, unbreakable items. Most of it's in bags and velvet cases, but I can still see quite a bit of gold, silver, and gemstones. He and Laine could live pretty well for a long time by selling just a fraction of what's here.

There's a knock on the door. I get up to answer it, expecting to see Carl or Mattie. I was definitely not expecting to see Natalia and Monarch Reginald.

"Is this a bad time?" Natalia studies me carefully.

"No..." I manage to recover a little, "No."

"We're actually looking for Lige Malin," Natalia explains, "We thought he might be with you and Laine."

I nod. "You might as well come in." I step aside so they can do that.

Laine and I aren't the neatest people out there, but we're not really messy either. Still, our suite looks very much like we've been living in it. And then there's the pile of treasure in the middle of the floor. Neither Natalia nor the Monarch attempt to conceal their bemused expressions as they glance around. Laine is doing her best not to laugh, but Duke Malin quickly gets to his feet, looking startled. I close the door as he bows.

Natalia studies the items on the floor, then turns to Monarch Reginald, "This answers one of your questions."

"So I see." The Monarch responds wryly, "Your grace, may I introduce Pleasure Society member Natalia Burren."

Natalia chuckles at the Duke's expression. "Lige Malin, is it not?"

"It is, my lady." Duke Malin bows again.

"Perhaps," Natalia addresses both me, "We should begin by seeing what we have here."

Monarch Reginald nods in agreement.

"As you wish," Duke Malin returns to sorting the items on the sheet, "I actually brought all that Lady Rose left in my care." He passes Laine two velvet cases and a large flat bag from underneath everything else.

Both cases are stuffed with jewelry, all gold and set with diamonds, rubies or jet. I can't help noticing all of it looks a lot like any jewelry Laine already owns.

"Looks like you and your mother share your taste in jewelry." I observe.

Laine shrugs and sets the cases aside.

The bag contains two neatly folded gowns. Both are simple, but made with rich fabric and expensive trim. One was once white, the other is a deep rich red. And I suspect both would fit Laine pretty well.

"Interesting," Natalia's voice is soft as she shakes her head, "What a woman fleeing for her life would pack."

"Oh?" Laine queries curiously.

"The red one was Rose's favourite court gown," Natalia explains, "I remember her wearing it to several important events. The other was her mother's wedding gown."

Duke Malin nods to himself. "I thought it odd Lady Rose had brought a dress she herself never wore."

"I'll never wear it either," Laine sets the yellowed gown aside. Then she holds up the other to study it. "I like this one though. It's not even completely unfashionable."

Natalia chuckles. "The more simple designs never completely go out of style. Believe me."

"These," Duke Malin picks up a heavy cloth bag, "I thought would be valuable simply for the gold." He pours a pile of coins onto the sheet.

Natalia picks one up to study it and her eyes widen in surprise. She passes the coin to the Monarch before speaking.

"Even I thought these all gone," She's shaking her head in amazement, "Estorika replaced its gold currency with paper in my grandfather's time. All the gold was collected up, despite an outcry from coin collectors and museums, and melted down for other uses."

"I imagine," Monarch Reginald returns the coin to the pile, "There are any number of collectors still who would pay handsomely for just one."

Duke Malin nods to himself. "This, I have no intention of selling." He uses a small key to open a small chest. Inside is a complete set of silverware, although in need of polishing.

"It's a shame the china and crystal are gone." Natalia observes softly.

"Even the sword cannot thwart time forever." Duke Malin closes the chest again, "These," He passes three velvet cases to Laine, "Belonged to my mother and grandmother."

Again, the cases are stuffed with jewelry, but this time there's a lot more variety. Silver, copper, all colours of gold... even the metal known as faerie silver... and every kind of precious and semi-precious stone. Including some I've never seen before. Natalia eyes several of the pieces curiously.

"Just how long has the Malin family had dealings with the Sedyr?"

"I do not know, my lady. Though I do know we sheltered both watchers and hunters many times over the centuries."

"And yet you still went after the Sword of the First?" Natalia raises an eyebrow in disbelief.

"A little knowledge can be a very dangerous thing indeed," Duke Malin responds, "Especially when coupled with the impatience and arrogance of youth." He sighs tiredly, looking absolutely ancient for a brief moment. Then he empties another bag onto the sheet. This one contains the pieces and board for the game Castles.

"My family's custom made set," Duke Malin explains, "If Laine doesn't want it, I'd just as happily be rid of it."

"May I take a look?" Monarch Reginald enquires.

"As your majesty wishes," Duke Malin replies, "The rest I brought with the intention of selling," He turns to Laine, "Unless something catches your fancy."

Laine and the Monarch spend several minutes sorting through the miscellaneous items left on the sheet. In the end, Laine sticks with the jewelry and dresses. Monarch Reginald, however, looks interested in several items.

"Negotiate later," Natalia advises, "You'll have plenty of time. We have more immediate business to discuss."

"Of course." Monarch Reginald takes the seat beside his son. He glances around the room before speaking again, "Whose suite is this?"

"Ours." Laine and I respond, not quite in unison. I quickly add, "Simply because of long engrained habit."

"I see," Monarch Reginald nods slowly, a hint of a frown appearing, "I don't know if you were told, but these are generally guest quarters, which I believe will be needed for guests before too long. Now you intend to remain here a while, am I correct?"

"I see little other choice at the moment." Duke Malin replies.

"I don't know if your grace is aware of this, but the upper levels of the old south tower were designated quarters for a younger son of the Malin family who moved to Norsecount. That line died out several generations ago and the rooms have been vacant since. However, they are the best I can offer your grace and your daughter."

"They will be fine, your majesty," Duke Malin bows his head, "Though I must insist on Lady Nerita remaining with us until her marriage."

Monarch Reginald's expression suggests he'd prefer that I stay with Laine and her father permanently. I wish I could get away with moving into Derian's rooms.

"As your grace wishes. Servants are cleaning those rooms as we speak," Turning to me and Laine, Monarch Reginald enquires, "What have you been assigned for servants?"

"A page and a ladies maid, your majesty." I reply.

"Actually, Nerita," Natalia interrupts, "It's been suggested that you should have a proper attendant. I'm thinking perhaps a graduate of Experiment Redemption, although she would need some extra training."

"You would place a Society trained woman in my court?" The Monarch frowns angrily.

"Hardly," Natalia's face turns hard, "On graduation she would come here for whatever training she would require. However, the young woman I have in mind doesn't graduate for two or three months yet."

"Then the matter can be discussed further later," Monarch Reginald returns his attention to Duke Malin, "Will your grace require a valet?"

"Likely," The Duke grimaces slightly, "Though I must admit to being long unaccustomed to dealing with servants."

Natalia chuckles softly. "I think your grace will find you have that in common with your daughter."

Laine rolls her eyes, but keeps quiet.

Monarch Reginald moves on, "Your grace has proved yourself well off, but until these items can be converted to ready funds, I imagine there are a few things you will require."

"Yes, your majesty, as what you see before you is all I own."

"Before you get into that," Natalia interrupts, "There is one more issue... an extremely important one."

"Yes, of course." The Monarch turns grim.

Natalia addresses me, "Nerita, you should recall the danger Sefu sensed at the ball over a week ago..."

I frown in confusion until I remember the incident. So much has happened since then I'd completely forgotten about it.

"What happened that night?" I query, "I know nothing 's bothered Sefu like that since."

"That I'm glad to hear," There's no change in Natalia's expression, "Unfortunately, the danger is not yet passed. It seems a certain anti-monarchy minority isn't content with the establishment of the Republic of Arawn."

Laine and I groan. Sefu raises his head, no longer at all sleepy.

"What's their problem now?" Laine scowls blackly.

"They appear to have a two fold agenda," Natalia replies grimly, "The first is the elimination of all known descendants of the Estorika nobility. President Gayre is, of course condemning such action and punishing those his people catch..."

"But they're somehow getting out of Arawn," I guess, "What else 're they after?"

"They would see this whole continent become like Arawn."

"Over my dead rotting body." Derian scowls dangerously.

Laine queries, "Just how many of these fanatics are there?"

"Any would be too many," I respond, "It only takes one to gather a following."

"And I don't care to know how much of a following they could gather," Monarch Reginald adds, "I've seen the devastation that is Arawn. I won't see such in my home."

"Cemen cannot handle another war," Natalia informs us, "The planet itself would destabilize."

"So what can be done about these nutcases?" I shift as Sefu rests his head on my knee.

"Most are very obviously just that," Natalia replies, "Easy to identify and easier to justify locking away. Channa is assisting General Verdas in identifying and tracking down the leaders and the more dangerous," She pauses, just for a second, "Though they will, I believe, have Ford's help."

Monarch Reginald looks confused. "Who?"

"Sorry," Natalia winces, "You met him today, although I gather he didn't introduce himself. Ford is quite literally Tory's other half... I've never seen so complete a bond. He's also the last descendant of Nicola Cenquasien and Jame Lun's younger child."

The Monarch nods grimly. "Of all Terantal's descendants, who will the sword act to protect?"

"The monarchs of Midkingsen and Ouestlun and their heirs, Angelita... although she is protected by Tory herself," Natalia turns to Derian, "Your highness and Princess Nerissa, and, of course," Now Natalia turns to Laine, "You, who have carried a portion of its power from birth."

"Not exactly," Laine scowls, "More like I'm still linked to it."

That would explain a lot about Laine. Still, I find it more interesting that Monarch Reginald isn't under the sword's protection. He doesn't seem surprised though.

"So the anti-monarchy fanatics are being dealt with," I return to the important subject, "At least inside Arawn. We just have to keep alert."

"Essentially," Natalia nods, "Although I'm sure Sefu will give you ample warning."

Duke Malin abruptly looks curious. "Lady Nerita, are you the only one Sefu would protect?"

"Depends a little on the situation," I respond, "He might protect Laine and possibly Princess Nerissa, although I can't begin to explain his attachment to her."

Monarch Reginald frowns. "Several reports claim he's been spotted running at her."

I grimace. "He's still a cub, your majesty, and over-enthusiastic in his greetings. He would not intentionally harm her highness. However, he has come close to knocking me off my feet and I doubt Princess Nerissa is as strong as I am."

"Not many women are." Laine observes dryly.

Natalia glances at the clock. "I believe we have covered everything. If you would please excuse me, I'm required elsewhere."

Both the Monarch and the Duke nod politely as Natalia leaves.

Once she's gone, Derian addresses his father, "Did you intend to ask about the substance mentioned in that proposal?"

"Oh, yes," Monarch Reginald turns to me and Laine, "How much can you tell me about protein paste? I believe it comes from Arawn."

Laine glances at me, "I think it was Tory who summed that one up in three words."

"Yeah, but if it's the description I think it is, it's not repeatable in polite company," I sigh, "Protein paste has been the dietary staple in Arawn for a long time now. It supposedly contains everything the body needs to maintain good health. It also, although fewer people know this, contains vaccines for a long list of ailments, some in live form."

Derian frowns. "That sounds dangerous."

"It probably is," I respond, "Production 's completely unregulated and people just don't care to speculate on it."

"Besides which," Laine adds, "Colour, consistency, and flavour leave a lot to be desired."

"I think I'll refer this one to the food and drug authority," Monarch Reginald decides, "I don't doubt they'll ban import."

Derian nods.

The Monarch turns to Duke Malin, "I believe your grace and I have business yet to discuss..."

11-10-48-06-04SM

What with one thing and another, only partly the negotiations between Monarch Reginald and Duke Malin, we don't actually get to see our new quarters until after breakfast today. I have to admit they're spacious though. We have the top three levels of the old south tower, which means we've got a spectacular view of both the rest of the palace and Monarch's Town. The first level is all common areas: Sitting room, private dining room, and a sort of recreation area... mostly intended for quiet activities, I suspect. The second level is two suites, one of which Duke Malin claims for himself. The third level is all one extremely spacious suite which Sefu and I'll be sharing with Laine for now. Four large windows, one in each room of the suite, allow us to see everything for kilometres.

Once we've decided whose stuff is going where, the next step is actually moving in. And that's where I run into trouble.

When we left South City for Experiment Redemption, none of us owned much more than would fit into a large backpack. While we were with Experiment Redemption, we were given a lot of stuff, but when it came time to leave, we were told to only pack what we'd need for the trip to Monarch's Town. So Laine and I've never attempted to pack up and move as much stuff as we currently own. It ends up being far more work than we expected and more chaotic than I can handle.

"Nerita?"

I look up to see Laine studying me worriedly.

"Fuck!" Fear flickers through her eyes, "You better find somewhere else to be."

"Like where?" I scowl.

"Upstairs," Laine is clearly thinking fast, "No one should really need to be in and out of our bedroom and you can lock the door."

"Laine?" The Duke's voice comes from the stairs, "Nerita?"

"Go!" Laine orders, "I'll explain."

As I start up to our new bedroom my field of vision begins to narrow. I hadn't realized I was this close to a full blown episode. Fortunately I don't encounter anyone on the way up. However, I stop short in the bedroom doorway.

"Tory...?" I can't help the edge of panic that enters my voice.

She gets up from the corner of the bed. "You can't hurt me."

I should've known that. I'm just not thinking very well. Even if I could move, which I can't, she's faster and possibly stronger than I am.

"How'd you...?"

"You think I haven't been watchin' for this?" Tory's expression is hard to read, "Unless you really want to continue like this."

"Can you actually help?"

"Yeah..."

"But?"

"What I can do could cause you to relive all or part of your life... includin' things you don't remember right now. I'd be right there with you an' there's a chance what we see could be projected."

"How far?"

"I can limit the effect to this room."

I don't really like the idea of my memories being projected for just anyone to see. Still, Tory isn't known for messing with people and Laine will keep anyone who might come up out of the bedroom. Tory can probably see as much of my past as she wants anyway.

"You're sure it would work?"

Tory nods.

"Do I really have a choice?"

She shrugs evasively. "Do you want this to end or not?"

"Yeah."

"Come sit."

I can move again, at least enough to walk to the bed and sit on it. As I do that, the door closes behind me. Tory seats herself facing me.

"Once this's over, I'm gonna put you to sleep an' tell Laine not to let anyone wake you."

I nod.

Tory reaches out to rest her finger tips lightly on my temples and her eyes close. My eyes close as well. I can feel her in my head and it's not really comfortable. But she obviously knows exactly what she's doing. Then the memories start.

Some are things I remember fairly clearly, whether I want to or not. Others are new, both good and bad. But it's all like I'm really there, living everything over again... watching my parents die all over again. It's no wonder I couldn't remember. Even now, after everything I've seen since then, it's horrific and almost more than my mind can handle. After that, the rest of my memories seem remote and out of focus.

"Nerita."

I open my eyes, only to find my surroundings distorted.

"I'm gonna put you out," Tory sounds worried, "You should sleep longer than normal an' I'm gonna keep an eye on you for a few days."

"'Kay." Somehow sleep sounds like a really good idea.

12-10-48-06-04SM

"Nerita?"

I don't really want to open my eyes, but Laine sounds concerned. Once she finally comes into focus, I can see that she's wrapped in her dressing gown, seated on the edge of the bed. I'm badly disoriented though and the room is only vaguely familiar.

"Ugh... where...?"

"Our rooms, remember?" Laine still sounds concerned, "You slept almost twenty-four hours..."

"But?"

"Seems like you've had one nightmare after another all night. Tory knows, but she wants to see how you deal today."

"Yeah... okay. How long 'til breakfast?"

"You've got time to shower."

"Are we expected anywhere today?"

"Court," Laine makes a face, "I think Derian and Nerissa 'd both like to see you, prob'ly this morning."

"How 'bout we see how I feel after I've showered and eaten," I'm having a hard time even sitting up, "Did you take Sefu out yesterday?"

"After lunch. But," Laine looks over me carefully, "We've got private telephone now and I was thinking maybe we could spend this morning tracking people down and seeing where things 're at."

"And straightening confused stories?"

"That too," Laine shrugs it off, "But you should get ready for breakfast."

The shower didn't do much to help me feel any better and the sight of food turned my stomach. Still, Laine's idea of tracking down our married friends sounds good.

Duke Malin seems preoccupied all through breakfast and disappears immediately after. Laine, Sefu, and I head into the sitting room, where the telephone is. She curls up at the end of the sofa beside the telephone table, but I sit on the floor below her with Sefu's head in my lap. Laine is the one actually hunting up numbers, dialling, and tracking people down.

It's been three days since Andrina left, but Haylie, who had the farthest to go, is the only one who might not have reached her new home by now. I don't feel up to talking to anyone so Laine does that as well. Still, from what I can hear of the conversations and Laine's comments between calls, it sounds like everyone is well... if a bit incredulous of Laine's version of the last couple days.

As Laine ends her conversation with Haylie, I can hear feet on the stairs below us. About the time Laine hangs up the receiver, Derian appears.

He studies me for a moment, clearly concerned. "Laine wasn't kidding when she said you're not well. Are you feeling up to visitors at all?"

"No, but come on in." I make no effort to move. Neither does Sefu. Derian crosses the room and settles himself on the floor beside me.

"Are you expected to be at court this afternoon?"

I grimace. "Last we heard."

"Will you be able to handle that?" Derian brushes a stray hair from my face.

"I'm gonna have to," I sigh, "Wouldn't be the worst thing I've ever had to deal with."

"That's true," Laine makes a face, "Who's next?"

"Lillian, and then Rowena."

Laine nods and starts hunting up the number.

"We're tracking down our friends," I explain to Derian, "Seeing how they're doing and passing along news."

He nods.

It takes a few minutes before Laine can talk to Lillian, although no longer than with anyone else. However, unlike the others, Lillian insists on talking to me directly.

Laine scowls as she holds out the receiver. "Nerita, she won't talk to me."

"Typical." I take the receiver, "Hello."

"Hey, Nerita," Lillian's voice sounds distant, "You okay?"

"Would I be having Laine do this if I was okay?"

Lillian doesn't respond to that, "There've been some really weird rumours... Tory 's back, isn't she?"

"Early morning of the tenth, although I didn't see her 'til court that afternoon."

"She had the stuff she promised Laine, didn't she?"

"She had two lockets for Laine and one for me."

"So you really are...?" Lillian swallows audibly, "Two lockets for Laine? Who were her parents?"

"Duke Lige Malin and High Lady Rose Nowellyr."

"Nerita!" Lillian obviously doesn't believe me.

"You really think I'd make that up?"

"I guess not," Lillian still sounds sceptical, "So Laine 's a duchess?"

"High Lady. Even if she were to inherit her father's title, it wouldn't be until his death and he's here with us at the palace."

"Shit. But what about your engagement?"

"His majesty was forced to announce it at court. Ford now has the Sword of the First and the Monarch was caught between it and a pissed off Tory."

"Not anywhere I'd want to be," Lillian's probably shuddering, "Any word on when you'll be married?"

"Not yet." I change the subject, "How've you been?"

"I'm starting to think Opal and I'll get along better than me, Violet, and Rosa."

"Edmund's sisters could use hobbies?"

"More like we're wishing they would marry," Lillian sounds irritated, "By rights Opal should be next to Emile and Lady Bowerstone in authority, but those two 're always in her way. I can accept my place here and no one except me, Edmund, and our personal servants are allowed in our private rooms."

"What'd that take?"

"Edmund said it first, right when we got here, and Lady Bowerstone agrees with him. But I can't talk long right now. You'll be okay, won't you?"

"I will be. You take care of yourself."

Once I've said good-bye to Lillian, I pass the receiver back to Laine, who hangs it up.

"Edmund's sisters 're becoming a problem?" Laine guesses.

"Sounds like they don't have enough to do with their time."

"So just Rowena 's left?" Laine reaches for the telephone again.

I nod.

"Seven, three... five, eight, zero, four... three, nine, two." That Derian has that number memorized isn't any surprise.

"Thank you." Laine tells him while she waits for someone to answer.

"Could you help me up?" I ask Derian as Laine asks for Rowena, "Those two can talk a long time and I'm not up to listening."

Derian nods and gets to his feet so he can help me to mine. I'm not very steady on my feet and end up in his arms. He studies me carefully, his concern clear.

"You really don't look well."

I take a deep breath. "What did Laine tell you?"

"Only that you weren't well," Derian guides me to a sofa across the room and has me sit next to him, "But I know Tory was here yesterday."

I nod. "She's been keeping an eye on me... probably for a while now. And if I'm not dealing better soon, I think she'll send Nikki."

"Then I hope she doesn't wait too long." Derian brushes a hand over my hair. I curl up against him and rest my head on his shoulder.

"Nerissa wants to come see you once she's done her lessons this morning," Derian's arm tightens around me, "I think perhaps it's better if she doesn't."

"I couldn't handle her on top of everything else today."

Derian nods. "I'll see what I can do about Nerissa. I'd much rather see you rest."

Unfortunately, while court audiences may be boring, they're far from restful. I'm actually okay for most of it, although I'm well aware of both Derian and Laine watching me. It's only towards the end that voices become distant and my vision begins to distort.

I'm remotely aware of Monarch Reginald dismissing the court. As people start to leave, Derian comes over and slips an arm around my waist.

"Let's get you out of here."

"Anyone else 'd be passed out," Laine informs him, "Nikki 's on her way."

Which means she's waiting for us in the corridor outside the throne room.

Nikki Genstang hasn't changed in appearance any more than her sister. Nikki and Tory are identical in figure and features, but Nikki has close cropped black hair, fair skin, and indigo eyes. They're very different in personality though.

"You didn't sleep well, did you?" Nikki studies me critically.

"Try constant nightmares." Laine responds.

Nikki nods to herself, then she turns to me, "Nerita, I'm gonna put you to sleep again, but a lot deeper this time."

"For how long?" Laine queries.

Nikki shrugs. "A minimum twenty-four hours... prob'ly a lot longer though. An' Nerita, I'll be keepin' an eye on you the whole time."

I nod. "Thanks."

14-10-48-06-04SM

I gradually become aware of a warm, furry body beside mine. Opening my eyes, the first things to come into focus are Sefu's tawny ones. That by itself is unusual since he usually sleeps on my feet.

"Nerita?"

I feel the bed shift as Laine sits on the edge.

"What happened?" My eyes are gummy and my neck is a little stiff.

"Nikki put you out," Laine replies, "Remember? She said you'd sleep longer than usual."

"How long?" I enquire warily, attempting to sit up.

"Almost forty-eight hours. If you're not feeling up to attending the masquerade tonight, Father 'll understand at least."

I shake my head. "I'll go. How long do I have to get ready?"

"A couple hours yet. You better eat and shower though."

Sefu hops off the bed as I slowly get up.

"Anything interesting happen while I was out?"

Laine thinks back while I hunt up my dressing gown and pull it on.

"Not really. Father 's been spending a lot of time talking with his majesty... Derian 's asked to be told as soon as you're awake... oh, and Angelita and Xylia 're coming tonight."

"Is someone on their way to tell Derian?"

"I sent Mattie for food, but that's it."

"I was talking in my sleep again?"

"Yeah," Laine looks amused, "Not that you've ever said anything I didn't already know."

"Even after this last week?"

Laine shrugs. "At least you haven't had any nightmares this time. How're you feeling?"

I take some time to think about that. "I'm okay actually."

Laine looks relieved.

I change the subject, "Any idea what his majesty and his grace have been talking about?"

"It's more a matter of what haven't they been talking about," Laine grimaces, "I haven't overheard anything that affects either of us, but that doesn't mean anything. Father seems to think I tell you everything."

I have to laugh. I know Laine doesn't tell me everything and I don't want her to. Some things she doesn't need to tell me and some I don't care to know.

"Any word from Tory?" I sit on the edge of the bed and Sefu comes over, looking for attention.

"No," Laine replies, "But Angelita said all of UnderGround Club 's getting pretty bored. I'd hate to be the hotel staff right now."

"Tory won't let them get too out of hand. That'd explain why Angelita 's coming tonight though."

Laine laughs. "That and 'cause it's a masquerade."

"Derian 'll be there, won't he?"

"The Monarch isn't giving him a choice," Laine studies me curiously, "You don't want him to know you're awake, do you?"

"So long as he doesn't know our costumes."

"He doesn't."

"Then let's see if he can pick me out of a crowd."

Laine slowly shakes her head. "You're definitely feeling better."

The masquerade is set to begin at six, which means we can show up any time between six and seven. However, Duke Malin, like Monarch Reginald, strongly believes in punctuality. So the three of us and Sefu are ready to go by six.

The old south tower is one of the few parts of the original Imperial palace remaining. Since the break up of the East Continent Empire, the palace has been both renovated and added onto numerous times and what was once the southern most part of the building is now somewhere in the middle. What that means for us is once we're out of the tower, we're practically at the ballroom.

Quite a few people are already gathered and I can see that the dress shop clerk had been right about the favoured costumes for this year.

There's a glittering dragon seated on the dais in the corner, flanked by a unicorn, a masked elf, and a rainbow feathered bird. Out on the floor, there're a variety of fantastic and mythological creatures.

Because Laine and I are tall and slim, we had decided to go as faeries as described in later versions of the east mythology. The dresses themselves are mainly layers of rainbow silk with bits of glittering stone. We're also wearing soft shoes and bejewelled masks with glitter gel through our hair and on any exposed skin. I left off my engagement ring so it can't give me away and, as soon as we enter, I send Sefu to keep Princess Nerissa company.

Duke Malin is dressed as a snow wolf complete with an elaborate, heavy headpiece.

A few people are wearing other kinds of costumes: Ordinary animals, historical fashions, various uniforms... all with masks, of course.

"There's Xylia." Laine spots the tiger before I do. We'd been watching for her since Angelita didn't say a word to Laine about her costume. We're just a little surprised to see two people accompany Xylia into the ballroom.

One is dressed in the original Imperial guard uniform, with the visor of the helmet down. My guess is a man and a big one... possibly Angelita's husband, Devin. The second could only be Angelita. She's wearing an early Imperial ball gown complete with hoop skirt; long, full sleeves; and low, square neckline. Her hair is gathered into a heavily jewelled hairnet and the mask covering the upper half of her face is decorated with feathers and more jewels. She's also wearing the jewelry she inherited from her mother, which gives her away as much as Xylia's presence.

"I'm not gonna ask where she got that," Laine shakes her head in disbelief, "I'd just like to know how she pulls it off."

I shrug. "You're not the only one."

It's been suggested numerous times by numerous people that part of my problem with Angelita is jealousy and I've given up denying it. No matter where she goes or what she's wearing, Angelita turns heads. When she wants to, she can look and act very much the princess she was born. If I'm lucky and let Laine pick my outfit, I might get a second glance.

The first dance begins shortly and I lose sight of Xylia and her companions in the crowd. Almost immediately a knight in gleaming chain mail invites me onto the floor and I accept.

I am keeping my eye open for Derian as the masquerade progresses. I have no idea what his costume is or if he's even actually here. I really hope he is, although I imagine the Monarch has been keeping him busy.

Then, about an hour into the evening, I find myself dancing with a man dressed in what I believe was the uniform of an Imperial forces commander. I can only just see his eyes behind the face plate of the helmet, but I'm absolute certain it's Derian.

"I see you're well again," The voice is definitely Derian's, "How long have you been awake?"

"Just long enough to eat, shower, and dress for this."

"After two days you couldn't've sent me word?"

I shrug evasively. "I knew I'd see you here."

"I had hoped to escort you." Derian informs me.

I chuckle. "Not this evening. Tonight, on the other hand..."

The face place of his helmet makes it hard to tell what Derian thinks of that. But, as the dance ends, he bends his head closer to mine.

"Tonight then."

The music changes and he slips away, but before anyone else can ask me to dance, I feel Laine's grip on my arm. I accompany her off the floor and over to a corner where the music is muffled.

"I see you and Derian found each other," Her eyes look directly into mine, "You're planning to sleep with him again, aren't you?"

I shrug evasively. "So what if I am? It's not like you've ever had trouble finding someone to sleep with."

"Nikki did tell you you're not actually pregnant," Laine reminds me, "And who knows when you'll be able to marry."

"Nikki also said conception was still possible, whether anything else happened or not." And, as I recall the conversation before Nikki put me to sleep, she'd seemed to think it was pretty likely.

Laine shakes her head. "I won't cover for you this time."

"So don't." I shrug it off.

"You're actually suggesting I find someone to sleep with?" Laine sounds sceptical.

"That's up to you. Sefu 's staying with me tonight and I'd kinda like to get back out there."

Laine nods.

Ten o'clock is unmasking time, but just before that, I notice the Imperial guard slip out of the ballroom. There's no sign of him as the music stops and the floor clears. Once everyone is back against the walls, the guards posted behind the dais step forward to assist the dragon in removing his headpiece. There's a distinct sheen of sweat on the Monarch's face as the guards set the dragon's head behind the dais.

Derian, who is standing beside his father, now removes his helmet and sets it aside. Next the unicorn steps onto the floor in front of the Monarch and removes its headpiece to reveal Princess Carina. The rainbow bird turns out to be Princess Letitia and the masked elf is Princess Delia. After them, a cat in a dress, a goldfish, and a faerie accompanied by Sefu step out of the crowd. Their headpieces and masks come off to reveal the younger three princesses; Elana, Kamilla, and Nerissa.

Then Monarch Reginald indicates for the nearest person on his left to step forward.

I don't recognize most of the people and no announcements are made of name or rank. Laine, Duke Malin, and Angelita are hidden in the crowd and I can't see any of them until the snow wolf steps forward to remove its headpiece. Like the Monarch, Duke Malin has obviously been sweating under his costume. I'm warm enough with just a mask.

My turn comes shortly after the Duke's. Stepping forward, I slip off my mask. Before I step back, I can see Princess Nerissa grin.

Laine is among the last to unmask, with only half a dozen or so left after her. Then, at the very end, Angelita steps forward, Xylia at her side. She takes her mask off and a murmur ripples around the room. I know people had been asking each other who she is all evening. They'd been wondering about the Imperial guard as well and evidently his majesty is too.

"High Lady Angelita," Monarch Reginald speaks for the first time, "A question, if We may."

"Yes, your majesty?" She turns to face him.

"Do you know the Imperial guardsman who was here?"

Angelita chuckles softly. "That's my husband, your majesty."

The Monarch nods to himself.

The music resumes and I make my way through the crowd to Laine. Angelita and Xylia reach her at the same time.

"Why didn't Devin stay?" Laine asks immediately.

"He's here on Tory's orders," Angelita grimaces, "So's Ford, but dressed like one of them," She indicates the guards behind the dais, "His majesty and the captain of the guard agreed no problem."

"Natalia told you what happened at the last ball?" I query.

Angelita shakes her head. "Tory knew from her ability. 'Sides, Natalia's skipped town."

I shoot Laine an irritated look. She hadn't told me that.

Abruptly Angelita changes the subject, "Who's Sefu been with all evening?"

Before Laine or I can answer, an irritated looking Princess Carina joins us.

"His majesty wishes to see you." She doesn't appear to be addressing any specific one of us.

"All of us or someone specific?" Angelita's voice turns cold.

Princess Carina shrugs indifferently and vanishes into the crowd.

"Who was that?"

"Her late majesty's oldest daughter," Laine replies disgustedly, "And she prob'ly means you."

"How 'bout if all three of us go and his majesty can sort it out?" I suggest. I should reclaim my tiger, who is with Princess Nerissa near the dais anyway.

The crowd is beginning to thin out. Many are still dancing, but a few have drifted out to the courtyard and some are leaving for the night. That makes it easier for the group of us to stay together as we approach the dais.

Monarch Reginald frowns on seeing us. "Carina was to bring you."

A guard leaves his post and disappears into the crowd. Four of the princesses are standing beside the dais; Princess Nerissa is seated on the edge of it with Sefu at her feet. Derian had disappeared briefly, but now appears at my side and takes my hand.

The Monarch studies Angelita's necklace curiously. "I see more was left than just the crown."

"Sort of," Angelita grimaces wryly, "All the pieces I've got are low carat gold and imitation stones. The crown was the only original piece left. This," Her fingers brush the necklace, "Was Mother's favourite."

Monarch Reginald frowns. "I know the crown jewels of Estorika were considered a joke..."

"Probably only Natalia or Tory would know what happened to the original pieces," Angelita shrugs it off, "The imitation ones look real enough."

"So they do." The Monarch straightens up as the guard returns with Princess Carina. There is no doubt she's in serious trouble, but the Monarch only gives her a stern look as she joins her sisters.

"Thank you, Conors." Monarch Reginald addresses the guard as he returns to his post. Then he turns back to Angelita, "Your companion's name is Xylia, is it not?"

"It is, your majesty."

He addresses the princesses, "I would like to introduce High Lady Angelita Mendus Straisen and her companion, Xylia," To Angelita, he adds, "These are the princesses of Norsecount: Carina, Letitia, Delia, Elana, Kamilla, and Nerissa."

The younger five curtsy as well as they can in their costumes and Angelita returns the gesture. Princess Carina stands stiffly, not looking at anyone specific. The Monarch notes her behaviour, but doesn't say anything. Instead, he goes to address Angelita again. However, before he can speak, she does.

"If your majesty would please excuse us, we need to go." She's watching the doorway from the corner of her eye. I glance over and spot Ford and Devin.

"Of course," Monarch Reginald nods, "Good night."

"Good night, your majesty, your highnesses." Angelita curtsies again, then nods to me and Laine.

Laine waits until she and Xylia are gone to query, "Since when does Tory set any kind of curfew?"

I shake my head. "I doubt it's anything to do with Tory. Angelita hasn't been staying out really late for anything in a while."

"Lady Nerita," The Monarch calls for my attention, "Might I enquire as to how long you have known Angelita?"

I glance at Laine, who shrugs, while I think back. "Eight... maybe nine years, your majesty."

"So you know her well?"

I shake my head. "She lived near me in South City for a little over a year. Then we met again at Camp Streton two years ago. We've never been friends."

Monarch Reginald frowns and turns to Laine, "What of yourself?"

"I may consider Angelita a friend, your majesty, although not a close one. But I doubt she would say the same of anyone, except perhaps Devin and Tory."

The Monarch's frown deepens, but he leaves the subject alone.

"Would my lady care to dance?" Derian's words are for my ears only. I nod and accompany him onto the floor.

15-10-48-06-04SM

Gentle fingers are brushing over my loose, tangled hair, but I don't want to wake up. Derian's bed is warm and comfortable and I can feel his body right beside mine.

"Nerita," His lips press against my ear, "You've barely time to get to the tower before breakfast."

I groan. Then I roll onto my side so I can look at him. "Will I see you later today?"

"This morning," Derian brushes my hair from my face, "Did his grace not tell you that Father has asked us and Laine to ride with them?"

I have to think back to last night. "He did."

Derian chuckles. "Although... his grace may not be pleased with you this morning."

I shrug lazily. "He'll be less pleased with Laine then. But if I'm lucky, she'll turn up before I do."

"You don't think she returned to your rooms last night?" Derian frowns.

"I know she didn't intend to."

His frown deepens. "She would take a lover under the current circumstances?"

I shake my head. "Any man can take Laine to bed once; none have spent a second night with her. Although I'll never understand how she can do that."

Derian nods to himself and changes the subject, "You may find you have another problem in that I doubt you want to wear that dress again."

I groan into the pillow. The glitter gel from my costume last night had gotten all over everything I touched. Derian and I had ended up showering together before going to bed and I'd really rather not shower again before breakfast this morning.

"Any ideas?"

Derian grimaces. "You may have to borrow something of mine."

I end up borrowing one of his shirts. It's just long enough to be decent, but I'm glad Derian can take me to the foot of the tower stairs without anyone seeing us. Unfortunately there's only one way up into the old south tower and it requires passing through the sitting room where Duke Malin is awake, dressed, and waiting.

"Lady Nerita," He emphasizes my title sternly, "Where were you?"

"I hope you don't seriously expect me to answer that." Besides which, I think the answer should be self evident.

The Duke doesn't press, "You wouldn't happen to know where Laine is, would you?"

"Where ever Laine wants to be. Although," I glance at the clock, "She should be back any time now."

Duke Malin doesn't look happy. "You'd best go prepare for breakfast. And please keep in mind we will be riding with his majesty at ten."

I nod and head up to the top floor. Sefu doesn't come with me. Probably because his breakfast should be in the dining room by now.

I'm properly dressed and working on my hair by the time Laine comes up. She's a mess of smeared glitter gel and I hate to think of what the bed she slept in last night looks like.

"Oh good," Laine looks relieved on seeing me, "I was hoping you'd be done with the shower."

I chuckle. "It's all yours."

She heads for the bathroom, but reappears in the doorway a moment later. "Whose shirt?"

"Derian's."

Laine doesn't ask anything else and, before long, I hear water running.

Once I'm finished braiding my hair, I head down to the dining room to find Sefu finishing his breakfast and servants setting the table. There's no sign of Duke Malin until the servants leave and Laine doesn't join us until we're nearly finished.

I don't know what's on the Monarch's mind this time, but Laine, Duke Malin, and I are appropriately dressed and on our way to the palace stables just before ten o'clock. Sefu tags along since there really isn't anywhere else he can go. Mattie refuses to go near him and he isn't fond of her anyway.

Derian joins us as we exit the palace, looking grim. He takes my hand, but allows Laine and the Duke to get a little ahead of us.

"I mistimed the sweep of the security camera at the foot of the south tower," He keeps his voice low, "And our people are trained to overlook nothing."

"Who all knows?"

"Only Father and the guard on duty at the time. The recording has been wiped from the system and I trust the guard, but Father's far from happy with me."

"Is that any change from the past few days?"

Derian shakes his head. "How much longer do you think Tory will wait?"

"I don't know," I shrug, "I don't even really know what she said to him."

"My impression is she wants us married soon... as in before the end of the month. But it's the middle of the month already and there's no sign of Father relenting."

"I'm not about to second guess Tory."

Derian chuckles. "Perhaps I'm impatient."

I'm not about to say anything to that. I know he isn't the only one.

The stable master, the Monarch, and two palace guards are waiting just inside the stable when we arrive. Sefu is now sticking right to my side; he doesn't like horses any better than they like him.

"Good morning," Monarch Reginald greets us, "I don't believe you've met the stable master, Fredric Trent. Trent, may I introduce Duke Lige Malin, High Lady Laine Malin, Lady Nerita Chassaven, and Sefu."

The stable master bows to each of us as we're named. Sefu, he studies curiously.

"Has he been around horses much?"

I have to shake my head. "Very little at all."

Fredric nods to himself. "Knowing Forrest, he would be opposed to tigers on principle. However, if my lady intends to make this her home it would be best if Sefu and the horses get used to each other."

Sefu glowers balefully at the stable master.

"That may be," I rest a hand on Sefu's head, "I just don't think inside the stable 's the best place to start."

"True," Fredric points out an open door across the building, "You'll be leaving through there for your ride."

Sefu slips out from under my hand and heads for the door. Unless there's a problem, I know he'll be waiting for me just outside. Fredric watches him go before turning to Duke Malin.

"I understand your grace hasn't ridden in quite a while."

The Duke grimaces. "Not since my teens."

Fredric nods and addresses me and Laine, "Forrest thinks highly of you, but it's my understanding you only learned to ride in the last year."

"Last December." I confirm.

"This way, please." Fredric leads us down the nearest aisle. Derian, the Monarch, and the guards head off in a different direction to get their mounts. Halfway down the building, Fredric stops in front of the stall of an older roan stallion.

"Your grace, this is Meteor."

"Thank you." Duke Malin studies the horse appreciatively.

Fredric leaves them to get acquainted and leads me and Laine farther down.

"My lady," The stable master addresses Laine, "Did Forrest speak with you before you left Arawn?"

Laine shakes her head. "Natalia Burren did, but I haven't heard anything more."

Fredric looks surprised. "I was under the impression you were told…"

Laine laughs. "Don't worry about it. When did Spirit arrive?"

"Just last night, my lady," Fredric stops in front of the stall, "I think she's eager for some exercise. I do need to speak with you later though."

"Of course. Her equipment?"

"I'll show you in a minute, my lady."

Laine nods and turns her attention to her mare. Fredric crosses to the stall opposite.

"And Lady Nerita, this is Dancer."

This mare, like Meteor, is older, probably nearing retirement. She's grey with a white mane and tail.

Fredric continues, "She'll likely have little problem with Sefu. But if you would please come with me."

Monarch Reginald, his son, and the guards are mounted and waiting when Laine, Duke Malin, and I join them. Sefu gets to his feet on seeing me, looking a little wary.

"You'll be fine." I keep one hand on Dancer's reins as I pat his neck. Then Laine and I mount. Forrest taught us the trick of mounting from the ground, but everyone around looks surprised to see us do it. Duke Malin, however, needs the mounting block.

"Shall we be off?" Monarch Reginald queries. When the Duke nods, one of the guards takes the lead. The Monarch and the Duke are next, then me, Sefu, and Derian, then Laine. The second guard brings up the rear.

Once we're on a trail, Monarch Reginald observes, "You must have ridden a great deal this past year."

"Every chance we got," Laine confirms, "Although the one time last June ended up being quite something."

"The actual ride wasn't the problem." I can't quite suppress a scowl.

"Might I enquire as to what happened?" Monarch Reginald sounds curious.

"Experiment Redemption allowed each of us to pick an activity to celebrate our birthdays," I begin, "Angelita, my cousin Lillian, and another girl known as Danika Gray all share a birthday... although I believe Danika 's a year younger. For this last one they got together and decided all three groups would go riding, have a picnic dinner, and then go on a hike."

"How many people?" Duke Malin queries.

"Twenty-nine between the three groups," I reply, "Plus the athletics coaches for all three groups, Forrest, and Channa and Shari of the Second Shield."

"You were certainly well protected," The Monarch observes, "But what happened?"

"The ride and the dinner went fine; it was the hike. I'm not sure how far along the trail we were, but all of a sudden we were told to turn back... that we were returning to Camp Streton early."

"It was Tory," Laine sighs, "She told Channa something felt off... though others were starting to pick it up by the time we got back to the vehicles. UnderGround Club and Alley Gang both have mixed blood members and then with Channa and Shari... Anyway, they were in a hurry to get everyone into vehicles and back to Camp Streton. No one thought to count heads until we had to turn in our gate passes to get inside the fence."

I grimace. "I still don't remember how Angelita and I ended up off the path and separated from everyone else."

Laine just shakes her head. "When we realized who was missing, a few people were pretty upset and it didn't help when the Second Shield were blocked from finding anything. Tory's abilities were still erratic at that point."

I scowl at the memory. "I should've stayed put and waited for the lodge staff to find me."

Both the Monarch and the Duke frown, but it's Derian who asks, "Why wouldn't Angelita have done the same?"

"She's paranoid. And UnderGround Club had encountered military in the area the previous winter. I don't know how much Sedyr blood she has, but she has an ability to communicate with animals and she'd met a winter tiger in the area before, so she went looking for it. I guess I just didn't want to be left alone out there."

Laine laughs and I scowl at her before continuing, "Except the tiger had been poisoned by men from the illicit military base in the area. It wanted help protecting its cubs and Angelita wasn't going to refuse. Then we discovered the base was being used for human experimentation... I hope I never see her that angry again."

"Human experimentation?" Monarch Reginald swallows hard, turning pale. Derian and Duke Malin don't look any better.

"Why do you think Angelita insisted on ethical standards for Arawn's scientists as a condition of giving up her birthright? At least half of UnderGround Club came out of someone's science project, along with probably three quarters of the participants in Experiment Redemption."

"What of the tiger and her cubs?" Duke Malin enquires.

"The mother died... we knew she would, but we found the cubs before that," I chuckle, "Where do you think I got Sefu?"

"How many cubs were there?" Derian frowns, "Obviously Sefu and Xylia..."

"Kasa, the other female, more or less belongs to Angelita's baby sister-in-law and President Gayre claimed the other male. I just don't know what he calls him."

Monarch Reginald frowns. "I've heard nothing of Angelita's husband having family."

"I'd've thought your majesty would've been told," I'm surprised, "Experiment Redemption 's reunited a lot of parents and children, including Devlin and Devin Straisen. But over a year ago now, Devlin married Rylle of the Second Shield."

"I'm not necessarily told of all the doings of the Second Shield," The Monarch responds, "Especially those who live primarily on the west continent."

"I doubt Rylle will return there," Laine observes, "Not when what family her husband has lives here."

"Rapidly expanding family at that." I chuckle.

Monarch Reginald frowns. "You think Angelita expecting already?"

Laine laughs. "I believe it was Channa said something about May..."

The Monarch looks sceptical, but changes the subject, "Surely President Gayre must be aware of events within his own borders."

"Oh, he is," I respond, "And he doesn't like a lot of things. It's just up until recently his power to change them 's been limited."

"So many say." Monarch Reginald doesn't say anything more to me or Laine. He and Duke Malin ride on ahead.

Derian sighs. "How I wish he would simply admit not everything is as he would like to believe."

"Why do you think the Sword of the First wants his abdication?" Laine responds, "Neither it nor Tory will wait on him much longer."

"When's the next court session?" I ask Derian.

"Tomorrow afternoon."

Laine nods to herself. "I have a feeling we'll see Tory there."

The trail ends in a golden meadow cut in half by a creek. Sefu goes bounding off for a drink and the horses spread out a little. When we reach the water, we dismount and allow the horses to drink. Sefu, having already drunk his fill, is now playing in the creek.

"I thought cats little liked water." Monarch Reginald watches Sefu splash around.

"Maybe house cats don't, but the big, wild cats love it. Winter tigers, at least, are strong swimmers," I grimace briefly, "Fortunately they dry quickly."

"No kidding." Laine comments sourly.

Derian eyes Sefu warily, although he doesn't say anything.

"We just might want to be mounted before he's finished," I recommend, "He will shake himself dry."

"How long is he likely to live?" The Monarch enquires.

"I'm not sure. There isn't much documentation on domesticated tigers. Although, research indicates they can live up to ten years in the wild."

"You've looked into the matter then?"

"When I first got him." I nod.

"It surprises me that those in charge of Experiment Redemption would allow participants to keep an animal." The Monarch strokes his horse's neck.

"I doubt they would've let just anyone do it," I respond, "They don't teach just anyone to ride either. But, actually, Sefu's been easy to care for."

Laine chuckles. "He's even grateful and loyal."

I shrug that off. "Yeah, well, people always complicate things."

Monarch Reginald studies me critically, just for a moment.

The ride back to the stable is quiet and people are waiting to help us dismount and put the horses away. Laine prefers to care for Spirit herself, as much as she can, but Derian pulls me away from the others.

"I want to show you something."

Sefu and I accompany him across to a paddock containing a mare and foal. Both are a beautiful silvery white with darker manes and tails. As we approach, the foal comes over to the fence, not seeming to mind Sefu at all.

"Rosebud," Derian grimaces as he indicates the mare, "Was Gabrielle's... for as much as Gabrielle ever rode, but she's of a good, long documented lineage and I kept her for breeding. Nerissa's mare is one of hers, although by Father's Maelstrom."

"And this little one?"

"Doesn't yet have a name. Her sire's my Evanescent."

I nod. "How old is she?"

"Less than a year... born last spring. Rosebud won't have another."

Sefu and the filly have been sizing each other up through the fence rails. Now Sefu sets his front paws on the top rail and turns his head to look at me.

"You can stay on this side of the fence." I inform him, earning myself a baleful look.

Derian chuckles. "I gather Sefu approves. What do you think?"

"She's beautiful." And, if I understood right, extremely valuable.

Derian slips his arm around me. "She's yours, if you want her."

"I do." I may not be able to ride her for years yet, but I'll be able to name and help train her. In the meantime, I suspect Sefu has found himself a new playmate.

16-10-48-06-04SM

I'm in the middle of getting dressed when there's a knock on the suite door. Derian quickly pulls on a shirt before going to answer it. I just continue dressing.

"Yes, Father?" I can hear Derian's voice clearly.

"I'm not disturbing anything, am I?" The Monarch sounds entirely too amused. Although it is an improvement on pissed off.

"I was just getting dressed. Why?" It's hard to blame Derian for being wary.

"I was hoping you and your lady might join me for breakfast... say in half an hour. That should be adequate time for her to go prepare."

"You mean after I let her know?"

"Whatever you feel necessary. I trust both of you will be punctual."

"Yes, Father."

I can hear the door close, then Derian returns to the bedroom.

"What's he playing at now?" I retrieve my hair elastic from the floor and slip it over my wrist.

Derian shrugs helplessly. "You know as much as I do, Nerita."

I nod to myself. "I'd better go change."

"Let me finish getting dressed and I'll go with you," Derian sighs, "Father obviously had the security cameras re-synched."

It only takes him a few minutes, then we head for the old south tower. We enter the sitting room just as Duke Malin comes downstairs.

"Nerita," The Duke looks concerned about something, "Did Laine say anything to you about going out last night?"

"No..." I can't help frowning.

"'Tis simply that she left the palace," Duke Malin explains, "And I wasn't aware she knew many in Monarch's Town."

"She could've gone to the Old Imperial Hotel. At least that's where Tory and Angelita and their friends 're staying."

The Duke nods, looking a little less concerned. "Are you in a rush for something?"

"Father 's asked us to join him for breakfast." Derian explains as I head for the stairs. Sefu disappears into the dining room, looking for his morning meal.

I'm just finishing with my hair when a flushed Laine enters our dressing room. I study her critically.

"Where were you?"

She gives me a surprised look. "Since when do you want to know that?"

"Since you don't generally leave the palace without a word to anyone."

Laine flushes bright red.

I chuckle. "You spent last night with Rylan, didn't you?"

"Nerita..." Laine is more completely embarrassed than I've ever seen her.

I shake my head. "I've got to go. Derian 's waiting for me."

Somehow, despite everything, Derian and I arrive exactly on time for breakfast. Sefu isn't with us because he was only just starting eating, but I'm not worried about it. Besides, I think Laine could use his company right now.

"Good morning," Monarch Reginald greets us cheerfully, "Please do come in." He doesn't seem to notice the slightly bewildered glances Derian and I exchange.

"Father," Derian sounds concerned, "What's going on?"

"All in good time. Breakfast is here, so please do come sit."

I'm starting to feel like I'm caught in some bizarre reverse world. Except Derian looks like he feels the same. We follow Monarch Reginald to the table and take the seats his indicates.

"Father," Derian tries again as we begin eating, "Are you well?"

The Monarch chuckles. "Certainly better than I've felt in quite some time. And no, I'm not losing my mind. At least not yet."

Derian nods, looking sceptical.

"However, I did have a couple very long, very interesting conversations yesterday evening."

"With whom?" Derian queries warily.

"High Lady Irina," Monarch Reginald replies, "She telephoned me, truth be told. Although I have invited her to come up for a time."

Derian winces. "Was that really necessary?"

"It's little to do with you," The Monarch turns stern, "You I've decided what to do about. Rather I'm hoping she will be of some assistance with the princesses."

"It's about time," Derian looks relieved, "Who else did you speak with?"

"Angelita and her husband," Monarch Reginald's amused expression returns, "Which was very interesting indeed."

I only just manage to suppress a wince.

The Monarch turns to look at me, "Perhaps you and Angelita have never been friends, yet she does hold you in a certain respect... You seem surprised..."

I grimace. "Angelita and I have a long history of fights going back to when we first met and I know she doesn't owe me any favours."

Monarch Reginald chuckles. "Has it never occurred to you that perhaps the two of you have different ideas of what constitutes a favour?"

"That would hardly be the only thing we don't see eye to eye on."

Even Derian looks amused by that. "Evidently one of those three said something to change your mind. So now what?"

"Tory had three major concerns when she spoke to me the other day: The first of which being your marriage."

"Which she would like to see by the end of this month." Derian finishes.

"That leaves little time for proper planning," The Monarch observes, "I don't suppose she could be persuaded to wait a little longer..."

I shake my head. "The thirtieth is fourteen days from now. Angelita had a proper, traditional wedding in nine. Although I'll admit that was Natalia's doing."

Monarch Reginald looks slightly affronted by that. "The thirtieth then, but planning will start this morning. I hope you two had no other plans."

Derian chuckles. "This morning is fine. But what of Tory's other concerns?"

"Her second related to Angelita and I have that matter well in hand," The Monarch replies, "You will hear of it with the rest of the court this afternoon."

"You've asked her to be present then." Derian guesses.

"Angelita and Tory both," Monarch Reginald confirms, "As for Tory's third concern... The Sword has spoken to you, has it not?"

Derian nods. "The first time I met Ford."

"The sword is allowing me to retain the throne until you have a confirmed heir. Provided I don't violate the Canon."

That explains a whole lot of what's been going on. It also means he could be off the throne in as little as nine months. I should probably talk to Nikki again.

A thought occurs to me and I address Monarch Reginald, "Exactly who is this High Lady Irina?"

"Widow of the late Monarch Tedrick of Ouestlun and a cousin of my first wife, Derian's mother."

I nod to myself. I'd known the second part from Derian, but I find the first more interesting. Now to see what kind of lady she is.

After breakfast, the three of us go to the Monarch's study, where Duke Malin and a professional looking middle aged woman join us.

"Your grace, Lady Nerita," The Monarch begins, "I'd like to introduce Florence Knight, events coordinator for the court of Norsecount."

Florence's curtsy is stiff, but her smile isn't. Duke Malin and I nod politely to her.

"Now," Monarch Reginald turns to the woman, "I have something of a challenge for you and your staff."

"A wedding, your majesty?" There's a hint of amusement in Florence's smile, "How soon?"

"The thirtieth of this month."

Florence doesn't flinch; she just produces a clipboard and pen. Somehow I suspect she's been expecting something like this.

"Here, your majesty?"

"Of course. Say perhaps two in the afternoon?" Monarch Reginald glances at me and Derian and we nod, "What else will you need to know?"

Florence consults her clipboard, "Wedding party. Your parents, my lady?"

"Have been dead sixteen years."

Duke Malin speaks up, "Would you permit me to give you away?"

I nod. "Thank you, your grace."

Florence notes that, "Bridesmaids?"

"Laine." I know she'd kill me if I even consider anyone else.

"And for your highness?" Florence turns to Derian.

"Marcellus Pelmont."

"I will arrange meetings to discuss clothes and rings for tomorrow," Florence is writing as she speaks, "Flowers, my lady?"

"Iris and lilies... and ivy."

"Thank you," Florence turns back to the Monarch, "Invitations will have to be kept simple and express couriered either today yet or early tomorrow."

"Whatever is necessary," Monarch Reginald nods, "What else?"

"The reception dinner," Florence addresses me and Derian, "Any requests?"

I shrug indifferently. "So long as it's real food, I don't much care."

"Something seasonal," Derian tells her, "Preferably local."

Florence nods and records that, "And, finally, guest list."

"We will have that for you by noon today," The Monarch replies, "Is that everything?"

"For this morning, your majesty. If you would please excuse me." Florence curtsies stiffly before leaving.

"Lady Nerita," The Monarch turns to me, "You have a birth record for yourself, do you not?"

"I do."

"If I could please get that from you so the necessary legal processes can begin..." He studies me carefully, "Might I ask your full name?"

"Nerita Chassaven," I grimace, "Unlike most born in the Old Quarter of South City, I don't have a second name and I don't know why."

Monarch Reginald nods to himself. "Would you object were the second name Amy be added?"

"If your majesty feels that necessary. And yes, I'll have my birth record for you this morning yet."

"What will Sefu do that day?" Derian enquires.

"Hang out with Nerissa," I respond, then turn to the Duke, "Do you know if Laine took him out this morning?"

"I believe she intended to."

"We do have one last matter to discuss," Monarch Reginald recalls our attention, "The guest list."

It's roughly three quarters of an hour before noon by the time I'm finally free to go look for Laine and Sefu. They're exactly where I thought they would be: Out in the fields. As soon as he sees me, Sefu abandons his ball and comes racing over. I have to brace myself and even then he nearly knocks me down.

"Easy, Sefu," I ruffle the fur of his head and neck, "You're getting too big for that. Now go get your ball."

He bounds off to do that while I cross the field to Laine.

"What 're you so happy about?" Laine looks a little irritated, "Where were you, anyway?"

"Wedding planning session... his majesty finally caved."

"How soon?" Laine is surprised.

"The thirtieth of this month. Do I have to ask if you'll be my bridesmaid?"

"Be a stupid question," Laine chuckles, "Let me guess: Marcellus 'll be best man?"

I nod. "Invitations 'll be out within twenty-four hours and they want to discuss clothes and rings tomorrow."

Laine nods to herself as Sefu joins us, his ball in his jaws.

"Actually," I accept the ball, "There's something I'd like to show you."

"Okay." Laine accompanies me and Sefu to the stable and inside.

It doesn't take me long to locate Fredric Trent. He's in the yard on the other side, helping the princesses dismount.

"She's over there." The stable master calls to me, indicating the paddock.

"Thank you." I lead Sefu and Laine over to where Rosebud and her foal are. Again, Rosebud shows no interest in me, but the filly comes straight over to us.

"Oh, wow!" Laine studies the foal, "Is this where you and Derian went after yesterday's ride?"

I nod. "This little one's mine. Moonbeam."

"From Derian?" Laine guesses.

"Since both sire and dam are his..." I set a hand on Sefu's head and force him off the fence, "Sefu, behave."

"A horse Sefu likes?" Laine is amused, "How long until lunch?"

I grimace. "We should probably head in."

Laine, Sefu, and I return to the stable to find the princesses gathering in the doorway. The six of them leave at the same time we do and Princess Nerissa leaves her sisters to walk with me.

"Lady Nerita, did Derian really give you Rosebud's foal?"

"He did."

"Did you already name her?"

"Moonbeam."

"Did Derian tell you my Sunflower is her sister?"

"I believe he mentioned that." I'm well aware of Princess Carina coming up behind me. She's lucky Sefu 's off ahead of Laine. Someone... possibly more than one... gasps as Princess Carina attempts to hit me from behind. Within seconds I've caught her arm and twisted it up behind her back. Although not too hard.

"Do you have a problem with me?" My voice is soft and even, but cool. Princess Nerissa takes off for the palace and Laine has managed to get a hold of Sefu.

Princess Carina sputters and struggles. She's surprisingly strong, but not nearly enough to do her any good. I gradually increase the pressure as I repeat the question in the same tone.

"Do you have a problem with me?"

No one around appears at all interested in interfering and Princess Carina continues to struggle.

"What're... you... you think..." She's managing words now, just not the one I'm looking for.

I keep increasing the pressure. "It's a yes or no question. Do you have a problem with me?"

She's gasping a little now, but manages to answer, "Yes!"

I release her, abruptly and completely, and she staggers. She doesn't fall though. After a moment, Princess Carina turns to face me, alternately rubbing her shoulder and her wrist.

"That's it?" Her surprise and disbelief are all too obvious, "You think that's the end of it?"

"Hardly," I shake my head, "I just don't think this's the time or the place."

Princess Carina retreats to where her sisters are standing while I turn to Sefu and Laine.

"Settle down, Sefu," From the corner of my eye I can see Princess Carina turn pale, "I'm fine. Let's go get you some lunch."

We arrive at the palace door to find Monarch Reginald waiting, looking thoroughly upset.

"I saw that from my window," He informs me, "I do hope you are not injured."

"I'm fine, your majesty. Although I do have a discussion to finish with Carina later."

"Very well," The Monarch nods, "You should be able to find her in her rooms at any time since," He raises his voice so the approaching princesses can hear, "Carina won't be leaving her rooms any time in the foreseeable future."

Laine waits until we're out of earshot to comment, "Ouch. Someone 's in serious shit."

I shrug. "We'll see what she has to say for herself when I get a chance to talk to her. Won't be this afternoon though."

Duke Malin, Laine, Sefu, and I are among the first to enter the throne room. Angelita, Xylia, and Tory are among the last. They join us near the front as Monarch Reginald and Derian enter and take their places.

At first it's all minor court business. Everyone present is bored stiff and Sefu stretches out on the floor at my feet. Then, late in the afternoon, Monarch Reginald straightens himself and raises a hand for silence.

"High Lady Angelita Mendus Straisen, approach."

Angelita steps forward and curtsies.

"We apologize for the delay," The Monarch begins, "There are very few vacant holdings and minor legalities had to be sorted out. However, now that those are out of the way, We are pleased to present your ladyship with those lands previously held by the late High Lord Yvon. We request your continued presence that the last details may be worked out."

"Thank you, your majesty." Angelita curtsies again and steps back.

"One final announcement," The Monarch stands, "We wish to inform Our court that Our son, Crown Prince Derian, will marry Lady Nerita Chassaven on the thirtieth day of this month."

I suspect Derian is as surprised by the formal announcement as I am.

"This audience is adjourned." Monarch Reginald finishes.

"Hey," Angelita immediately turns to me, "Congratulations."

"Thanks."

"Better you than me." She adds as the Monarch indicates for her and Tory to accompany him. Laine groans, but for once I'm willing to agree with Angelita.

I spot Derian's signal for me to join him and manage to make it to his side before we're swamped with well wishers. It seems like forever before the throne room empties and Laine, Sefu, and Duke Malin can join us.

"Congratulations," The Duke chuckles, "If you will excuse me."

Derian nods. "Thank you, your grace."

After Duke Malin leaves, I rest my head against Derian's shoulder. His arm tightens around me.

"Tired?" He queries softly.

"Very."

"I know they could be a while," Laine tilts her head toward the door Tory and Angelita had disappeared through, "But I'd like to talk to Tory before they leave."

I glance over her curiously. I'm not about to ask though.

"Shall we go?" Derian asks me.

"Sounds good."

17-10-48-06-04SM

It's nearly time for the meeting to discuss wedding clothes and rings before Laine turns up. She's flushed and breathless as if she's been running.

"You're late."

"No shit," Laine begins stripping even before she reaches our dressing room, "Please tell me you can give me a hand."

"Yeah," I go with her, "You two oversleep?"

"No, UnderGround Club left Monarch's Town this morning. The plan is for them to go to Seeri Meadow, look around, get settled in, and then some 'll be back for your wedding."

"Good thing I don't need to talk to Nikki then." I grimace.

Laine chuckles. "I'm guessing you're not pregnant yet. Does that mean you'll actually be sleeping here?"

"For the next few days anyway. Derian isn't entirely happy about it."

"Tough shit." Laine doesn't sound at all sympathetic.

"Let's just see how fast we can get you ready."

Laine, Sefu, and I are only just on time and the last to arrive. Already present are Derian, Duke Malin, Monarch Reginald, and three men I've never seen before. The Monarch glances at the clock on the wall as Laine and I sit.

"Derian," He begins by turning to his son, "Did you speak with Marcellus yesterday?"

"I did," Derian nods, "And he agreed. He also suggested wearing our dress uniforms this time."

"Of what rank?" One of the strange men queries.

"Marcellus and I are both colonels with the secondary reserve."

Duke Malin looks surprised at that. "Your highness has served in the militia?"

"Tradition requires all princes of Norsecount to serve a minimum two years with the primary reserve," Derian explains, "Although most simply take an officers commission and retire after."

"I gather your highness didn't?"

"It's a bit of a long story," Derian replies, "Suffice it to say Marcellus and I started as privates; I served two years, Marcellus served three; then we transferred to the secondary reserve."

"Dress uniforms will be acceptable," Monarch Reginald states firmly, "However, I believe his grace still needs appropriate attire."

"I do." Duke Malin confirms.

The stranger who had spoken notes that.

"And for the ladies?" The second man enquires.

Laine turns to me, "Would you like to have my grandmother's gown? I'll never want it for myself."

I nod. "Sure. It's just the gown though, isn't it?"

"Yeah."

The second man begins writing. "Then my lady will need a veil and shoes, among other things. And for your bridesmaid?"

"I've got a formal gown I've never worn," Laine replies, "And anything I need to go with it."

"Which one?" I query dryly. I happen to know Laine has a number of dresses she has yet to wear.

"I'll show you later."

"And rings?" The third man speaks up.

"Will have to be purchased, if not custom made," The Monarch responds, "And if they are to be made, I would see them delivered no later than the twenty-fifth."

"Yes, of course, your majesty."

"Could custom rings be made to match the ring my lady has in that time?" Derian queries.

"Yes, your highness. Such a task would be my highest priority."

Derian glances down the table at me and I nod. Then he turns back to the third man, "In that case, it had best be. I trust you have the design."

"I do, your highness."

"Is there anything else?" Monarch Reginald glances around the table.

The second man addresses me and Laine, "I will need to see the gown my lady spoke of."

Laine nods. "No problem there."

No one else speaks and the Monarch dismisses everyone.

After lunch, I leave Sefu with Laine and find my way to the rooms I've been told are Princess Carina's. Shortly after I knock, I can hear a muffled, "It's open."

I let myself in and close the door behind me. Then I glance around. The room, which I'm guessing was originally a sitting room, is only very dimly lit. It's also been thoroughly trashed.

Princess Carina appears quickly, wrapped in a dressing gown, and scowls. "Where's your tiger this time?"

"Busy," My eyes meet and hold hers, "What's your problem?"

"With what? You?"

"It's as good a place to start as any."

Princess Carina's scowl deepens, but she seems to be having trouble deciding what to say. She doesn't try to look away though.

"Who do you think you are?"

I know she doesn't want me to answer that so I wait for her to continue.

"Everything was fine and then you showed up... you and your friends and that animal... and now everything 's all crazy..." One of Princess Carina's hands is holding her gown closed, but the other is tightly clenched at her side, "You're not even anybody important or anything, but you're always around... everything was going just fine... and then you come taking over everything..." Her voice drops so low I can only hear, "...Should've been mine..."

That strikes me as weird and I can't help raising an eyebrow. Princess Carina catches it immediately and understands the unspoken question.

"Everyone knows Derian isn't really my brother. His majesty 's just too stubborn to come out and admit it. If he would then..."

Obviously my amazement at what I'm hearing is showing in my face because Princess Carina trails off in confusion.

"What?"

I slowly shake my head. "I thought you smarter than that. Either I'm wrong, which I doubt, or it was someone else's idea originally."

"What do you mean?" Princess Carina demands.

"Whether you're his majesty's daughter or not, your mother was still married to him, making him your stepfather, at the very least. Marriages between step-siblings 're frowned on everywhere I know of. Besides, his majesty seems to prefer whispers behind his back to open scandal that he could be pressured into doing something about."

Princess Carina's face is hard to read as she considers that. Then, abruptly, she drops onto the edge of a chair, looking thoroughly defeated.

"It was Mother's idea," Princess Carina admits softly, "It always sounded wrong, but I could never figure out why."

I cross the room to sit in the chair beside hers.

She sighs and slumps back before continuing, "I always knew Mother's head was twisted around funny. Letitia 's the same... worse actually. That's probably why Sefu doesn't like her."

I allow my surprise at that to show. "I've never been sure which of those four he doesn't like."

Princess Carina grimaces. "Letitia doesn't like animals of any kind and they don't like her. A lot of people can't stand her either. Except Delia, Elana, and Kamilla. They worship her." Princess Carina shudders.

I frown. "You mean twisted as in insane?"

"In ways..." Princess Carina breaks off to study me critically, "You might actually believe the stuff that goes on that no one sees."

"Does Nerissa even know about that?"

Princess Carina shudders again. "I hope she never does. I've always made them leave her alone... as much as I could. Nerissa 's always been different from them... it's just," Princess Carina slumps farther in her seat, "I've never liked little children. I just never seem to understand what they want."

I nod to myself. That explains a whole lot.

"But what about you? You're not like them either and you're smarter and tougher than you let on."

"Fat lot of good that does me," Princess Carina scowls, "I'm never going to be allowed to go anywhere or do anything more than I am now."

"Maybe, maybe not. His majesty may be a little stuck on the status quo, but it's costing him big time."

Princess Carina studies me curiously. "You know what's going on?"

"As much as I need or care to. But that's a whole long story and not what I'm concerned about right now."

"Which would be?"

"You play the court butterfly well and yet..." I glance pointedly around the dim, trashed room, "What would you do if you could get away from this?"

Princess Carina looks surprised by the question. "I don't know... possibly leave Monarch's Town. Maybe even Norsecount."

"Would you want to marry?"

"Maybe... I don't know," She shrugs, "I do know I don't ever want children. Why even ask? You can't help me."

"Maybe not," I concede, "But did his majesty tell you he's invited High Lady Irina of Ouestlun here?"

Princess Carina scowls. "No. Lady Irina may mean well, but the last thing I need is a mother figure. It's been hard enough escaping my own mother's influence."

"Your mother decorated your rooms?"

Princess Carina nods. "Not just my rooms... for all six of us. And she appointed all our personal servants and she made up a whole lot of ridiculous rules for us... What we can and can't do, what we can and can't wear... And of course we can't make any changes..."

"How old are you?" I query curiously.

"Twenty-three. My birthday's in March."

Making her about a year older than I am and ten older than Nerissa.

"You've lived here the whole time?"

"Only since Mother died. It's been like his majesty doesn't have any idea how to deal with us."

"That much's obvious. But then there's a lot he seems incapable of dealing with."

"Yet he's not a bad monarch..." Princess Carina frowns.

"Just old and set in his ways."

Princess Carina studies me critically. "You don't want me or my sisters to continue on here, do you?"

"I don't see how it's to anyone's benefit."

She chuckles sardonically. "There is one benefit to being confined to my rooms right now."

"Not having to go to Letitia's ball?" I've heard both Derian and Nerissa complain about that one as well.

"First off," Princess Carina grimaces, "It's Letitia's twenty-first birthday. Second, all of us are always supposed to dress like you saw on the thirtieth. Nerissa loves it, but..."

"She would," I chuckle, "I don't know of many others though."

"They'll want your wedding gown to look similar." Princess Carina informs me.

"Maybe if they had more time," I respond, "Which they don't."

Princess Carina looks disgusted. "Is there anything you won't get?"

"I don't have a choice about attending the ball this evening. Or any other event in the foreseeable future."

"True," Princess Carina concedes, "The greater the position the greater the hassles. Or so Grandmother Martrency claimed. Mother's mother," Princess Carina explains, "Although the complete opposite of her daughter in every way. I lived with her on and off as a small child."

"My father used to say similar things. Except our family's position came with far fewer privileges."

"Your family retained some power?" Princess Carina frowns.

"Not exactly. We had our responsibilities to the people around us and a certain degree of respect. And, invariably, a certain number of enemies."

Princess Carina chuckles. "I think I would prefer not to be counted among them."

"That depends entirely on you."

Princess Carina nods. "Don't count on seeing me or Nerissa this evening."

Dinner is part of this thing tonight. That's why Laine and I make sure to have a snack before getting ready. We've never been impressed with formal dinners.

Duke Malin wants us ready for five, which's when it's supposed to start. Laine and I are a little late, but Derian ends up being even later.

"I do apologize, your grace." Derian bows his head to Duke Malin.

"Accepted," The Duke frowns sternly, "Shall we go?"

I take Derian's arm as the five of us head down to the ballroom.

Princess Letitia is standing just inside the doors, greeting people as they enter. Flanking her are princesses Delia, Elana, and Kamilla. Evidently a means of escape was found for Nerissa.

Derian nods to the four of them. Laine and I curtsy, although perhaps not as deeply as strictly required. Sefu begins to growl, but stops when I rest a hand on his head.

Duke Malin bows. "Happy birthday, your highness." Then he guides us across the floor to where Monarch Reginald is seated.

"Your grace is late..." The Monarch begins sternly.

"Because I was late," Derian doesn't give the Duke a chance to speak, "Captain Sevyn wanted a word with me."

"Very well," Monarch Reginald remains serious, "Have you or your lady seen Nerissa at all today?"

Derian frowns warily. "No."

I shake my head.

"As you can see," The Monarch gestures around the room, "Nerissa is not here. Nor is she to be found in any of her usual haunts. None of the staff have seen her... indeed no one has and her rooms are empty, yet the guards are certain she is somewhere within that wing of the palace."

Derian's frown deepens, but we're interrupted by others coming to pay their respects. Duke Malin and Laine move off, but Derian and I are expected to stay and be polite. At least Sefu remains at my side. Probably to let me know what he thinks of the people we're introduced to.

Until tonight I really haven't met many people here in Norsecount. Not formally anyway. I've seen most of them before, either at the dances I've attended or court. Sefu's reactions help me remember more than I would otherwise. There're very few people my tiger likes. He's indifferent to most, but he never dislikes anyone without good reason.

Finally the ballroom doors close and the dancing begins. Sefu waits near the dais while Derian and I dance the first couple together. Derian is worried about his sister though and after the second dance, we return to the dais.

"You spoke with Carina this afternoon, didn't you?" Derian's voice is low enough only I can hear him.

I nod. "She's interesting to talk to."

"I generally don't."

"I learned a few things," I continue, "But I suspect I know where Nerissa might be and why. I just haven't seen or spoken to her today."

"I've never noticed that Carina particularly cared what happened to any of her sisters," Derian looks wary, "Although I'll admit I don't know her well."

I shrug lightly. "Keeping in mind too... If Nerissa were in danger, we'd hear from Ford."

Derian nods and relaxes. Or at least until we can hear Sefu growl over the music. I immediately kneel down beside him.

"What is it?"

He just growls again, lower this time.

I look up at Derian. "Whatever it is, it's not really close."

"Still," Derian is clearly concerned, "If there is a problem, either the guards need to know or they'll be reporting something soon."

The three of us head around the dais. The four princesses have gathered on the other side of it and the Monarch is speaking with a group of people I'm not sure I've met.

"Is something wrong, Lady Nerita?" Monarch Reginald addresses me immediately.

"Sefu thinks so, your majesty."

Before anyone can respond, a guard appears and speaks softly to the Monarch, who nods quickly. Sefu has stopped growling, but he hasn't relaxed at all. Monarch Reginald gives the guard an equally soft order. Then the guard leaves. Derian pulls me off to one side as the Monarch returns to his previous conversation.

"Do you know anything about these anti-monarchy fanatics that could help?"

I shake my head. "I know what I needed to to protect the people of the Old Quarter. But even if you are facing ex-military, they'd be trained and armed differently from the Arawn city patrols."

Derian nods grimly. "You should know... if the situation worsens too much they could call the secondary reserve to active duty."

Including Derian.

"Is that why you were late?" I lace my fingers through his.

"It is."

19-10-48-06-04SM

High Lady Irina is expected to arrive sometime this morning, but Sefu has way too much energy and needs to get out. Laine and Derian are both busy so I end up asking Princess Nerissa to come with us.

She's unusually quiet though, almost sombre. Even Sefu's high spirits don't seem to cheer her up.

"Hey," I wait for the girl to look at me, "Is something bothering you?"

"Is Lady Irina really coming here?"

"So his majesty says."

Princess Nerissa's shoulders slump. "Derian and Carina both think I should foster with her. But Lady Irina lives in Ouestlun. I don't want to leave Norsecount. Not when you and Derian are getting married and he's home more..."

"You and Lady Irina are both invited to the wedding," I point out, "In fact, I'm hoping you'll look after Sefu that day."

Princess Nerissa brightens. "Really?"

"Really."

"Do you think I'll really have to foster with Lady Irina?"

"I don't know. Even if you do, I doubt it'll be as bad as you think."

Princess Nerissa scowls. "Why does everyone treat me like a child?"

"In all honesty, your highness, because you act like a child."

The girl's scowl deepens and she glares at me. Then she turns and flees to the palace. Sefu, who has just returned with his ball, watches her go with a puzzled expression.

I kneel down to rub his head and neck. "She'll be fine, Sefu. She just needs some time."

On returning to the top of the old south tower, Sefu and I find Laine talking on the telephone. She glances up when we enter.

"Who?" I query.

Laine places a hand over the mouthpiece. "Angelita."

I start to nod, then a thought occurs to me, "Did anyone tell her President Gayre 's sending an ambassador?"

Laine shrugs. She returns to her conversation as I head up to our suite to change before lunch. I've been invited to eat with Derian, the Monarch, and High Lady Irina, so I should shower as well.

I'm just finishing in the bathroom when Laine comes up.

"Apparently Angelita didn't know about the ambassador," Laine grimaces, "Anyway, she actually called me."

"So they've got telephone service?"

"Three lines," Laine confirms, "They've got four houses in the village since there's no keep. They're just only using three for the moment."

"Did you get her number?"

Laine nods. "She said we'd only reach her or Devin on that line. Apparently the second line 's for Logan and Nikki and everyone 'cept Fae 's on the third."

I can't help frowning. "Fae left the group?"

"All Angelita said was Fae returned to Eltdar Phimq to get married."

I nod to myself. "Any word as to who'll come with Angelita?"

"I didn't ask," Laine flushes slightly, "Anyway, aren't you invited elsewhere for lunch?"

"Yeah, and I've got twenty minutes before Derian comes looking for me."

Monarch Reginald is waiting when we arrive at the same time as another woman.

I would guess that she's in her late fifties or early sixties, although her hair is mostly still black. She's my height, slim, stately, and well dressed with the deep tan and dark eyes common to natives of Ouestlun.

"Please, come on in," The Monarch calls on seeing us, "Thank you for coming."

The dark woman smiles, looking a little bemused. All four of us enter and she half closes the door.

"Lady Irina," Monarch Reginald addresses her, "If I may introduce Lady Nerita Chassaven and her companion, Sefu."

She looks a little wary on seeing my tiger, but he's studying her with the curious expression that means he's not sure what to think of her.

"Lady Nerita," The Monarch continues, "I would like you to meet High Lady Irina of Ouestlun."

I curtsy appropriately, which she acknowledges with a gracious nod.

"This way, please." Monarch Reginald indicates the table, which's already set for four. He sits at one end, with Lady Irina on one side and me and Derian opposite her.

"Lady Nerita," The Monarch addresses me as we begin to eat, "What happened this morning that has Nerissa so upset?"

"I gave her an honest answer to a semi-rhetorical question."

Both Derian and Lady Irina wince.

Monarch Reginald nods to himself. "Would that more people did such with her," Then he sighs, "Only after she locked herself in her rooms did I discover she has somehow acquired all the keys."

"Even from her maid?" Lady Irina frowns.

The Monarch nods. "Speaking of whom, she's had an accident similar to the one suffered by Carina's maid after Victoria's death."

"If that was an accident..." Derian shakes his head, "To my knowledge Nerissa forbid her maid to enter her rooms years ago."

"If the Princess Nerissa is indeed committed to my care, I will find her an appropriate attendant." Lady Irina tells the Monarch.

"Thank you, my lady," Monarch Reginald responds, "And I'm beginning to believe time in your care will do Nerissa a great deal of good."

Lady Irina nods.

"Now," The Monarch turns back to me, "I understand you spoke with Carina yesterday. I trust she was better behaved than the day before."

"She was."

"She actually spoke to you?" Lady Irina raises an eyebrow, "Not an hour ago Carina rather unceremoniously told me to go away... you're not surprised."

"No, I'm not. From what she had to say, I got the impression she'd simply like to be treated her own age."

Monarch Reginald frowns sternly. "I've seen little evidence of her acting her age."

"Your majesty, she's older than I am, living under rules made when she was a child."

Lady Irina studies me critically. "How old are you?"

"Twenty-two... born in January."

"Nearly a year younger than Carina," Lady Irina nods to herself, "Had you your way, what would you see done about her?"

"For now I'd like her where Laine and I can keep an eye on her. If things continue the way they are, she'll find worse trouble than she already has."

"Certainly true," Lady Irina nods again, then addresses Monarch Reginald, "As for the other four... Did Victoria not leave her daughters a small property?"

"She did."

"Then I suggest the necessary arrangements be made to move them there. To keep them at court benefits no one."

"I will take that under consideration," The Monarch's expression is hard to read, "Have you any other concerns at present?"

"Only that the upcoming wedding seems rather rushed..."

"My lady," My eyes catch hers, "If you want to go out to Seeri Meadow and argue that point with Tory, go ahead. I just doubt you'd have any more success than his majesty."

The Monarch frowns. "You think them in Seeri Meadow already?"

"Angelita called Laine this morning. Not only are they there, they've got homes and telephone service."

"Of whom are you speaking?" Lady Irina frowns.

"Lady Nerita knows these people best." The Monarch informs her.

I sigh. "You've heard of the Second Shield and the Sedyr, haven't you?"

Lady Irina nods. "It's said it was the Second Shield who originally dreamed up Experiment Redemption. Although I wouldn't care to guess their motives."

"They were looking for someone," I can't help an amused smile, "I just don't think they were quite expecting what they found."

"I think that would be understating the case." Monarch Reginald observes wryly.

"UnderGround Club was originally a mercenary crew out of lower Central City. Eight people, all with interesting abilities, if not unusual pasts. And then they added two members while at Camp Streton."

Lady Irina nods slowly. "Unusual how?"

"I don't know everything," I warn her, "But roughly forty years ago there was a group of scientists known as Mountain East Development. I don't know what they were doing originally, but they found samples of DNA from four races: Pure human, Sedyr, Lendin, and one other. They tried one experiment with some of it and created Rylan Tobin."

"Would that not be considered highly unethical?" Lady Irina looks shocked.

"Ethics kind of got lost early in the civil war, along with human rights and respect. Anyway, MED was dissolved and the remnants became GenTech. Their sole purpose was to tinker with the DNA MED found. Tory and Nikki Genstang are the only survivors of hundreds of attempts. It's interesting though, in that FTK, who're running Experiment Redemption, are a group that broke away from GenTech a decade ago."

"This is the same Tory I've heard spoken of recently?"

I nod. "You'll hear more of her yet. She's the one the Second Shield were looking for. She's also the leader of UnderGround Club."

Lady Irina nods. "You've mentioned three. Were others in the group from experiments?"

"Logan Hysan has to be. There's no other way a pure human could survive to grow up. And we know Devin Straisen escaped one of the military's projects."

"That's half. And the others?"

"Pharessya Norst 's from the Sedyr community and I doubt she has much human blood. Angelita Mendus Straisen 's a whole long story by herself..."

"The former princess of Estorika?"

I nod. "Shawnda Silver, Ford, and Kyle are all from lower Central City, but that doesn't make them normal by any standard."

"I see." Lady Irina nods thoughtfully.

We eat in silence for a time. Finally Lady Irina addresses me again, "To have participated in Experiment Redemption, you must have been part of a group yourself... yet..."

"They classed us as a gang for convenience," I respond, "And I suspect they considered us something of a headache."

"Did you have a name for yourselves?"

"The girls of Black Oak Court... commonly shortened to Black Oak Court."

"Please tell me that is not a reference to Lost Cities." Lady Irina looks pained.

"It was Laine's idea," I chuckle, "But my aunt had been reading Hortense to us. Must've been twelve years ago now."

Lady Irina frowns. "What kind of woman reads such to a ten year old child?"

"First of all, my aunt wasn't considered entirely sane. Just relatively benign. Second, ten year olds in Arawn have to function on the level of a fifteen or sixteen year old anywhere else. Although I'll admit some of what my aunt read to me made more sense when I read it myself a couple years later."

Lady Irina shivers. "You were the leader of your group then. How did that come about?"

"It's quite a long story and I'd have to go back to the end of the civil war."

"I think we have time enough for that," Monarch Reginald tells me, "I must admit a certain amount of curiosity myself."

I nod. "The war didn't end with victory on one side or the other. It ended because the mines and wells ran dry. While they could recycle a certain amount, they couldn't maintain previous production levels."

"So they stopped fighting because they had to?" Lady Irina looks both horrified and fascinated.

"More or less. But just before the official declaration, both sides forcibly relocated large numbers of people. Literally went through the cities and took away people at random."

"Why?" Monarch Reginald swallows hard.

I shrug. "I don't think there was an official reason. Just rumour and speculation. But the end result was chaos... most notably panic and a break down of the basic family."

"Unbelievable." Lady Irina shakes her head sadly.

I move on, "Then came the military unification and an attempt to impose martial law. The problem was only those with money or military connections were considered citizens and protected... for as much as Arawn's military protects anyone."

"How much of the population did that actually include?" Monarch Reginald queries.

"Maybe a third... if that. But not a single person in the Old Quarter of South City."

Lady Irina frowns. "Yet surely there must have been some order."

"The same as there had been for the previous century or so. I just wish the city patrol masters had learned to leave us alone."

Derian studies me curiously. "How much of that was your family and how much was this John Simeon?"

"John Simeon kept our records and judged disputes as necessary. So births, marriages, deaths, legal transactions... The Old Quarter 's never had more than a thousand permanent residents at any given time."

"And your family?" The Monarch enquires.

"We looked after the people. That meant keeping the military and scientists out, for which they hated us," I grimace briefly, "But it also meant ensuring an adequate food supply... primarily protein paste; keeping an eye on the elderly, ill, and orphaned; lending a hand as necessarily... Almost all my memories of Father are of accompanying him while he worked. Inside our home it was Mother and Father's sister who looked after me."

"How often did you accompany your father?" Lady Irina queries.

"Most days... it really depended what he was dealing with. He and Mother both died when I was six."

"How then did you come to follow in his footsteps?" Lady Irina frowns, "Evidently you did. Yet no six year old child could be capable of so much."

"After Father's death, the two who had been assisting him split the work between them and I was left in the care of my aunt. I was pretty well known though, from being seen with Father, and people would ask me to help them. At first it was little things... tasks and errands any small child could be entrusted with. And I liked to visit some of the people who couldn't get out of their homes. As long as my aunt could find me when she wanted me, she never seemed to mind."

Lady Irina nods to herself.

"It didn't take long for me to end up working with Father's assistants," I continue, "Then, just before my eighth birthday, one of them vanished and I took over almost everything that didn't involve leaving the Old Quarter or dealing with outsiders. I had free access to all John Simeon's records and files by then."

"What about your own education?" Lady Irina frowns.

"John Simeon taught me to read, write, and figure and my aunt used to read all kinds of books to me... although most of it was pre-war history and mythology."

"How old were you when you took on the remainder of your family's responsibilities?" The Monarch returns to the previous subject.

"That came gradually and I always had help from others, but when I was nine, Father's other assistant died. By then my reputation was such that no one cared to question me."

"At nine?" Lady Irina looks very sceptical.

I chuckle. "A few city patrol masters thought that too. But between the lower city, which was rough compared to Port or Central, and repeat visits to the Old Quarter, South City went through twenty-seven patrol masters in fourteen years."

Derian frowns. "It never occurred to anyone that might be indicative of a problem?"

"Oh, they knew there was a problem," I shake my head ruefully, "It just never occurred to them to change tactics. Anyway, the summer I was nine, my aunt went out one day... I don't even remember why... and came home with Laine."

Monarch Reginald nods to himself. "That was the first time you met her, was it not?"

"First time I'd seen or heard of her. She was half feral and it took months for us to find out what little she knew of herself and her family. We figured she was about thirteen, but she just kind of attached herself to me."

Lady Irina frowns in confusion. "That would make her twenty-six..."

"Give or take a couple centuries." I chuckle.

"I believe his grace and I worked her birth date out to ten, oh four, thirty-seven, oh three, oh four." Monarch Reginald adds.

Lady Irina looks sceptical, but moves on, "She was the first you and your aunt took in?"

I nod. "The first of many, not just the nine who left South City with me. Laine 's just the only one not born in the Old Quarter."

"Might I ask where your aunt is now?" Lady Irina queries.

"She died just before I turned sixteen and my only living blood relation is a first cousin on my mother's side, who came with me."

Lady Irina looks thoughtful for a moment. "How is it that you were able to leave at all?"

"There was someone who had no intention of leaving that I trusted to take my place... and John Simeon insisted it was important I take the opportunity to get out. Besides which, I wasn't about to just trust FTK with the ones who did want to leave."

"And you haven't heard anything of those you left behind?" Lady Irina frowns.

"Tory briefly mentioned seeing John Simeon when she went back into Arawn to get the lockets for me and Laine, but, beyond that, no. Until very recently all communication in Arawn has been word of mouth, military radio, and, for those with the right connections, limited internet. There hasn't been telephone or radio service in centuries."

"I gather they have electricity, at least."

"Amazingly enough, they do," I grimace, "But the power plants weren't maintained properly and the dam on the Riverre blew last winter."

"I think," Monarch Reginald looks grim, "I'm beginning to see why Angelita chose to give up her birthright."

"Complete chaos or not, she wouldn't've if she didn't trust President Gayre."

Derian frowns. "Why would she trust the President when she trusts so few others?"

I shrug. "All I know is they seem to understand each other."

The Monarch frowns abruptly. "He too has a tiger companion, does he not? How did that come about?"

"After Angelita and I found the cubs, she took Xylia and left me with the other three. When she came back, she had a whole group with her, including Natalia, Tory, and President Gayre. He was pretty angry... apparently he'd seen the mess Angelita made of the military base when she put an end to their experiment..."

Monarch Reginald's frown deepens. "One woman took on an entire base?"

"Angelita's other ability, above and beyond communicating with animals, is what Becky Riverson calls empathic projection. And not only can she project emotions on others, she can amplify what a person is already feeling. After what I saw her do that day, I don't ever want to see her that upset again."

The Monarch nods to himself. "So President Gayre took one of the cubs for himself?"

I nod. "He's evidently been looking after it himself too. A winter tiger's first loyalty is to its main caregiver and the cubs weren't yet weaned when we found them."

"Sefu 's still a cub then?" Lady Irina queries.

"And still growing," I confirm, "Males, like Sefu, can get up to three hundred kilograms."

Derian raises an eyebrow. "And you claim he sleeps on your feet?"

"Not for very much longer."

Monarch Reginald frowns. "I was under the impression he's trained to stay off furniture."

I sigh. "Everything except my bed. And I don't know why I can't train him to stay off that."

"He'll learn." Derian responds.

The Monarch chuckles and addresses me, "Lady Nerita, would you happen to know anything about household locks? I will not leave Nerissa locked in her rooms, whether sense can be talked into her or not."

"I can pick locks, although I would prefer that to be a last resort."

"Fair enough," Monarch Reginald turns to his son, "I believe you are the only one who hasn't tried speaking to her."

Derian grimaces. "She hasn't been entirely happy with me in days, but I will try."

"Thank you. If you three would please deal with Nerissa. I intend to have a few words with Carina."

We'd long ago finished lunch, so we leave the table and head for the wing of the palace containing the princesses' suites. Lady Irina, Derian, Sefu, and I stop at Princess Nerissa's door while Monarch Reginald continues to Princess Carina's.

Derian knocks. When there's no response, he knocks again. "Nerissa!" There's still no response.

Then Sefu takes a swipe at the door with his paw. When there's no response to that either, he looks up at me with worried eyes. I sigh as I take a small, blackened metal case from my skirt pocket. Opening it, I remove my lock picks. I set the case on the floor for the short time it takes me to open the simple household lock. Once that's done, I return the lock picks to the case, which goes back into my pocket.

"How did you come to learn that?" Lady Irina studies me with undisguised interest.

"It's handy when a child accidentally locks themselves in somewhere... or a person living alone falls ill... among other things."

Derian opens the door, but Sefu is the first one inside. He isn't in the outer room when the rest of us enter. Derian and I wait while Lady Irina goes looking for Nerissa and Sefu.

"What else do you have on you?" Derian keeps his voice soft.

"A few useful little tools. I'll show you some other time."

He nods.

A moment later, we can hear muffled voices. Then Lady Irina calls, "Lady Nerita!"

It doesn't take me long to find what is obviously Princess Nerissa's bedroom. And even less time to identify the problem.

"Sefu! Get over here!"

He looks momentarily torn between me and Princess Nerissa, but evidently recognizes my tone as one he shouldn't ignore. The girl glares at me as Sefu comes to my side.

"Come on." I encourage Sefu to come with me by means of a hand on his neck. Lady Irina gives me a grateful look as I guide my tiger from the room and back to where Derian is waiting.

"I have to take him right out of here." I tell Derian, who nods and accompanies us into the corridor.

"How did he come to be so protective of Nerissa?" Derian frowns slightly.

"I honestly don't know," I kneel down beside Sefu to rub his head and neck, "But he's as attached to her as Laine."

Derian's frown deepens. "What was said between you and Nerissa?"

"I gather she's feeling picked on, but what she asked was why everyone treats her like a child."

Derian nods to himself. "I find it hard to think of her as anything else. Although that could be partly attributed to the sixteen years between us."

I shrug. "What do we do now?"

"Wait to see if either Father or Lady Irina need anything more of us."

That could be a bit of a wait, depending how co-operative Carina and Nerissa are.

"Is this whole wing just for the princesses?" I continue to rub Sefu's head and neck.

"Traditionally," Derian replies, "Well, including the crown princess and monarch's consort."

I can't help shaking my head. "It always seemed to me that separate rooms for married couples only invites trouble."

Derian chuckles. "That's all too often the case. Incidentally, I believe Mother shared Father's rooms. I know Victoria didn't."

Lady Irina enters the corridor, steering a sullen looking Nerissa by the shoulder.

"Derian, should his majesty ask, we will be in my rooms."

Derian nods. Sefu stares balefully after Nerissa as Lady Irina leads her away.

After that it's still a long wait before we see Monarch Reginald. He looks distinctly bemused as he approaches us.

"Lady Nerita, would you know where I might find Duke Malin? I've a favour I wish to ask of him."

"I believe he and Laine were keeping to our rooms this afternoon."

"Thank you. I trust Lady Irina has Nerissa well in hand."

"She seems to." Derian responds.

The Monarch nods to himself. "Do either of you know when Pelmonts expected to arrive?"

Derian and I both shake our heads.

"Very well," Monarch Reginald nods again, "I don't believe there is anything else I need of either of you this afternoon." He heads off down the corridor.

Derian waits until we're alone, "Then I've got a few hours free. Would my lady care to look around the palace? For as long as you've been here, I don't believe you've seen much of it."

"Sure." It's not like I have anything better to do anyway.

20-10-48-06-04SM

Because Duke Malin and Laine didn't tell me they were going riding yesterday afternoon, Monarch Reginald couldn't speak with the Duke. So I'm not surprised when Carl appears as Laine, her father, and I are finishing breakfast.

"Your grace, my ladies, his majesty wishes to know if he might come speak with you in half an hour."

Duke Malin glances questioningly at me. I nod and he turns to the page, "As his majesty wishes."

"Thank you, your grace." Carl bows, then leaves.

Shortly after that, Laine, Sefu, and I go up to our suite to prepare. Neither of us says much and we're back downstairs just as feet can be heard from below. Monarch Reginald appears a moment later, accompanied only by the guard called Conors.

"Good morning, your majesty," Duke Malin bows, "Please, be seated."

"Thank you, your grace."

Conors remains standing by the stairs, but the rest of us seat ourselves. I can't help noticing how old and tired the Monarch looks.

"Your grace, I must request of you a favour," Monarch Reginald begins, "May I commit the Princess Carina to the care of yourself and your daughter temporarily? I have already spoken to her on the matter."

Duke Malin considers the idea carefully, "As your majesty wishes. We do have rooms enough for one more."

"Thank you, your grace," Monarch Reginald looks relieved, although only momentarily, "Lady Nerita, have you any intention at all of using the rooms reserved for the crown princess?"

"No, your majesty."

"Good. Then, with Nerissa entrusted to Lady Irina and the other four moving to the property left them by their mother, that wing can undergo a much needed renovation."

Laine nods to herself. "So Carina 'll only be here while the work 's being done?"

"That is the current plan. Although," The Monarch sighs, "Carina doesn't have a ladies maid and it could be some time before someone suitable can be found."

"No rush." Laine shrugs it off.

"Lady Nerita," Monarch Reginald turns back to me, "How is Miss Conors working out?"

"She and Sefu don't like each other, your majesty." From the corner of my eye I notice the guard at the stairs stiffen slightly.

"I see..." The Monarch frowns.

"Truth is, your majesty, I won't need a personal servant until next month."

"And yourself?" He addresses Laine.

"I neither need nor want any kind of attendant," There's a cool edge to Laine's voice, "I don't intend to continue living at court past the end of this month."

Evidently she's already discussed that with her father.

"Then neither of you would object were Miss Conors reassigned... perhaps to either Carina or Nerissa?"

"Might I suggest Nerissa, your majesty?" I know he'll at least consider the idea, "If Lady Irina hasn't already found someone."

Monarch Reginald nods. "One last thing: Lady Laine, when did you last speak with Angelita?"

"Yesterday, your majesty. I believe she intended to contact you."

"She hasn't yet. Do you have a telephone number she could be reached at?"

"I do."

"If I could please get that from you."

"Sure." Laine gets up to get that for him

"Thank you," The Monarch turns to Duke Malin, "If your grace would please accompany me, there are just a couple matters to attend to before Carina moves up here."

"Of course, your majesty."

Monarch Reginald and Duke Malin leave. Then Laine and I go change clothes again so we can take Sefu out for some exercise.

Last night Pelmonts accepted an invitation to have lunch with us today and they reach our floors of the old south tower a little before noon. Laine, her father, and I aren't especially dressed up for this. Neither are Marcellus and Rowena, but Lord Pelmont is a little overdressed. I guess that's not really a surprise.

"Hey, come on in." Laine calls when they hesitate in the doorway.

Rowena enters first and glances around. "You really did get nice rooms."

Laine shrugs it off. "I'd like you to meet my father, Duke Lige Malin."

Our guests bow or curtsy as appropriate.

"Father, Lord George Pelmont and his son and daughter-in-law, Marcellus and Rowena."

The Duke bows his head briefly. "I'm honoured."

Rowena looks bemused, but we'd warned her Duke Malin is old fashioned.

"Please, be seated for the moment," The Duke continues, "Lunch may be some time yet."

Lord Pelmont looks uncomfortable as he takes the nearest chair. Duke Malin sits near him, but Marcellus accompanies the rest of us across the room. The Duke is good at putting people at ease, especially if left to do it on his own.

Laine claims a chair while Marcellus and Rowena sit together on a sofa. I settle myself cross legged on the floor so Sefu can rest his head on my knee. I don't know why, but he's wanted extra attention today.

"Derian wasn't invited?" Marcellus seems surprised.

"He'll be here... if he can," I respond, "Not that I've seen him yet today."

"At all?" Rowena raises an eyebrow.

"As in not since yesterday evening." I give her a stern look and she drops the subject.

"What has been happening here?" Marcellus enquires, "I last spoke with Derian the evening of the sixteenth."

"Wedding plans," I grimace, "Of course. I'm just happy there's someone else to look after the worst of that."

Rowena chuckles. "For all the rush, people're expecting it to be the biggest event of the year."

"I know exactly how many invitations went out," I inform her, "I specifically told Florence Knight, in his majesty's hearing, I don't want to know how many 're actually coming."

Marcellus laughs. "Sounds like something Derian would say. But what of the princesses? Derian gave me the impression they're finally to be dealt with."

"Oh, they are. Lady Irina 's here, but she's got her hands full with just Nerissa."

"Nerissa is to foster with her?" Marcellus nods to himself.

"That's already a done deal. They just won't leave for Ouestlun until next month."

"Now to see if Nerissa gets over herself between now and then," Laine grimaces, "Is she currently speaking to anyone?"

"Sefu... but I think that's about it."

Marcellus looks surprised. "I thought nothing could keep her quiet."

"She's decided everyone 's picking on her," I grimace, "Lady Irina 's doing the best she can and the rest of us 're leaving it to her. Besides which, I'm more concerned about Carina at the moment."

"Is that why his majesty asked Father to take her on?" Laine isn't happy about that one.

"I want Carina where I can keep an eye on her... before she gets herself into trouble his majesty can't cover up."

Rowena raises an eyebrow, "She's moving up here with you guys?"

"Today." Laine confirms sourly.

"His majesty wants that wing of the palace empty. The other four are leaving court permanently. But it sounds like that whole wing 's going to be gutted and redone."

Marcellus nods to himself. "It's about time."

Feet can be heard coming up the stairs, then Derian appears. Something is clearly bothering him, but he turns first to Duke Malin.

"Good morning, your grace... Lord Pelmont."

"Good morning." The Duke responds. Lord Pelmont bows his head.

Then Derian comes over to claim the chair directly behind me. I move back until I can rest my head on his knee.

"You look far too serious," Marcellus doesn't try to conceal his concern, "Or has something new come up?"

"Not new... exactly," Derian sighs, "At least not unexpected. How was the trip here?"

"Much the same as usual. Certainly more quiet than our week at Matllind."

Derian chuckles. "You expected anything else when you're there so seldom?"

Marcellus grimaces, but before more can be said, servants appear with lunch.

Pelmonts and Derian don't stay long after lunch, although Derian promises to come see me later. No sooner are they gone than Carina arrives with the first load of her belongings. She's moving into the suite opposite Duke Malin's and he's supervising that. Laine and I don't have anything to do, so we go out to the stable to visit our horses.

We return to the old south tower to find Carina waiting for us in the sitting room.

"Laine," Carina hesitates uncertainly, "His grace suggested I ask your help in updating my wardrobe..."

"I can do that," Laine agrees readily, "How about we start now by seeing what you have."

Carina still looks uncertain, "My things are pretty messy..."

"Best time," Laine responds, "That way only what you'll wear again gets into your closet."

"Okay." Carina leads the way to her new rooms. Sefu continues up to the top floor, probably for a nap, while Laine and I accompany Carina into her dressing room.

All her belongings are in the right rooms, but nothing has been put away yet. There's no sign of the servants who've been helping her; apparently they're off on a break.

"What's the next formal event you have to attend?" Laine enquires.

"The reception for the ambassador from Arawn," Carina makes a face, "Because I didn't attend Letitia's ball, I don't get a new dress for that."

"Well, let's start with that."

Carina's expression suggests she'd rather die than be seen in the lacy lavender confection she dredges from the bottom of a basket.

Laine cringes. "Do you own a formal gown that doesn't look like that one?"

Carina starts to shake her head, then pauses thoughtfully, "There's this one..." She tries several bags, boxes, and baskets before finding what she's looking for, "It was my grandmother's... Letitia got all Mother's clothes... I've just always thought it a bit old fashioned."

Laine studies the gown critically. It's a silvery grey-blue of quality fabric, simple lines, and minimal ornamentation.

"Can you wear it?" I enquire.

"Like it was made for me." Carina confirms.

"Good," Laine nods to herself, "We'll see what we can do with it once we see what else you've got."

Carina sets the gown aside and I separate out her other formal dresses to get them out of Laine's way.

"Is there anything else in this mess you wouldn't wear if you had a choice?" Laine queries.

Carina shakes her head. "I left that kind of stuff in my old rooms."

"Good. Let's get this put away and see what you'll need."

Which turns out to be a fair bit. Carina doesn't think twice about trashing things she doesn't like and I suspect she'd ditched two thirds of her wardrobe. I know Laine intends to take her shopping at the first opportunity, but I'd just as happily skip that trip.

After clothes come shoes, most of which aren't too bad, followed by jewelry, all of which turns out to be pearl.

"That was one of Mother's standing orders," Carina explains somewhat disgustedly, "The six of us were only supposed to have pearl. Nerissa has other stuff because Derian gave it to her."

Laine shakes her head. "None of this's even valuable. Would you keep any of it if you could get something else?"

"This," Carina picks out a string of pearlescent beads, "I strung them together myself, but they're originally off a doll's dress I had as a child."

"Then put them away and leave the rest in the box for now," Laine advises, "We've got a few days to see what else we can do."

There's a knock on the outer door and all three of us go out to see who it is. Carina lets the Monarch in, along with two guards carrying a large chest. They set it down and return to the corridor.

"I gather," Monarch Reginald begins dryly, "Given the amount of stuff left in your former suite, you'll need a few things."

"Mostly clothes, your majesty." Carina flushes slightly.

He nods. "Earlier I was reminded of something, although you must keep in mind it is a guess on my part. Have you heard mentioned the name of Travis Adarion?"

Carina shakes her head.

"He was a good friend of mine from childhood, but he left Norsecount shortly after Victoria and I married, on what always seemed to me a rather weak pretence. He was thought to be the end of the Adarion family and, after his death in Ouestlun near on twenty years ago, most of his possessions and the family holdings were sold or given away. Except for these few things I felt compelled to keep."

Carina frowns. "Your majesty thinks he might've been my father?"

"A guess, as I said before, based on certain similarities," The Monarch smiles wryly, "But it would now be impossible to prove for certain. Still, I'll let you look through these things and keep what catches your fancy."

Carina swallows hard. "Thank you, your majesty."

Monarch Reginald unlocks the trunk, which turns out to contain a wide variety of things, including sapphire and emerald jewelry and several small portraits, one of which could be Carina.

"Travis's mother," The Monarch identifies the woman, "And the last High Lady Adarion."

In the end, Carina leaves very little in the trunk.

"I would prefer," Monarch Reginald adds before leaving, "That you not speak of this widely. Although perhaps Lady Irina may know something of the last years of Travis's life."

"Yes, your majesty." Carina waits for him to leave the room before slumping in the only uncluttered chair.

Something is still bothering Derian when he comes looking for me after dinner. He doesn't seem interested in talking around Duke Malin and Carina, so we take Sefu and wander the palace corridors. As we walk, I lace my fingers through his.

"Rough day?" I query softly.

"Very," Derian sounds tired, "Some days it's as if everything hits all at once. And then it was reported Nerissa 's on a hunger strike."

I slowly shake my head. "That'll only last so long."

"I know." Derian is silent for several long minutes, "So his grace agreed to take on Carina. How long do you really think that'll last?"

"Only until she figures out a way out of here."

"With or without leaving a trail of scandal behind her?" Derian queries warily.

"Hopefully without. That's why I want to be able to keep an eye on her."

Derian chuckles. "You do have a way with people."

"You think I'm gonna change?"

"I wouldn't want you to." He squeezes my hand and neither of us speaks for a time.

"Does the name Travis Adarion mean anything?"

My question prompts a laugh from Derian and I glance up at him in surprise.

"Father finally told Carina about that?"

"And gave her a few things from the family..." I trail off to study Derian curiously, "What do you know about him?"

"Father and Travis Adarion were very close friends," Derian sounds tired again, "Much like me and Marcellus. But Victoria couldn't leave anything alone..."

"His majesty doesn't seem to blame..."

"Father blames Victoria," Derian's voice turns hard, "He knew what she was... even then. It helps though, that he believes Travis dead."

"How many know otherwise?"

"Barely a handful. Carina ought to..." Derian sighs, "Lady Irina might tell her, were Carina to ask."

I can't help being amused by that and Derian gives me a sharp glance.

"His majesty did suggest Carina could ask Lady Irina about her father," I explain, "Although whether she will is another matter."

"And not really our business."

"I know that."

21-10-48-06-04SM

The outer door of Lady Irina's suite is open and I can see her seated at a writing desk. I knock anyway.

She glances over immediately, "Yes, Lady Nerita?"

"I was hoping I could ask you about something."

"Of course," Lady Irina turns away from her desk, "Please, come in and close the door."

Once I've done that, she queries, "What is it you wish to ask about?"

"I received this invitation this morning," I cross the room to show it to her, "I don't want to offend anyone, but still..."

Lady Irina studies the stiff paper card with a thoughtful frown. "If it's Lady Covak's motives you mistrust, I hardly blame you. However, there's more to be gained from accepting."

"I wasn't planning to turn it down. I just prefer to have some idea what I'm walking into beforehand."

Lady Irina chuckles. "I think this time will be more questions than anything else."

"And every answer 'll be twisted around sideways," I grimace, "I won't pretend to be anything I'm not though."

"Some will certainly look for ways to use what you say against you. However, others will find it a refreshing change,"

Lady Irina looks me over critically, "Do you own a nice pantsuit?"

"Somewhere in the depths of my wardrobe."

"I strongly recommend you find one. You do well enough on formal occasions; however, it's obvious you're unaccustomed to skirts for everyday."

I can't help chuckling. "Not for lack of trying on the part of Experiment Redemption's etiquette instructor. Thing is, in Arawn, respectable women don't wear skirts."

Lady Irina frowns at that. "Laine…"

I shake my head. "She wasn't considered respectable… or at least not where I grew up."

Lady Irina sighs and shakes her head. "All I can say is this: Go, dress carefully, and watch what you do and don't say."

"Thank you." I nod.

She returns the card. "And best of luck."

I nod again and pocket the invitation. Lady Irina turns back to her desk as I start for the old south tower.

About halfway there, I encounter Laine.

"What'd she say?"

"I'll be fine except she doesn't think I should wear a skirt."

Laine bursts out laughing. "D' you explain that one?"

"Only briefly. She can believe me or not as she likes."

"Well, we'll see what we can do with what you've got." Laine shrugs it off.

I change the subject, "How'd clothes shopping with Carina go?"

"Better than you thought it would. And she should be fine for clothes for a while."

"Now that you've spent some time with her, what do you think?"

Laine grimaces wryly. "That'd be why our positions are what they are."

22-10-48-06-04SM

I really don't want to wake up. There's just something about being warm and comfortable and wrapped in Derian's arms. But I can feel him toying with a strand of my hair. I half open one eye to look at him. Derian looks amused, wry, and apologetic all at once.

"We overslept," He explains softly, "It's nearly mid-morning."

I groan. "Fuck." Then a thought occurs to me, "No one's come looking for either of us?"

"You left Sefu with Laine." Derian reminds me.

"Still..."

He shrugs lazily. "Evidently we're not wanted for anything this morning. Can't say as I mind."

I don't mind either. I better get up now though. Just because no one has come looking for me doesn't mean I won't catch hell from someone... most likely Laine.

I sigh and rest my head on Derian's chest. He tangles his hands in my loose hair.

"Do you have plans for this afternoon?"

I have to think about that. Then I remember the invitation and groan, "Tea." I lift my head.

Derian looks a little disappointed, "With whom?"

"Lady Covak."

He nods to himself. "Beryl Covak 's an officious gossip, but..." He emphasizes the word, "She's also somewhat old fashioned and less close minded than many."

I shrug lightly. "I don't have the luxury of not dealing with people just because they're pains in the ass."

Derian grimaces. "Maybe Norsecount really has been too long without a proper lady. Anyhow, we'd better get you back to the tower."

The invitation is for three, but even with Carl to guide me through the palace, I'd rather be early than late. That means being ready to go around two thirty. At least Laine took Sefu out this morning, so he should be fine through this. People around here need to get used to seeing him with me anyway.

Despite everything, it's five to three by the time Sefu and I arrive at the Covak family's suite. The outer door is open, but the only person visible is Georgiana Pelmont Covak, who I got to know a little at her brother's wedding reception.

She smiles on seeing me, "Lady Nerita... good afternoon. Please, come in."

As Sefu and I enter the sitting room, Lady Beryl Covak appears through a doorway on the far side. I've been introduced to her before; I've just never really spoken with her.

"Lady Nerita," Lady Covak smiles politely, "I am glad you were able to come."

I nod politely and guide Sefu away from the doorway, well aware of the two ladies who've just arrived. Dorothea Pelmont Varien, I've met before. It's her companion I don't think I've even seen.

"Lady Nerita," Dorothea inclines her head politely, "I would like to introduce you to my mother-in-law, Lady Marigold Bowerstone Varien."

I bow my head appropriately.

"My lady," Dorothea continues, "If I may introduce Lady Nerita Chassaven and her companion..." Dorothea glances at me, "Sefu, correct?"

I nod.

"A pleasure to meet you." Even without having heard the name, I'd've guessed Lady Varien was related to Lady Bowerstone. Probably her sister.

"Please do come in," Lady Covak calls, "Sit anywhere you like."

I end up sitting in a chair between the sofa Georgiana is sharing with her sister and the chair Lady Varien claims. Sefu curls up around my feet and promptly goes to sleep.

Another three ladies join us after that. Lady Ruby Skystar Gravenor, I've been introduced to a couple times now. Her daughter, Titania Gravenor Carun, and daughter-in-law, Olicia Javion Gravenor, I haven't even seen. Sefu naps right through all the introductions, which I take to mean he doesn't care one way or the other.

"Lady Nerita," Dorothea sounds curious, "Do you know who worded the media announcement of your engagement?"

"Natalia Burren." I suppress a grimace.

Georgiana frowns. "Surely Lady Natalia ought to know better..."

"I certainly thought she would have," I respond, "Seeing as she has spent a lot of time in Arawn in the last couple years."

Lady Gravenor slowly shakes her head. "To encourage his highness to do such a foolish thing..."

"Natalia had very little to do with the matter... beyond the wording of the announcement." I correct.

"Certainly true," Georgiana observes, "She could have introduced the two of you, but I don't believe she even offered."

"She didn't intend to," I point out, "It was Prince Derian who asked Marcellus and Rowena for that."

Georgiana and Dorothea both wince at the memory.

"Marcellus ought to have left that to his wife," Georgiana slowly shakes her head, "Though I doubt even that would have prevented yourself and his highness talking half the night."

I can't help chuckling. "According to the guard log, we came in from walking the gardens at one."

Lady Covak smiles, looking amused. "'Tis easy enough to lose track of time in conversation."

"Yet for an engagement to come of such so quickly," Lady Gravenor frowns, "Surely there was a great deal more to the matter."

"Is it ever any other way?" Lady Varien responds quickly, "'Tis enough for me to see the beginnings of long needed change."

"Only if it's change for the better," Lady Covak observes, "And that remains to be seen."

Lady Varien shrugs lightly and changes the subject, "Lady Nerita, it's said you come from South City, Arawn, yet what or where is that?"

"South City was built on the remains of Hailmark," I explain, "I believe the Old Quarter, which is where I was born and lived the first twenty years of my life, was originally Terrace Gardens."

Lady Gravenor frowns. "Was Terrace Gardens not a housing project for the poor?"

I shrug lightly. "Where better to hide than among those who owe you the most?"

Lady Varien nods to herself. "Had you a home there?"

"My family had a house, but many families in the Old Quarter do."

"Your immediate family or more than one or two generations?" Dorothea queries.

"At least as far back as anyone 's been keeping records again... so roughly a hundred and sixty years, if not longer."

Lady Gravenor frowns. "Who was there to keep records at all?"

"I'm talking about the community records for the Old Quarter, not anything official. Although my guess would be my family 's had a home there throughout the civil war."

Georgiana studies me curiously, "Are you the last of your family?"

"On Father's side."

"And on your mother's side?" Lady Varien queries.

"I have one cousin."

Lady Varien frowns abruptly. "Why does it seem I've heard mention of that before?"

"Lady Bowerstone knows," I respond, "Since Lillian is her daughter-in-law."

Most of those present look slightly baffled, but Lady Varien studies me critically. Then she chuckles.

"I'm beginning to see what Lily meant when she said you have a way with people."

I shrug lightly.

Lady Gravenor frowns again. "You hardly look twenty, yet you..."

"I'm twenty-three in January," I respond, "I was twenty when I left South City more than two years ago."

"That makes you a great deal younger than his highness," Lady Covak observes, "Although I imagine you know that."

I nod in confirmation.

"Would not the Lady Angelita have been a better choice age wise...?" Lady Gravenor trails off on seeing me shake my head.

"Angelita was twenty-one last June," I explain, "And her marriage before leaving Arawn was only part of her means of evading his majesty's plans for her."

"Yet she seems very well brought up," Lady Covak observes, "For what little the court has seen of her. Still, 'tis the first I've heard of Imperial Blood shirking duty thus."

I have to shake my head at that. "Angelita 's done far more in the way of her 'duty' than anyone who knows her would've expected. She could have remained safely hidden among her friends and left the provisional government and the military to continue fighting for power. She knew full well that any attempt to restore the monarchy would have led to renewed war; that the anti-monarchy sentiment is too strong and too many blame the monarchs for the war and the desolation it left behind."

"It's been five hundred years," Lady Gravenor sounds sceptical, "And fifteen or twenty since the war ended."

"Arawn will remain a wasteland for hundreds, if not thousands of years... short of a miracle. When people wake up every day to that, they want someone to blame. The monarchs are a convenient target."

Lady Varien frowns deeply. "Why not the military?"

"Would you take on people who could destroy your whole life in moments?"

Lady Varien swallows hard as she considers that, "I suppose not."

Georgiana studies me carefully. "Yet you did, unless I'm mistaken."

"For more than ten years. The martial law they imposed granted citizenship to very few and basic human rights to no one. The common law of the Old Quarter was better than that. One of the responsibilities I inherited from Father and later passed on to a trusted friend was the protection of the residents."

"You're accustomed to a certain degree of power then." Lady Gravenor studies me critically.

"Power usually entails privileges to balance responsibility, but the privileges of my family's position were few and far between. At best there were others to help with the work and a certain degree of respect."

Everyone else in the room shivers.

"You may yet set Norsecount on its ear," Lady Varien observes, "Though many of the upper nobility will make such difficult."

I shrug. "I find that kind of thing easier to deal with as it comes up. Besides which, I know I've only begun to figure out where things are at here."

Lady Varien chuckles. "Few enough would admit to that."

Lady Covak adds, "So far you've done quite well in that regard."

It's nearly dinnertime before I get back to the old south tower. Since Derian had asked me to have dinner with him, I'm not surprised to find him waiting with Laine and her father.

Laine glances over me, "You look wasted."

I roll my eyes. "And you wouldn't be?"

Derian chuckles sympathetically. "Who else did Lady Covak invite? I imagine Georgiana was present."

I nod as I cross the room to sit beside him. "Dorothea as well, along with her mother-in-law. And then Lady Gravenor and her daughter and daughter-in-law."

Derian nods to himself.

25-10-48-06-04SM

So far Rowena isn't impressed with the life of a married woman at court. I suspect, once she returns to Matllind next spring, I won't see her often or for long. In the meantime, she's been hanging out with Laine and Carina. It seems, between time spent with Derian, wedding preparations, and an unending stream of minor issues, I'm constantly busy. Still, Laine and Rowena always did get along well and Carina fits in with them better than even I suspected. Now if only Lady Irina was having the same success with Nerissa.

However, my main concern for today is the reception for the ambassador from Arawn. We've had no word at all of who President Gayre is sending. I still can't think of anyone he would entrust the job to. I guess I'll find out this afternoon with everyone else.

Angelita won't be here for it though. She wanted to be, but couldn't get away from Seeri Meadow in time. Instead, she arrives tomorrow and it sounds like she has her own business to take care of while she's here. She didn't say who, if anyone, is coming with her, but I think Laine is hoping Rylan will. Never thought I'd see Laine actually missing a guy like this.

For as well as Carina has been doing lately, she has been avoiding the Monarch since she and Laine went clothes shopping. Carina seems especially nervous as we head to our rooms to prepare for the reception this afternoon.

Laine got the shower first and, by the time I'm finished with it, Laine is half dressed and working on Carina's hair. So far it hasn't been a problem that none of the three of us has a ladies maid... we'll see how today goes.

When I enter the dressing room, I study what Laine is wearing with a raised eyebrow. "Even I know you wouldn't wear that under your new dress."

Laine chuckles. "I'm gonna wear Mother's gown and save the new one for another time. There, what do you think?"

Carina studies her reflection in the vanity mirror. "I like it. Thank you."

She finishes dressing while Laine and I do each other's hair. Then Laine helps her with her jewelry while I dress. Eventually all three of us and Sefu are ready to go downstairs.

Laine goes first, then Carina, who's more nervous than ever, and Sefu and I follow. We reach the sitting room to find Derian waiting with Duke Malin.

The Duke sucks in a sharp breath on seeing his daughter and I suspect she looks more like her mother than usual. Lady Rose's dress fits Laine perfectly, but it's cut lower in the neck and back than is usually Laine's style.

Derian pays little attention to Laine, but is caught off guard on seeing Carina. Actually, I'm not sure he recognizes her immediately. She still looks every bit a princess, just a grown up one.

Carina flushes as both Derian and Duke Malin glance over her. "I hope his majesty won't be upset..."

Derian quickly shakes his head. "Don't worry about that."

"We'd best go," Duke Malin adds, "It's been asked that we arrive before the ambassador's party."

I take Derian's arm as the six of us leave the tower and head for the reception hall off the main entrance. There, we find Monarch Reginald waiting with a handful of the highest ranked among the nobility. The Monarch greets us quietly, but doesn't comment on Carina's appearance, and quickly turns his attention to greeting Pelmonts, who arrive next.

Lady Irina and a rebellious, but unusually grown up looking Nerissa are nearly late. Evidently Lady Irina doesn't approve of fussy faerie tale dresses either and Nerissa isn't happy about it. I just hope she behaves better than she has been recently.

Since word came of the ambassador's impending arrival, what was once the embassy for Estorika has been redecorated with the colours and symbols of Arawn. We'd had a report that his party had arrived at the embassy around noon, so they've had time to rest and prepare for this.

Now they arrive, all five of them, precisely on time. I immediately recognize John Simeon, who hasn't changed in two years, and I can't quite repress a grin. Laine, who is beside me, and Rowena, who is nearby, aren't even trying.

"Check out who's with him!" Laine's voice is so soft I can barely hear the words.

I look over the rest of the party. There's a man in a modified military uniform; a second, younger, man in a neat, dark blue suit; an elderly woman with a cane; and a young woman I have to study very carefully to identify. But once I do, I can't help the grin. I never expected to see her again.

"You know these people?" Derian's voice is also extremely soft and nearly cut off by the herald at the door.

"Presenting John Simeon, Ambassador to the Monarch of Norsecount from the Republic of Arawn. Also his staff: Ms Priscilla Terrence, Mr Zachary Walnir, and Miss Catarine Varlok. And Captain Samuel Jarevar of the Arawn Militia Reserve."

That last one is the real surprise. Obviously there've been some huge changes in the month or so since I left Arawn. On the other hand, I'm sure I'll hear all about it from John Simeon and Cattie.

Monarch Reginald steps forward and spreads his arms wide, "We welcome you to Norsecount..." The speech that follows is an old, traditional stand-by, although not insincere and mercifully short.

At the end, John Simeon bows just deeply enough to be respectful. "Thank you, your majesty. On behalf of President Gayre, we offer your majesty these tokens of good will."

Cattie passes John Simeon a neatly wrapped parcel, which he crosses the room to present to the Monarch. I can't see exactly what is inside the cloth wrapping, but the Monarch nods gravely.

"Our deepest gratitude to yourselves and President Gayre," Monarch Reginald hands the gift to one of his guards, "If I may introduce you to but a small part of my court. Beginning with my son and heir, Crown Prince Derian Regan of Norsecount."

"Your highness." Again, John Simeon's bow is only just respectful.

"However, I believe you already know his fiancée, Lady Nerita Chassaven."

"A great many years." A brief, fond smile flickers over John Simeon's face as he studies me.

The Monarch recalls his attention, "These are the princesses of Norsecount, Carina and Nerissa, and with them, a guest of Our court, High Lady Irina of Ouestlun."

"Your highnesses, my lady." John Simeon bows again.

Monarch Reginald moves on, "Duke Lige Malin, with his daughter, High Lady Laine Malin, whom I believe you already know."

"Yes, of course." John Simeon never was fond of Laine, but only those who know him well would spot his surprise at her new name and rank, "Your grace, my lady."

The Monarch continues through the upper nobility present, "And lastly, Lord George Pelmont with his son and daughter-in-law, Marcellus and Rowena. I believe you know the lady."

"Since she was very small." John Simeon smiles fondly.

Throughout all this, the four who had entered with John Simeon have been standing awkwardly just inside the doorway. I don't know about the rest of them, but I'd guess Cattie is feeling pretty out of place. Now, Monarch Reginald indicates for Derian and Lady Irina to accompany him and John Simeon over to them. I go as well since my fingers are laced through Derian's and he isn't letting go. That means Sefu, who has been overlooked so far, comes along as well.

The military captain spots Sefu and swallows hard. "Is that a winter tiger?"

The Monarch can't quite suppress a wince. "Yes, it is."

John Simeon chuckles softly. "I'd heard word of a domesticated one here. However," He turns serious again, "If I might be permitted to introduce my staff: Ms Priscilla Terrence, Mr Zachary Walnir, and Miss..." He catches the look Cattie shoots at him, "Cattie Varlok. And also Arawn's militia representative, Captain Samuel Jarevar."

Monarch Reginald, Lady Irina, and Derian all nod politely, but I catch Sefu's growl and have to grab a handful of the back of his neck. I already knew he wouldn't like John Simeon, but I suspect he doesn't like Captain Jarevar either.

"Behave!" My voice is soft, but sharp. Sefu glowers at me, although he quits growling. I catch John Simeon's questioning glance and nod.

The Monarch, evidently sensing the problem, quickly finishes this round of introductions, "I would like to introduce my son, Crown Prince Derian; his fiancée, Lady Nerita Chassaven; her companion, Sefu; and High Lady Irina of Ouestlun."

The ambassador's party all bow or curtsy as appropriate. Then Monarch Reginald and John Simeon guide Zachary Walnir and the militia captain to another part of the room. Derian takes a step to accompany him, but this time I'm not releasing his hand.

"Lady Nerita..." Priscilla seems hesitant, "John Simeon thought perhaps you might be able to answer a question for me..."

I nod. "Perhaps."

"You are a graduate of Experiment Redemption, correct?"

I nod again.

She continues, "Only recently did I hear that Experiment Redemption might be able to reunite me with my missing youngest son, but I went too late. They confirmed he had been with the program, as leader of his group, but had graduated and left Arawn. They wouldn't, or couldn't, tell me more, so I was hoping you might have known him. I'm told he still uses the name I gave him: Rhett Terrence."

I suppress a grimace. "Yes, I knew him, but I don't know where he would be now. However, there's someone arriving tomorrow who should be able to help you."

"Thank you." Priscilla bows her head appreciatively.

"Ms Terrence," Lady Irina calls for her attention, "Come and I will introduce you around."

Priscilla nods uncertainly and accompanies Lady Irina.

Cattie, who's been studying Sefu curiously, now looks at me, "How long've you had him?"

"Since June. He was just a tiny cub then."

"Oh, wow." Cattie grins.

"Give him some time to decide what he thinks of you," I warn her, "Anyway, I should introduce you to a few people." I turn to scan the room for the people I have in mind.

Laine and Rowena are easy enough to spot. They're standing with Marcellus. Carina and Nerissa are nearby. As Derian and I guide Cattie across the room, I catch Carina's eye. She nods and steers her sister over to Laine.

"Where did his grace go?" Derian asks Laine when we reach the group.

Laine shrugs. "His majesty summoned him."

"His grace?" Cattie raises a sceptical eyebrow.

"My father," Laine explains, "Duke Lige Malin."

Cattie shakes her head in disbelief. "You always were a little weird."

"She's now High Lady Laine Malin." I inform Cattie.

Laine and Rowena both laugh at Cattie's expression.

"Cattie," I recall her attention, "I'd like you to meet Princess Carina and Princess Nerissa of Norsecount and also Rowena's husband, Marcellus Pelmont."

Cattie swallows hard, but manages an appropriate curtsy.

For the benefit of those I've just named, I continue, "This is Cattie Varlok," Catching a couple of their expressions, I add, "You'd be wasting your breath to address her as anything else."

Derian appears somewhat amused, but Marcellus frowns.

"Why does that name sound familiar?"

"You've probably met my third cousin, Amalia." Cattie grimaces.

"Who is married and unlikely to return to Monarch's Town before the twenty-ninth." I inform Cattie.

"Someone actually married her?"

Most of us burst out laughing.

"Many here would say the same of him." Marcellus explains once he recovers enough to speak.

"Okay..." Cattie looks bemused by that, then she turns back to me, "And the others?"

"Married and scattered," I reply, "But we knew that would happen even before we left Arawn."

Cattie nods to herself. "So when's your wedding?"

"The thirtieth of this month.'

Cattie studies me critically, but before she can ask another question, Laine changes the subject.

"What could've possibly made both of you leave?"

"Long story," Cattie grimaces, "And probably better if you hear it from him."

I nod to myself. "What happened to my house?"

Cattie grins impishly. "Mellie and Ross and their children live there now. Though they've promised I can stay there any time I need a place."

"Children?" Rowena raises an eyebrow, "Did they come first or the wedding?"

"The wedding... sort of."

Laine, Rowena, and I all have to shake our heads at that. Nerissa doesn't seem to understand, but Derian, Carina, and Marcellus look bemused.

Sefu is still trying to make heads or tails of Cattie and, for once, ignoring Nerissa, who's getting noticeably frustrated. She's definitely too used to having Sefu's attention. Then, abruptly, she attempts to escape her sister's grasp on her shoulder. Carina immediately tightens her grip and Derian frowns sternly. At that, Nerissa scowls outright.

"I suggest you rejoin Lady Irina." Derian keeps his voice low, but it's not really a suggestion.

Nerissa continues to scowl. All of us watch as she goes; most of us to make sure she reaches Lady Irina.

Laine slowly shakes her head. "What's it going to take before she learns?"

Derian sighs. "Nothing too drastic, I would hope. And yet..."

"We'll see what happens." I squeeze his hand.

The reception lasts two hours, at the end of which Laine is nowhere to be seen. That's a little odd because I doubt she left with a guy. I know she hasn't even been looking around since the two nights she spent with Rylan. I'm not gonna worry about it just yet and maybe I'll hear what's up later.

I'm standing near the door with Duke Malin, John Simeon, Cattie, and Sefu when Carina comes over to join us.

"Are you ready to go?" Duke Malin asks Carina, who nods fervently.

Cattie studies me curiously, "Where're you living?"

"Here. We've got the top three floors of the old south tower."

John Simeon shakes his head ruefully. "Would you mind if she stayed a while? I shouldn't need her before tomorrow afternoon."

"Fine by me." I respond.

Neither Duke Malin nor Carina so much as look like objecting and Cattie grins.

"Will you need anything from the embassy?" Duke Malin enquires. Cattie glances at me and I shake my head.

"She'll be fine."

"Then we should go." Duke Malin takes a step closer to the door.

Carina frowns. "Where's Laine?"

"She said she needed some air." The Duke replies.

That sounds odd to me, but I don't ask and Carina just accepts it.

The four of us and Sefu leave the reception hall and head for the old south tower. On our second floor, Duke Malin goes into his suite, but Carina hesitates at her door.

"Just come up," I tell her, "I think you left some stuff anyway."

"Oh right."

We continue up to the top floor and go into the dressing room. I immediately hunt up clothes for Cattie to change into.

"Yours or Laine's?" Cattie studies the t-shirt and track pants critically.

"Mine, actually. We got a ton of clothes and shit from Experiment Redemption... for all kinds of stuff."

"So you guys graduated, right? How long were you there?"

"A little over two years," I sit so I can remove my shoes and jewelry, "You'd've hated it though. Andrina nearly snapped a couple times."

Cattie shivers. "You said she's married now?"

I chuckle. "Fallen for him too. Interesting case though."

"Who?" Carina is also removing her shoes and jewelry.

"Nikolai Gris."

"D' you know him?" Cattie queries.

"Very little," Carina shakes her head, "I just know all the court gossip and old stories... and some of the facts."

"Considering the facts in that particular case, I can imagine the gossip." I shake my head.

"Oh?" Cattie looks very serious.

"Laine could explain it better. Andrina 's happy with the whole deal though."

"Must be some case then," Cattie laughs, "But what about the rest? The marriages must've all happened pretty fast."

"All within the first eight days of this month, although a couple were double ceremonies," I start pulling pins from my hair, "First were Andrina and Nikolai and Amalia and Nathan Skystar..."

Cattie frowns. "What about him makes it so amusing?"

I chuckle. "He has a reputation comparable to hers... keeping in mind the cultural differences between countries."

"It's been suggested Lord Skystar was hoping marriage would force Nathan to settle down." Carina observes.

"They picked the wrong girl then," Cattie makes a face, "'Cause I'm guessing Amalia hasn't changed."

"Considering she went and put the barbell back in her tongue the day they married..."

Carina frowns, studying Cattie, "Do you not like this girl?"

"Never did."

"Anyway," I recall their attention, "That was the first of this month. On the second, Danya married Zale Pondurst."

"How'd that get past Agatha Pondurst?" Carina looks surprised.

"I gather Lord Pondurst decided he'd had enough of her bullshit," I shrug, "But last time I spoke to Danya, it sounded like he's far from the only one."

Carina rolls her eyes. "If Lord Pondurst wasn't so set on ensuring the family would continue none of his sons would've been allowed to marry."

"Sounds like a real lovely lady," Cattie observes dryly, "On the third?"

"Lillian and Edmund Bowerstone."

"I heard about that one," Carina sets her hair combs with the rest of her belongings, "Opal... that's Edmund's sister-in-law... told everyone who'd listen she'd never been so offended as at the reception."

"That happens sometimes when Laine gets pissed off," I respond, "Not that I'd particularly want to live with the rest of the women in that family."

Carina shrugs. "Generally they're not too bad."

"Then, on the fifth, Ilaria married Kilian Xelloverd."

"Is Old Josephina Xelloverd on her side?" Carina queries.

I nod. "Elizabeth as well. And Ilaria got even more jewelry out of the deal."

Cattie rolls her eyes. "As if she needed any more."

"Anyway, Rowena and Marcellus married on the seventh..."

"With Derian as best man." Carina adds.

"And Nadine as bridesmaid. If you can imagine how she handled that."

Cattie laughs. "The eighth must've been a double ceremony."

"Haylie and Raymond Tremauld and Nadine and Lysander Rossa."

"I thought I'd heard Lady Tremauld had married off the last of her grandchildren." Carina, now finished pulling her hair down, reaches for her brush.

"So they're all living with their husbands' families," Cattie nods to herself, "And you'll be married in a few days. But what about Laine? I'm guessing she hasn't changed any."

"She has and she hasn't..." I grimace, "Some of it's knowing more about who she is and where she's from."

Cattie nods again. "Duke Lige Malin, huh. And the rest of it?"

"Laine Rose Malin, born ten, oh four, thirty-seven, oh three, oh four to Duke Lige Malin and High Lady Rose Nowellyr at his family's estate."

It takes a minute for Cattie and Carina to process that. While they think, I change from my gown to jeans and one of Laine's t-shirts.

Carina frowns. "Didn't Laine say she's twenty-six?"

"For any practical purposes she is. But the rest of it's a little..."

"Fucked up?" Cattie supplies dryly.

"That's about how Laine describes it." I retrieve my hairbrush.

"What will she do once you're married?" Carina shakes out her dressing gown.

"Move to Seeri Meadow."

Cattie raises an eyebrow. "Why am I thinking there's a guy involved?"

I laugh. "Not just any guy... one she spent two nights in a row with."

"Really?" Cattie sounds distinctly sceptical and I don't blame her.

I shrug. "All I know's she's been turning bright red when he's mentioned and she's actually been behaving since he left town."

"Until now..." Cattie begins.

I shake my head. "Laine left the reception by herself. I saw that much. I think this's just something bothering her."

Cattie looks sceptical, "You really think Laine would change her ways that fast?"

"That could be what's bugging her," I shrug, "But until she's ready to tell me..."

Cattie grimaces. "You're same as ever. Are you getting better at all?"

I laugh. "Oh, yeah."

Cattie studies me critically, "They actually found something that worked?"

"Something like. Good thing too 'cause I've got too much to deal with as is."

Cattie gives me a weird look, "You're crazier than ever."

"She is marrying Derian." Carina observes wryly.

"Different problem." I respond.

Cattie glances back and forth between us, "I know I missed something there."

"Derian 's been married before," I explain, "Twice, actually."

"Okay..."

Carina scowls. "Anything you've heard doesn't begin to cover that mess."

"I haven't heard all that much," I respond, "But even that says a lot."

Carina chuckles sardonically. "I suppose it would."

"Anyway," I change the subject, "I gather the real big changes 're a recent thing, so what happened after we left?"

Cattie thinks back, "I guess the first thing was finding out Mellie was pregnant. Ross was set and determined to marry her, but you remember his uncle..."

"So you let Ross move in."

"Once they were married," Cattie nods, "He took over looking after the house itself pretty quick... and the baby, once it was born."

"Boy or girl?" I query.

"Boy... Titus Ross. Then, just before John Simeon and I left, they had a girl that they named Milicent Nerita."

I nod to myself. Nerita has become a popular second name in the Old Quarter in recent years.

"I don't think I had any worse problems than you ever did," Cattie moves on, "By last December the group was up to ten and we got another invitation from FTK."

"How many went?"

"I sent eight, under Nathania, and there's been no more word than there was from you."

"As Black Oak Court?"

"Of course."

"Then I might be able to find out where they're at."

"That'd be kinda nice."

Carina, who has been frowning thoughtfully, speaks up, "I can understand your friend not wanting to leave her husband and child, but what about you?"

"Partly the same reason I didn't go with Nerita the first time and partly because there wasn't anyone I trusted to take on the job Nerita left me."

"I'm guessing you didn't give them much choice," I reach down to rub Sefu's fur, "How much worse did things get?"

"Not too much worse, actually. It got harder to keep the patrols out, but not impossible. Still..."

"So who went with Nathania?"

"Winifred, Jasmina, Vlaria, Tiana, Natika, Monica, and Allison."

"Monica and Allison Galacia?" I query warily.

"Their mother died," Cattie looks pained, "You think anyone else'd've taken them?"

I sigh deeply, then explain for Carina's benefit, "There're twins and then there're identical twins, but these two take it way too far. They're so fucking irritating!"

"No shit." Cattie rolls her eyes.

"Teddy sent Tiana?" I don't care to discuss the Galacia twins further.

"Teddy's dead," Cattie responds flatly, "I know I should tell Rowena, but the reception wasn't the time or place."

I nod.

Cattie stretches out first her neck, then her shoulders. "Any chance of a real dinner?"

I laugh. "Yeah, should be soon, too."

26-10-48-06-04SM

I don't know what time during the night Laine turned up, but Cattie, Sefu, and I had fallen asleep sprawled on top of the blankets and there wasn't much room left. Still, it's something of a surprise to wake and find myself in the middle of the bed. Cattie and Laine are sound asleep, but Sefu yawns widely. He hops off the bed, allowing me to slip off the end, then follows me into the dressing room.

As I finish pulling on jeans and a sweater, I hear a tap on the door frame at the top of the stairs. I go out to find Carl standing on the top step.

"Lady Nerita, is Lady Laine available?"

"She's still asleep. Why?"

"There's a lady asking to see her."

"Did she give a name?"

"No, my lady."

A thought occurs to me, "Is there a winter tiger with her?"

"There is." Carl swallows nervously.

"Just send her up."

"As you wish, my lady." Carl bows before retreating down the stairs. I return to the dressing room to brush out my hair.

Before I'm finished, I can hear feet on the stairs followed by a tap on the door frame.

"In here."

Angelita appears in the dressing room doorway a moment later with Xylia just behind her.

"Hey, Nerita."

I continue working my brush through my long, thick hair. "You must've only just got here."

"Half an hour ago," Angelita leans on the door frame, "At least I've got rooms in the palace this time."

"Who all came out with you?"

"Shawnda an' Rylan. They're out cold, but I slept nearly eight hours in the vehicle. I was hoping you guys 'd be up 'cause I've got a question for Laine."

"It's gonna have to wait," Now finished, I set my brush down, "I'm not waking her when I don't know how much sleep she's had."

"Yeah, fine." Angelita moves out of the doorway so I can pass her, "So who 'd President Gayre send as ambassador?"

"John Simeon."

"Oh fuck," Angelita makes a face, "How many staff?"

"Four... including a captain with the Arawn Militia Reserve."

"Really?" Angelita raises an eyebrow as she follows me down to the sitting room two floors below, "Anythin' else I should know?"

I shrug. "I imagine you'll see him and his people while you're here."

Angelita grimaces, then sighs. "Has he heard about me?"

"Whatever President Gayre knows. I haven't really had a chance to talk to him yet."

"I don't mind." Angelita claims a chair and I sit beside her. Sefu and Xylia have found a ball and are batting it around the room.

"Oh yeah," Angelita remembers something, "I was told to ask you where I can take Xylia out for exercise."

"If you can hang around for breakfast, I'll show you."

"Sure. I doubt Shawnda or Rylan 'll move before noon."

I get up to send a message to the kitchens and return to my seat just as Carina comes downstairs. She stops short at the bottom and studies Angelita with a thoughtful frown.

"Yes, you've met... briefly, at the Masquerade."

Carina flushes instantly, but Angelita laughs.

"A lot 's been happening everywhere."

"Oh yeah," I'm a little annoyed with myself, "We've got a guest as well."

"Anyone I'd know?"

I shake my head. "Cattie Varlok 's from the Old Quarter... she's part of the ambassador's staff... but she was stuck looking after her grandmother when you lived there."

"Related to Amalia?"

"Third cousins... not friends."

Angelita nods to herself.

Duke Malin appears shortly, followed by Cattie.

"Has Laine even moved?" I ask Cattie.

"She's in the shower," Cattie grimaces, "Looks like she had a bad night."

"That sometimes happens." Angelita observes.

Cattie studies her curiously for a moment, then glances at me.

"That's Angelita Straisen," Turning to her, I add, "This's Cattie Varlok."

We're just sitting down to breakfast when Laine finally comes down. She looks almost hungover and she's clearly not impressed with the number of people at the table.

"You sure you should be up?" Angelita looks sympathetic.

Laine scowls. "Just fuckin' leave me the fuck alone!" She turns and leaves the room. A moment later feet can be heard headed upstairs.

"Whoa." Cattie shivers.

Duke Malin starts to rise, but I catch his eye and shake my head. Hopefully Laine will go back to bed and sleep it off. Until she's feeling better anyone who tries talking to her is likely to get hurt.

Breakfast is quiet after that and afterwards Carina and Duke Malin go on with whatever they had already planned for this morning.

I turn to Cattie, "We're taking Sefu and Xylia out. I don't promise there's much to do if you stay here."

"Do you think Rowena would be up?"

I shrug. "Get the page to send her a message, if you want."

"I guess." Cattie doesn't look too certain about the idea.

I turn to Angelita, "I just need to get one thing from upstairs, then we can go."

She nods.

Up on the top floor of the tower, I look into the bedroom to see if Laine actually went to bed. She is there, sprawled across the bed, but all too clearly not asleep.

"Laine."

She doesn't even move. I'm just not sure whether she didn't hear me or I'm being ignored. Taking a chance on the first, I take a seat on the edge of the bed. Laine still doesn't move. Not even when I reach out to touch her shoulder.

"Laine?"

I'm starting to think I really am being ignored when Laine finally lifts her head. Her face is tear streaked, which both is and isn't surprising. In all the time I've known Laine, I've never seen her cry. But I've also never seen her snap at anyone like that either.

"My head's so completely fucked up right now," She rolls onto her side, "Angelita's not upset, is she?"

I shake my head. "You think she's never had a bad night?"

Laine's expression twists wryly. "Father's prob'ly not too happy though."

"Not especially, no. But Angelita came up looking to ask you something anyway," I don't give Laine a chance to respond, "For the moment, maybe you should get some more sleep. I told her I'd show her where she can take Xylia for exercise."

Laine sighs. "I'm not gonna get back to sleep anytime soon. What're Cattie and Carina up to?"

"Don't know about Carina, but I left Cattie trying to decide whether or not to bug Rowena."

Laine nods slowly. "I'll be..." She's interrupted by a knock at the top of the stairs.

"You might as well go see who it is." Laine grimaces.

I leave the room and find Carl on the top step.

"My lady, his majesty requests that Lady Laine and yourself attend a meeting scheduled for one o'clock."

"We'll be there." I return to the bedroom where Laine is now sitting up.

"Meeting for what?"

"Probably an exchange of information," I shrug, "We'll see who else's there."

Laine nods. "I'll be fine. You should go though."

I go into the next room to change shoes before leaving our suite. Both tigers were waiting with Angelita and they get to their feet on seeing me.

"How's Laine?" Angelita also gets to her feet.

"Complaining about her head feeling fucked up."

Angelita nods to herself. "D' you tell her I'd like to talk to her?"

"Yeah."

"Thanks."

We leave the tower and I guide her along the shortest route through the palace. Not that there's any real short route from the old south tower to the stable door, as it's called.

"Lady Nerita!"

Recognizing the voice, I stop and wait for Lady Irina to catch up. As she gets closer, she starts to look uncertain.

"I had hoped to ask a favour of you..." She sounds out of breath.

"Such as?"

"It's simply the physician has ordered daily exercise for Nerissa and no one is available to take her riding this morning. I thought perhaps she might join you and Sefu..."

I glance at Angelita, who shrugs indifferently.

"Fine by me."

Lady Irina still looks uncertain, but I think I know why.

"These are High Lady Angelita Straisen and Xylia," Turning to Angelita, I add, "This is High Lady Irina of Ouestlun."

Lady Irina inclines her head graciously. "Pleased to meet you." Then she returns her attention to me, "Then, if you don't mind, I'll send Nerissa to join you."

"And when we come in?" I query.

"I would hope she'll return to her rooms to prepare for lunch," Lady Irina replies, "Though it would hardly be fair to hold you... or anyone else... responsible if she doesn't."

"Thank you." I nod.

Lady Irina returns the way she had come while the four of us continue on outside.

"I'm told there're trails," I explain as we pass through the gardens, "But I'm not sure where or which ones. We usually stick to the fields."

Angelita nods. "Before I came out here Nikki not too subtly suggested too many long walks aren't a good idea."

I raise an eyebrow. "Since when does Nikki tell you to do or not do anything?"

"Since she came into her healing ability an' I've been having stress related issues."

"And it's still too soon to just admit you're pregnant?"

That earns me a brief, black scowl. However, Angelita doesn't try to deny it. Instead, she throws the ball she has with her well across the nearest field. Both tigers take off after it.

I'm keeping an eye open for Princess Nerissa, who quickly comes out to join us.

She's dressed more appropriately than usual, but looks thoroughly unimpressed. Evidently I haven't been forgiven yet.

"Good morning." I study the girl carefully as she approaches. She barely glances at me and doesn't seem to notice Angelita at all.

Sefu, having finally wrestled the ball away from his sister, comes bounding over to us, but stops short on seeing the princess. He studies her for a moment, then drops the ball at my feet and goes over to butt his head against her hand.

"Hi, Sefu." Nerissa brightens a little and kneels down to hug him. I scoop up the ball and throw it for Xylia.

"What's with her?" Angelita keeps her voice soft.

I don't bother. I've had enough of the attitude and Nerissa needs to learn to get over herself.

"She's just decided everyone around her's out to pick on her."

Angelita shakes her head. "She's a little spoiled, isn't she?"

"Certainly too used to no one paying enough attention to where she goes and what she does."

"She's what? The youngest?"

I nod. "By quite a bit."

Nerissa's head jerks up at that and I can only just hear her muttered words, "I'm only two years younger than Kamilla."

Angelita frowns. "How old 's Carina?"

"More or less a year older than I am."

"And Derian 's even older," Angelita nods to herself, "Sefu 's sure gotten attached to her."

I shrug it off. "Not so much I'm gonna worry about it."

Angelita looks thoughtful for a moment, then studies me curiously, "Have you had an episode since you've had him?"

I scowl at her. "Stress test."

She makes a face. "That asshole could've set off anyone... well, 'cept Tory. Apparently she asked if he was related to some of the people she had to put up with at GenTech."

"Tory 's atypical in a lot of ways," I remind Angelita, "But I'm guessing she doesn't tell you everything she's into."

Angelita rolls her eyes. "Never did. I'd've thought she'd have to send Nikki to help you."

I shake my head. "I don't even carry the gene for it. Near as I can figure I was mimicking my father's symptoms... that's Tory's area."

Angelita nods to herself.

Xylia drops the ball at Angelita's feet and looks at Sefu and Nerissa in concern. Angelita kneels down to rub her tiger's head and neck. Because she can communicate with animals telepathically, Angelita only rarely talks to Xylia out loud. There's times when I wish I could do that, but Sefu is generally pretty good about listening.

"Sefu," I stoop to retrieve the ball, "You're supposed to be chasing this thing, remember?"

He looks irritated at the interruption. He does need the exercise though and he knows I'll bounce the ball off his rear end if I have to. Not that I've needed to in two or three months.

I throw the ball and he chases after it halfheartedly. Nerissa drops back into the grass, looking stormy. I almost wish I dared bounce the ball off her.

Angelita gets to her feet as Sefu returns with the ball. He gives it to her and, when she throws it, Xylia races him for it. That turns into another game of keep away out in the field.

"Nerissa!"

The girl hesitates mid-step. Evidently she thought she could slip away while I was watching the tigers.

"You do not want to walk away from me."

She hesitates a moment longer, then breaks into a run. Angelita and I watch until the girl disappears into the stables.

Angelita turns to study me, "You're not gonna go after her?"

"I'm not the one she's gonna catch hell from."

"Mind if I go?"

"Suit yourself," I shrug, "Just make sure to introduce yourself to the stable master. His name's Fredric Trent and he knows Forrest."

"Thanks." As she heads for the stables, Angelita calls Xylia to her. Sefu, now in possession of the ball, returns to me.

It's late morning and Sefu is getting tired when Angelita and Xylia escort a subdued looking Nerissa out of the stables. Sefu spots them, but returns to me to wait for the three of them to cross the field. As they get closer, the girl starts to look uncertain. However, once they reach us, she takes a deep breath.

"Lady Nerita, I want to apologize. I've been behaving badly and I'm sorry." She bows her head.

I'll admit to being a little floored on this one. At least I know she's sincere because, whatever was said, I know Angelita wouldn't've suggested a formal apology.

"Thank you, your highness."

Nerissa is happier when she looks up, although not quite back to her old self.

"I better go see if Shawnda 's up," Angelita tells us, "I'll see you later."

Nerissa waits until she and Xylia are gone to ask, "Who's Shawnda?"

"A girl she knows... Shawnda Silver."

Nerissa frowns. "I thought Lady Angelita said all her friends are grown up."

"Shawnda only turned sixteen last summer," I explain, "We should start inside. Sefu 's tired and I've got a meeting after lunch."

"You too?"

"Me and Laine... and Sefu."

"I have lessons anyway," Nerissa grimaces, "Lady Irina gave my main tutor a real scolding the other day..."

I let the girl continue to talk until we reach her rooms. At the door, Nerissa hesitates and looks up at me.

"I talk a lot, don't I?"

I can't help laughing. "Yes, sometimes you do. I don't mind though."

She looks like she's about to say something, but seems to change her mind. Then she goes into her rooms and Sefu and I head for the old south tower.

The one o'clock meeting turns out to involve eight people and two tigers. And most of the people are from Arawn. Laine, Sefu, and I arrive to find Angelita and Xylia waiting with Monarch Reginald. Then John Simeon enters, accompanied by Priscilla and the militia captain. And, finally, Derian slips in just barely on time.

"Good afternoon and welcome," The Monarch begins, then addresses John Simeon, "Now, I believe you, sir, have much you wish to tell us?"

John Simeon nods gravely. "A lot has changed in Arawn in barely six weeks. So much it's almost unbelievable..."

"I met with President Gayre on September thirteenth," Angelita speaks quietly, "How soon did you begin to see changes?"

"The President's announcement meant almost nothing at street level... at least at first," John Simeon replies, "But on the sixteenth the martial law was replaced with the new Republic Law, which is a slightly modified version of Terantal's Canon."

"And that meant any more than the announcement?" Laine queries.

"Again, not at first," John Simeon admits, "Although that was partly because the patrol master at the time was fighting the restrictions it imposed on his activities."

"So what was the real catalyst?" I enquire, "You never were one for blind faith in government policy. Neither 's Cattie."

John Simeon sighs. "You wouldn't have left things any other way.

"After the sixteenth there were rumours of other changes, but it wasn't until October second that we actually saw any difference. That was the day General Stephen Verdas and Channa came looking to talk to me."

"About your records?" Laine queries.

"Not initially. They'd run into problems with the patrol master and realized that things that should've changed hadn't. What they wanted me to do was organize a meeting of everyone living in the Old Quarter, which ended up including many from the lower city as well.

"At that meeting, the night of the second, General Verdas read out and explained the Republic Law as it applied to us and spent a long time answering questions. Then they were sent home to think about it, with instructions to return at the same time the next night."

Angelita nods to herself. "And in the meantime?"

"General Verdas and I had a long discussion on matters past, present, and future," John Simeon replies, "The meeting the next night was nearly double the previous one. Many more from the lower city came and even a few from the upper city. General Verdas answered more questions, but primarily he wanted us to register as citizens of Arawn."

"They sent a general for that?" Derian sounds surprised.

"President Gayre has few people he dares trust with the errand he sent General Verdas on."

"Besides," Angelita adds, "The people of Arawn aren't trusting. I doubt they'd've believed anyone of lower rank."

"And not everyone believed the General, for all he's well known to be one of the President's most trusted advisers," John Simeon continues, "However, registering as a citizen is a simple enough process. General Verdas and Channa each had a portable terminal, which was linked to a federal database. Each person was asked to enter a DNA print and their name, with the option of adding any additional personal information they knew. The information was encoded on a personal ID card then and there."

"So no waiting periods?" The Monarch waits for John Simeon to nod, "Amazing what can be done without an entrenched bureaucracy."

"I'm sure that will come in time," John Simeon observes, "In the meantime these ID cards are intended to serve all the functions of the multiple cards other countries issue. Any and all services accessed may require DNA verification in an attempt to discourage identity theft."

The Monarch nods approvingly.

"I was the first and Cattie Varlok the second," John Simeon moves on, "And no one left the meeting without registering. After that, all the records in my possession were scanned into the system. President Gayre is quite serious about reconstructing the records as far back as possible."

"And those who would never register voluntarily?" Angelita enquires.

"Those with cards are citizens with rights protected by law and the newly established courts. Those without aren't considered to have rights and may be forcibly registered... at which point they can file a complaint, but no one can be removed from the database once entered."

"And to prevent someone from registering a second identity?" Derian sounds curious.

"An alert comes up if the same DNA is entered twice. There's an override for identical twins, but both twins have to be present and that's the one thing that does create delays."

"Especially if they've been separated," Angelita observes, "And may not even know they have a twin."

John Simeon chuckles. "President Gayre openly admits that one of his goals is the re-establishment of the basic family. As soon as a new print enters the system, it's compared to every other print in the database, looking for first degree relations. Since October third, we've seen and heard from people we thought long gone."

"There must've been improvements in communications then." Angelita figures.

John Simeon nods. "The beginnings of a telephone network, publicly accessible internet, and several civilian radio stations.

"They've also completely overhauled the Ocean Falls power plant, the dam on the Riverre, and the Mount Trie wind farms."

Monarch Reginald frowns. "I was under the impression Arawn had limited resources."

"We do and we don't," John Simeon replies, "We have people and the means to recycle a great deal. We just can't purchase outside assistance."

The Monarch nods to himself. "What else has been happening?"

"The establishment of an ethical code for the scientific community named Regina's Code, which has most of them screaming."

Angelita looks amused. "Good to know President Gayre kept his word."

"Regina's Code is very strict, as well as retroactive," John Simeon explains, "Procedures on live animals are greatly restricted and even more so for human subjects. Also, human subjects, past as well as present and future, must receive compensation."

"No wonder they're screaming," Laine observes, "Is anyone taking advantage of it?"

"Many," John Simeon replies, "With court cases already being won on both sides. So far, in all cases, the judges are being scrupulously fair.

"President Gayre also has people scouring the country for illicit projects. Only FTK has been allowed to proceed without first proving their compliance with Regina's Code."

"Probably because FTK already follows their own, stricter, ethics," Angelita figures, "Which would be why Cemen Group chose them."

John Simeon nods. "However, President Gayre would like to see FTK independent of Cemen Group and Experiment Redemption phased out. Even now a school system is being established, although borrowing heavily of Experiment Redemption's methods and materials."

"I can't see the head of Cemen Group objecting," Angelita is amused about something, "Since her underlying objective 's already achieved."

Laine snickers, but the others frown.

"You suspect a motive beyond assistance where it was most desperately required?" Monarch Reginald queries.

"Altruism 's a neat concept," Angelita responds, "But since when 's Natalia altruistic?"

"Certainly true," The Monarch grimaces wryly, "Although I wouldn't care to guess her reasons for doing anything."

"The Second Shield were tasked with finding the final focal point," Laine speaks quietly, "I just doubt anyone was prepared for Tory."

"Even Sedya herself wasn't," Angelita chuckles, "Natalia doesn't seem to want anything to do with her now."

"That explains much," Monarch Reginald observes dryly, "But what other changes are happening in Arawn?"

"Production of our dietary staple, protein paste, while it cannot be halted, is undergoing major changes. Until now it's been unregulated, but restrictions are being imposed on ingredients and additives and export has been forbidden."

"Our food and drug authority has already banned import." The Monarch responds.

"As it should be," John Simeon nods, "Several scientific groups have put forward proposals for studying its long term effects. However, President Gayre is more interested in research towards enabling us to raise crops and food animals. Should any of that be successful, we may look to negotiate for seed and livestock."

"We will keep that in mind," Monarch Reginald replies, "But what of Arawn's military?"

John Simeon turns to the militia man beside him, "Captain, if you would."

"Yes, sir," Captain Jarevar addresses the Monarch, "On September twenty-eighth Arawn's army was officially disbanded and split into two groups: The Arawn Militia Reserve, in adherence to the guidelines set out in the Pleasure Society Treaty, and the Republic Police Force."

"They're retraining military as civilian police?" Angelita sounds sceptical.

"Based on psychological profile," Captain Jarevar clarifies, "As that training is successfully completed, the city patrols will be phased out.

"Also, all armaments not suitable for militia or police use are being gathered up and recycled. Your majesty, we are giving you a list of models and identifying marks and we ask that, should your people find any, they be destroyed, at the very least."

Monarch Reginald nods. "Thank you, Captain."

"Are you still losing supplies at the same rate?" I enquire.

"Slightly higher," Captain Jarevar admits, "Men as well, primarily those with noted anti-monarchy leanings."

"Speaking of which," John Simeon looks grave, "Republic law strictly forbids continued anti-monarchy activity. Those convicted in Arawn are sentenced to a life of manual labour... President Gayre sees no reason to waste manpower.

"As for those who escape Arawn, they are unlikely to be registered citizens of Arawn and may be dealt with as you see fit."

"And should we choose deportation?" The Monarch enquires.

"They will be assigned manual labour, just like the rest."

Derian frowns. "You make that sound like they couldn't be put to any other use."

"Those who feel compelled to continue anti-monarchy activity at this juncture are presumed unfit for any other assignment." Captain Jarevar sounds like he's quoting official government policy.

Angelita bursts out laughing. "Is that presumption based on their intelligence or their sanity?"

"Both," John Simeon replies, "Although they're no less dangerous for that. All too many are ex-military and Arawn is centuries ahead of any other country in both arms and tactics."

"So we've been warned." Monarch Reginald looks grim.

"Your majesty," Captain Jarevar speaks up, "Should you wish it, my orders permit me to share such information, along with advice on counter-measures."

"Thank you, Captain. We will keep that in mind."

John Simeon glances from Captain Jarevar to Priscilla, "I believe that covers matters in Arawn for the moment."

Monarch Reginald frowns slightly. "Did Ms Terrence not have a question she wished to ask?"

"It's not official business, your majesty."

"Be that as it may, perhaps someone present may have an answer for you."

"I only wish to know what became of my son, Rhett, after he left Experiment Redemption."

"He's somewhere in Ouestlun," Angelita grimaces, "It shouldn't take much to find out exactly where."

John Simeon frowns. "You're certain it's the same young man?"

"Rhett Terrence, right?" Angelita waits for Priscilla to nod, "He was well known at Camp Streton, believe me."

"But not well liked?" The Monarch guesses.

"Oh, he could be charming..." Laine makes a face.

"But in the end only concerned with himself?" Priscilla doesn't wait for an answer, "His father was like that."

"I'll still get you the information," Angelita promises, "Tory would know, if anyone does."

"Thank you."

"Lady Angelita," The Monarch turns to her, "You said you came out on business. Could that be dealt with now or would you prefer another time?"

"Now's fine."

"I presume this is business relating to your holding. What is the situation in Seeri Meadow?"

"Messy, just as your majesty warned me, although not as bad as it could be," Angelita replies, "Between what the village already had and what Natalia sent in the guise of wedding and housewarming gifts, this winter shouldn't be too bad."

"Good to know. What of the people and the village itself?"

"Aside from the keep, all the buildings are in good shape; however, the farm equipment's in rough shape and no one had a working personal vehicle. The only proper tradesman in the village was the blacksmith," Angelita sighs, "The mayor's been doing his best, but his health is failing. Other than that, there's one semi-retired physician... oh, and Old Yvon's bastard son, who's the only one in the village who doesn't know that."

"And you would be well within your rights to turn him out." Monarch Reginald observes.

"I can't afford to. So long as the villagers feed him, he'll do the labour of any three of the village men."

"That sounds to me like labour issues." John Simeon frowns.

Angelita nods. "On top of under population."

"And likely child labour issues." The Monarch adds grimly.

Angelita nods again. "From what I've seen, most of the village children work at least as long and hard as the adults and general educations levels rival any lower city in Arawn."

Derian frowns. "Where's your NRP representative?"

"Dead... since last winter," Angelita grimaces, "The mayor wrote up the reports and mailed them to headquarters... or thought he had. He's never heard back and Tory thinks they never left the village. I intend to deliver the mayor's duplicates myself while I'm here."

Monarch Reginald nods. "If you don't have copies of the child labour act, we can provide some."

"Thank you, your majesty."

"What else is happening?"

Angelita sighs. "A couple things. We are doing what we can: I seem to divide all my time between paperwork, petty disputes, and supervising the village stables."

"There's no stable master?"

"Not currently."

"And your husband?"

"He's been trying to turn some of his projects into cash flow. In the meantime, Ford, Rylan, and Kyle are helping with the last of the harvest... and, according to the mayor, each doing the work of any two village men... Tory 's mainly helping me, Nikki 's working with the physician, Shawnda 's filling in where she can, and our mechanical prodigy thinks he's in paradise."

The Monarch raises an eyebrow. "You brought your own mechanic?"

Angelita nods. "Tory originally took Logan on because he can drive anything with wheels and an engine and if he can't fix it, it's not worth fixing. The only problem is we're going to lose two or three families as soon as their vehicles are running."

"Why?" Monarch Reginald frowns.

"Two, I can understand. There's an older couple who want to move closer to their daughter before their first grandchild arrives. The other is a young family with a premature baby who needs better medical care... although they hope to return eventually."

"Both common enough situations. But what problem do you have with the third?"

Angelita scowls outright. "It's a couple with one son that they wait on hand and foot. He's the only child in the village who doesn't do so much as household chores. But last year they bought him a pony, which is kept in the village stables."

"At your expense?" John Simeon queries.

"Certainly not at theirs. Even that wouldn't bother me if one of the three of them were doing the stable chores for it. Instead, they've been having one of the village orphans, a six year old, do all the work without any compensation at all," Angelita's scowl deepens, "That I won't tolerate... especially when I'm looking after my mare myself. I told them either they look after the pony or they're not keeping it at my expense."

"And they threatened to leave completely?" Derian guesses, "They'll hardly find sympathy elsewhere."

"Does your highness want to come explain that to them?"

"It would hardly be worth the effort," The Monarch observes, "But what of these orphans? I would guess they've been little better than slaves."

Old pain flickers over Angelita's face, "For the most part they work no harder than the other children and the villagers have been feeding, clothing, and sheltering them. It's not too bad, given the circumstances.

"There're three of them: The foundling, Kayli, who's about eight and two boys, Peter, who's six, and Zane, who's five."

Laine frowns. "Wouldn't Tory be able to find out where Kayli 's from?"

Angelita shakes her head. "Tory said it's kind of like Kayli appeared from nowhere. Anyway, I know that they should be my responsibility, but most of the villagers fear upper nobility and all the children were warned to give Xylia space. Besides which, all three of them adopted Tory the first time they met her."

"You sound relieved." Laine observes dryly.

"Peter and Zane are very shy and far too submissive," Angelita grimaces, "It's a constant battle to keep the less scrupulous from taking advantage of them. Especially now that Tory's taken them in."

"You're covering their expenses and the villagers still expect them to work?" The Monarch guesses.

Angelita nods. "Neither Tory nor I object to letting them run minor errands occasionally, but even in Arawn they'd be considered too young for some of the work they're asked to do.

"And then there's Kayli. She's no less submissive, but she's not at all shy and she never quits with the questions. Tory doesn't seem to mind... most of the time, but I doubt I could handle her."

I frown. "Could Tory adopt these children without being married?"

"Not without special permission," Monarch Reginald replies, "But what would prevent her marrying?"

"That's a long and complicated explanation," Angelita sighs, "And as she put it, she's as married as she's going to get. But she would like to adopt the children."

"That, I think, is a discussion best saved for another time," The Monarch observes, "Is there anything else?"

"Not that I know of, your majesty."

He glances around the table, but no one else speaks, "Then I believe that is all for now." He gets up and leaves the room, but no one follows.

There's silence for a minute, then Derian addresses John Simeon, "President Gayre must have had everything planned in advance, to make so many major changes so quickly."

John Simeon nods. "He's been planning and preparing for years. But also fighting the military for power enough to implement anything."

Angelita chuckles. "So far it sounds like he's done better than I hoped he would. Anyway, Ms Terrence," Angelita turns to the elderly woman, "If you would come with me, it shouldn't take long to answer your question."

Priscilla glances at John Simeon, who nods. After she leaves with Angelita and Xylia, he turns to me.

"I'll need Cattie back at the embassy. Do you know where she is?"

I glance at Laine, who grimaces.

"Where ever Rowena is. I'll find her and let her know."

"Thank you, Laine."

No sooner has she left the room than a big man in the uniform of the palace guard appears in the doorway.

"Captain Samuel Jarevar? I'm Han Sevyn, captain of the palace guard and commanding officer of the Norsecount Militia Reserve."

Captain Jarevar can't quite conceal a wince at the combined titles.

"His majesty just informed me that you would be willing to share information that could help us with our current situation."

"Yes, of course."

"Would it be possible to begin now or is it necessary to set up a time?"

"Now is fine." Captain Jarevar accompanies Han from the room. That leaves me with John Simeon, Derian, and Sefu.

John Simeon gets to his feet. "Nerita, is there a place we could take a short walk? I've been sitting far more lately than I'm used to."

"Sure." I'd been wondering when John Simeon was going to ask to talk to me. Derian catches my eye, his expression hard to read. I shake my head.

Sefu accompanies me and John Simeon, although clearly not happy about it. I know he'll never like John Simeon, but I'll settle for him behaving.

This late in the fall the palace gardens aren't much to look at, but the sun's shining, so it's not too chilly. We walk silently for a few minutes while John Simeon looks around.

"I have to admit you're doing better than I thought you would. Still..."

"My father had Taireem's Mania, didn't he?"

John Simeon glances at me sharply, "Why do you ask?"

"I know exactly how my parents died."

John Simeon swallows hard, "Yes, your father suffered Taireem's Mania. He considered it a family curse and had hoped it would end with him."

"It did."

"Then how...?" John Simeon looks both confused and relieved.

"I don't have the gene mutation that causes true Taireem's, but there's a pseudo form... that's what I had."

John Simeon frowns. "Had?"

I nod. "That's all over and dealt with. I'll never have another episode... good thing too."

"Certainly better than I dared hope," John Simeon relaxes visibly, "And Andrina?"

"She's just fine. She was one of the first to marry."

"And you're to be married in four days... or so said the invitation delivered to the embassy for us," John Simeon studies me carefully, "Cattie and I will be there for sure... Still..."

"I know what I'm doing. Besides," I can't help chuckling, "Arguing with Tory 's a waste of breath."

"So I've discovered," John Simeon chuckles as well, "Although she seemed to think you headed for some trouble."

There's nothing I can do to stop myself from flushing. He studies me with a bemused expression, then shakes his head.

"I do need to return to the embassy."

I nod.

We head back into the palace and through to the main entrance. Cattie and Priscilla are already waiting. There's no sign of the militia man, but that's hardly surprising. John Simeon, Cattie and Priscilla leave quickly and Sefu and I set out for the old south tower.

As we enter the first corridor, Derian joins us.

"What is it about John Simeon that Sefu mislikes?"

"I don't know," I rest a hand on Sefu's head, "But I don't think anyone's ever really known much about him... beyond what's common knowledge."

"That's precious little, given what I've heard," Derian frowns, "Yet you've known him all your life... worked with him much of that time."

I shrug. "It is weird. The man had no private life to speak of: He lived in his study, which also housed our records, and the bedrooms in his house were always full of those with no where to go. Most of the years I worked with him, I had free access to anything I wanted in his house, attic to cellar."

Derian's frown deepens. "You said he wasn't the first in his position. Do you know anything of his predecessors?"

"There've been five men like John Simeon. Each came to the Old Quarter as a young man and left as an old one... each named John something... each doing the same work from the same house. Yet those who remember the most recent three claim there's no physical resemblance. No one's ever known where they come from or where they go."

Derian just shakes his head. "But Sefu doesn't like him at all..."

"Neither do feral children. It's interesting though... What do you think of Ford?"

Derian's frown returns at the apparent change in subject, "He's a likeable enough man... certainly an interesting one."

"So's Rylan Tobin," I observe, "But animals don't like either of them."

"You think there's a connection?" Derian's frown deepens.

I shrug lightly. "Maybe it's just coincidence."

"You don't believe that."

"I don't know enough about any of them to know otherwise."

27-10-48-06-04SM

For those of us without telepathic ability, contacting Natalia Burren is easier said than done. Fortunately the information I'm hoping to get from her isn't urgent. I end up leaving a message at the Pleasure Society embassy here in Monarch's Town. But even the staff there aren't sure how long it'll take her to get back to me.

In the meantime, it's three days before my wedding and I'm starting to wish it was over already. Guests are starting to arrive now, although not many yet. Maybe I don't know exactly how many are expected, but I can't avoid all the rumours flying around. Especially since I seem to have become popular with the middle nobility.

That's easy enough to explain though... as Marcellus pointed out. First of all, I am middle nobility... set to marry into the monarchy, which is a rare occurrence. Secondly, my friends married into the middle nobility, which is thoroughly knit together by blood and marriage, and they've been surprisingly well received. I suspect rumours of pregnancies still too early to be officially announced help. And, thirdly, ladies Covak, Varien, and Gravenor took a liking to me the afternoon I had tea with them. Now if only the upper nobility were so easily won over.

For the first time in days, I have an afternoon to myself. However, everyone else is busy with something. I'm too restless to just sit around the south tower, so Sefu and I head out for a walk.

The palace gardens are pretty much dead for this year, although they do look pretty in the morning frost. But it's sunny today and too warm for the frost to last. So Sefu and I go looking for a trail instead. We end up on one that winds through the forest behind the palace, and turns out to end closer to the front entrance than the rear.

As Sefu and I approach the steps, two vehicles pull in. The first stops just long enough to disgorge three of the most vicious old gossips of the upper nobility. These three have taken an especial disliking to me and they're very lucky Tory was able to cure me.

They head up the steps as their vehicle leaves and the second parks in its place. Only one lady gets out; one I'm sure I've never seen before. She's accompanied by two servants who immediately set to work unloading baggage while she pauses on the bottom step to survey the palace entrance.

The three at the top of the steps turn to see who's behind them and it's instantly obvious that they don't like the new arrival.

"Were you not banished from court, Lady Ayson?" The woman's voice is loud enough to carry to the street beyond the gates. All the guards in the vicinity turn to look and Sefu growls low in his throat.

I haven't stopped walking and now mount the first step. The four ladies notice me at the same time.

"This isn't your concern, girl..."

I know better than to say a word to those three, but my eyes meet those of the speaker. Even at this distance, she flinches and looks away. Then she and her friends head into the palace.

"Who might you be?" The lady on the bottom step sounds more curious than anything else.

"Lady Nerita Chassaven."

She studies me carefully, "The same as is to marry the Crown Prince?"

I nod.

"I am High Lady Chelsea Deruna Ayson... although I don't doubt you've heard something of me before now..."

"Only briefly, during a discussion regarding the wedding guest list."

That clearly surprises Lady Ayson, "Would you walk with me? That is if your companion doesn't object."

Sefu's been studying her quietly, his expression almost sad.

"If Sefu objected to you, I'd know already. So certainly."

"Thank you." Lady Ayson starts up the steps and Sefu and I accompany her. She doesn't speak again until we're through the main entrance way.

"Perhaps I was never officially banished from court, but I've most certainly been out of favour a great many years," Lady Ayson sighs, "I was a schoolmate of Victoria Martrency, who later became his majesty's second wife, and once foolish enough to think her my friend."

I keep silent and wait for her to continue.

"But a few unguarded words regarding a poorly arranged marriage," Old pain flickers over Lady Ayson's face, "Words that were deliberately and maliciously twisted... I'd always been half aware that Victoria had a vicious... almost insane streak in her."

"Likely insane," I observe dryly, "Given what Princess Carina has said of the woman. But continue."

Lady Ayson nods grimly. "Victoria delighted in the discomfort of others. Yet never did I dream such a small thing could be warped into such a terrible, foolish problem."

I nod to myself.

"At least it seemed a small thing at first. Still, words said cannot be unsaid and mine were twisted and tangled beyond the influence of any to repair. I left court... buried myself away in my work and my children. But now," She glances over me and Sefu, "Such tales as visitors and winds have been carrying... I had to see matters for myself. And then came the invitation to his highness's wedding..."

I nod again.

"You're not of the Chassaven family of Norsecount, are you?"

"No, I'm the last of the Estorika line. High Lord Chassaven 's twice refused to acknowledge that, even though his majesty has."

"I take it you're little liked by the upper nobility here?"

"Those that I've met so far."

"Few with power and influence like threats to that power and influence," Lady Ayson observes, "'Tis those without such that welcome change."

"Or at least those discontent with the status quo." I respond.

She chuckles. "I would guess you to be a great deal older than you look."

"Somewhere between my appearance and my experience," I shrug evasively, "I'm younger than Princess Carina."

"I suspect she ought not be a princess, given that the pictures I've seen of her most closely resemble the late High Lady Adarion."

"His majesty thinks otherwise... even now."

"And never allows mention of Travis Adarion, I'm sure."

I shake my head. "His majesty believes Travis Adarion dead twenty years. Some people care little to speak of the dead."

That earns me a sharp look from Lady Ayson.

"Yet is not death a common part of life?"

"In places, too common."

She nods to herself and changes the subject, "How long have you lived at court?"

"A month now."

"With a sponsor?"

"With a friend and her father for the moment."

"A school friend?" Lady Ayson sounds wary.

"More like a foster sister."

"Ah," Lady Ayson stops at a half open door, "I really must thank you. I am, as I said earlier, somewhat unpopular here. And I am pleased to have met you."

I bow my head briefly. "You're welcome, my lady."

She smiles before disappearing through the door. I remain in the corridor, trying to decide where to go. Sitting around the south tower still doesn't appeal, but neither does another walk.

"Lady Nerita."

I look down the corridor to see Lady Irina approaching. She joins me and Sefu quickly.

"The guards reported Chelsea Ayson's arrival," Lady Irina studies me critically, "I hardly thought she'd dare return to court."

I shrug evasively, "I really hadn't heard of her before today."

"Yet you've seen the results of her wagging tongue." Lady Irina responds sharply, starting back down the corridor. Sefu and I accompany her.

"It takes more than one woman's complaints to create a problem on this scale."

"You believe whatever tale she told you?"

"She believes it," My voice is cool, "Which I think is more important."

"You may yet get yourself into serious trouble."

"That's inevitable."

Lady Irina looks disgusted and vanishes down the next side corridor.

28-10-48-06-04SM

"Nerita."

I lift my head from Derian's chest to look at him.

"Do you have any plans for today?"

I spend a moment thinking about that, "Nothing urgent. Why?"

"Would you be interested in going into town with me? There's a lady I'd like you to meet."

"Okay..." I study Derian curiously.

He brushes his fingers through my hair. "We're not going anywhere fancy... in fact, old jeans 'll be just fine."

I have to raise an eyebrow at that, "How're we getting out of the palace?"

Derian chuckles. "I'll show you."

"I'm guessing I should see if Laine 'll tiger sit."

"That's up to you. I'd like to leave after breakfast."

Which means we have to get up and dressed because I have to return to the old south tower to eat and change.

I arrive at the same time as Laine, who has been spending her nights with Rylan, and we find Duke Malin and Carina just sitting down to breakfast. Sefu, who had been with me, immediately heads to the corner of the dining room where his morning meal is waiting.

The Duke eyes me and Laine disapprovingly as we take our seats. I think it's more because we were late. He seems to have realized neither of us much cares what he thinks of where we choose to sleep. Carina, on the other hand, looks slightly jealous. Still, neither of them says more than good morning.

After breakfast, Carina accompanies me, Laine, and Sefu up to our rooms. I have to get changed, so I head straight to the dressing room. Old jeans and one of Laine's t-shirts are easy enough to find, but I'm going to need a jacket and I can't seem to find the old denim jacket I still have from South city.

"Nerita," Laine is watching me with a bemused expression, "What're you looking for?"

"My jacket. Derian asked me to go out with him and said to dress casually."

Laine raises a sceptical eyebrow, "You do remember what kind of shape that jacket 's in, right?"

I shoot her a look of irritation, "Just tell me where it is."

Laine shakes her head as she comes up with it for me, "He say where you're going?"

"Only that there's someone he wants me to meet," I start to get changed, "Is it gonna be a problem if I leave Sefu with you?"

Laine clearly doesn't like that idea, "You're sure you don't want him with you?"

"I'd kinda rather not call attention to myself. A winter tiger walking anywhere people are..."

Laine nods. "Yeah, fine. I'm gonna take Spirit out... he'll have to come along."

Carina takes a deep breath, "Would you object if I came as well? I'd like to speak with you."

"Sure," Laine nods, "I'd like to go as soon as I'm changed though."

"Yes, of course." Carina leaves us so she can get ready.

Laine waits until we can hear her door close, "Why am I thinking you and Derian 're gonna get yourselves in trouble?"

I chuckle. "Only if we get caught."

Laine just shakes her head and turns her attention to getting herself ready to go riding.

Once I'm finished getting dressed, I head downstairs to find Derian waiting for me in the sitting room. He's also dressed in old jeans and a casual shirt, but the jacket in his hand is old brown leather.

Derian looks over me approvingly. "You're ready to go?"

I nod and let him take my hand.

Once we're out of the tower, we take a series of back corridors and staff only doors to the cellars below the kitchens. Derian opens a half concealed door in a distant corner and guides me inside a stone passageway. Neither of us speaks for a while and the only sound is his soft footsteps. Then I catch the curious look he gives me.

"I've never truly believed any person could move completely silently... 'til now."

I laugh softly. "I doubt you've been around many people for whom it's habitual."

Derian raises an eyebrow at that. "And you have?"

"Every child in Arawn, especially in the cities, learns three basic survival skills early on... those who don't seldom survive."

Derian looks wary, "Why am I thinking we have different ideas of basic survival?"

"Because we grew up in very different circumstances. In Arawn, children learn to fight at least enough to defend themselves and to move and hide without making any sound."

Derian nods to himself, then frowns, "That's only two."

I grimace wryly. "Children in Arawn also learn to pick pockets."

"As all too many children here learn to beg." Derian sighs grimly.

"Begging 's a waste of time and breath when those who would give have nothing themselves."

Derian shivers. "Even the children of the Old Quarter?"

I nod. "There was more order to life in the Old Quarter, but food and clothes and such had to be obtained from outside and we had, if anything, less money than those living elsewhere. And neither the military nor the provisional government distributed aid of any kind."

"Not even the protein paste?" Derian frowns.

"Protein paste production was outside the control of either. Contracts were in place to provide an number of people in each inhabited area with a set amount per batch. But it wasn't free... just cheaper than the underground."

"You held such a contract?"

"My family and those authorized to represent us... The only contract in or for the Old Quarter."

"How did you pay for that if you had little money?"

"The whole community contributed... each individual or family gave what they could when they could. Not just for food either. Few cared to venture into the lower city even to obtain clothes and personal items."

Derian raises an eyebrow. "They entrusted you with a great deal."

I shrug it off. "What good is all the money in the world when it's worth your life to try to get food, shelter, and clothing?"

Derian shivers, but doesn't try to say anything to that.

Shortly, we reach the end of the passageway and climb a ladder, which leads into an empty, windowless, concrete room. There's a door in the far wall and on the other side of it we find ourselves at the foot of a set of stairs leading up to the alley between two warehouses.

"You should know," Derian laces his fingers through mine as we leave the alley, "That passage is actually intended as an escape route for the monarch's family in case of trouble. Father knows of it as I do, although I'm not sure he knows I occasionally use it."

I nod to myself.

Derian is silent for a moment before asking, "Did you tell Laine where we're going?"

I shake my head. "Only that I'd be with you."

He nods and changes the subject, "What did you say to Lady Irina yesterday? She's highly offended over something."

"Did she mention the circumstances?"

Derian shakes his head.

"Sefu and I went for a walk in the palace grounds yesterday afternoon and found ourselves on the main steps as ladies Huntley, Vorsen, and Minotte returned and Lady Ayson arrived."

Derian groans. "So that's what the guard thought it so important Father hear."

"I didn't say a word to any of the first three and they went inside quickly."

Derian looks somewhat sceptical, but doesn't interrupt.

"You know I'd never met Lady Ayson before... I couldn't've. But I'd only even heard her name mentioned once... and then only briefly.

"But you did speak with her?" Derian queries.

"Enough to hear what she had to say of herself. Lady Irina didn't see us together and couldn't've heard what was said, but she seemed to think I should take her view of the situation."

Derian sighs and shakes his head. "Outside her home and country Lady Irina can be all too officious and judgemental. You should know that she never visited Norsecount between Mother's death and Victoria's... in fact not even for several years after that."

"So all her knowledge of the situation is second hand," I nod to myself, "Do you know how many children Lady Ayson has?"

"Four of her own," Derian replies immediately, "But the former Lord Ayson was neither a good man nor a faithful husband and she's taken it on herself to assist and protect those of his bastard children as she knows of."

I can't quite suppress a scowl, "Their mothers weren't mistresses?"

"Certainly not willing ones," Derian confirms my guess, "Yet Chelsea Ayson was only heard to complain the once. She's kept quietly to herself since leaving court... even when her former husband was convicted of the abuse of a Society ward travelling through the village. A sentence in Cold Pass Castle for such carries the additional penalty of the loss of all titles and lands and the annulment of marriage."

"She didn't say anything of that... only of her original reason for leaving court."

"There were, and still are, those who thought Father should've banished her. He would've sooner banished Victoria, who always was the greater problem."

We've been walking through an industrial area, but now come to a wider road with a strip of grass and trees down the middle. As we step out from between the last of the warehouses, we get hit with a strong wind. It isn't enough to make walking difficult, nor is it especially cold, but I can't help shivering.

"Nerita?" Derian releases my hand so he can slip an arm around me, "Is something wrong?"

I sigh. "Just my imagination playing tricks on me."

He frowns. "You look as though you'd seen a spirit."

"More like heard one... or several."

That clearly surprises him, "What do you mean?"

I shake my head. "It's nothing more than my imagination... well, and a bit of superstitious nonsense."

Derian's frown deepens. "Superstition is common enough on this continent, but I thought those from Arawn less prone to it."

"It isn't that we're less prone to it so much as we don't share the same superstitions. Although perhaps the origins of ours, being more recent, are more easily explained."

"But you don't believe?"

"I know better. Still..." Now that we're across the street and in between buildings, this time apartments, the worst of the wind is blocked again.

Derian considers what I've said for a time while we continue to walk.

"Connections have been drawn between the wind and spirits before..."

"But perhaps never so directly as in Arawn," I respond, "To us, to show respect for the dead is not to bury them... not even to allow them to be taken to the morgues. Even if there was a place to bury the dead, either would only result in the bodies being stolen for science."

Derian nods, not looking surprised by that. "Hence Angelita's one request of President Gayre. Yet you wouldn't keep the dead among you."

"In a way, we do. To protect and respect the dead, the body is burned and the ashes taken by the wind. Yes, it is a funeral pyre, but we long ago learned ways to ensure that nothing but ash remains."

"And the dead are literally taken by the wind." Derian doesn't seem as bothered by the idea as many people are.

"Besides, most people in Arawn are born and live their lives half underground. Why would we want to condemn the dead to that permanently?"

That does get a shudder from Derian, but I have to wonder if there isn't more to it in his mind. I'm not about to ask though.

"Good day, sir!"

Derian and I look over to see a street vendor at his cart. Derian immediately steers me over to him.

The vendor smiles warmly. "It's been some time since you were by."

Derian shrugs lightly. "As business allows. I trust you've been well, sir."

"As well as ever. Is this your lady?"

"My fiancée," Derian nods, "Though we will be wed soon."

"My congratulations, sir... my lady," The vendor bows his head briefly, "And again, good day to you."

We move on, but more slowly. We're now into a neighbourhood that looks something like my home would've before the war. Each street is lined with neat townhouses with flowerbeds and shrubs on each side of each door. It's clearly a lower class neighbourhood, but one where the people care for each other and their homes. Many people are out, mostly women and children, many of whom greet me and Derian politely, although familiarly, as we pass. Derian returns the greetings and it's obvious he comes here often. What is equally obvious is they either don't know who he is or don't care. I suspect the former.

"Well, young man," One late middle aged matron with a stern expression and a twinkle in her eye stops us, "It's about time you found yourself a lady."

Derian can't quite conceal a pained look and I suppress my amusement.

She glances at my left hand, "I hope you're to be wed soon."

"Very soon." Derian confirms.

The matron's expression softens, "My congratulations to you both and I do wish you well."

"Thank you." Derian bows his head politely. I do the same. Then we're allowed to move on, although still slowly.

But not long after that, we start seeing more people out and many faces at windows. I glance at Derian and he chuckles.

"I've never understood how word spreads so fast here, yet it does."

I just laugh softly.

"My lady..." At the soft, timid voice, I turn to see a small girl approaching. She looks a little scared and her hands are clasped behind her back. I kneel down to her eye level.

"Hello."

The girl smiles shyly. "People 're saying you're to be wed soon..."

I nod. "In just a few days."

She brings her hands out from behind her back and holds out a white flower. "This's for you."

"Thank you." I accept the flower, to her obvious delight. She quickly bobs her head and retreats. Then Derian helps me straighten up.

"A hope rose," He identifies the flower for me, "No woman from this neighbourhood would be married without one in her hair or bouquet. They're said to bring happiness to the bride."

I nod and slip the flower into the end of my braid as we continue walking.

Eventually, Derian guides me up the steps to the door of a house that looks the same as the others around it. He knocks and it takes a minute before the door opens.

"Good day, sir," The girl in the doorway can't be more than sixteen, "She kept saying you'd come today."

Derian chuckles. "I gather she's expecting me then."

"Of course, sir," The girl steps aside, "If you and your lady would please come in. She's in the living room."

"Thank you." Derian ushers me inside. The girl leaves the house, closing the door behind her. Then I follow Derian into the living room. There, we find an older woman seated in an armchair, wrapped in blankets.

"Ah, Derian... there you are." The woman smiles broadly. He crosses the room to accept a hug and kiss her cheek.

"I am sorry it's been so long," He begins, "I hope you've been well."

"Oh, never better," She laughs gently, "You've no cause to worry over me. Violet 's such a help, you know, despite having her mother's wagging tongue. But I see you've brought a young lady... you will introduce her, I hope."

Derian chuckles. "I have every intention of it. I'd very much like you to meet my fiancée, Nerita Chassaven. Nerita," He turns to me, "This is Kendra Percival. She was my mother's ladies maid."

Which explains a whole lot of the situation.

"So this's your lady," Kendra studies me critically, "'Tis about time you found one worth bringing to see me."

Derian sighs and indicates for me to sit with him on the sofa. Kendra continues to study me.

"A hope rose? That'll be from one of the girls here," Kendra nods to herself, "And my lady's ring? This must be an interesting tale indeed. Were you allowed your own choice this time?"

"No," Derian shakes his head, "Although I did actually propose. That just wasn't where things began."

"Oh?"

"Things began with Angelita looking to thwart his majesty's plans for her," I lace my fingers through Derian's, "She suggested this marriage to Natalia Burren and Tory, who both took a liking to the idea."

"Angelita as in the former princess of Estorika?" Kendra looks surprised, "How long have you known her?"

"Many years... long before she even considered telling anyone who she was. But it was Natalia who first presented the idea to his majesty."

"And his majesty agreed?"

Derian shakes his head. "Father wouldn't even consider the idea. I met Nerita when I came home to be best man at Marcellus's wedding, where he married one of her friends."

Kendra nods to herself. "I thought I'd heard he'd remarried. Without interference, I hope."

"There was no time for interference," Derian replies, "I only just had enough warning to finish my business and get home. Although, given what I've seen of his new lady, I doubt interference would be attempted more than once."

Kendra raises an eyebrow. "Then this lady must be nothing like his first."

"Certainly very little... which I think just as well. This one can hold her own with his sisters."

"So you came for Marcellus's wedding and met your lady there," Kendra returns to the original topic, "You didn't propose without his majesty's permission, did you?"

"Yes, I did. But even when Father confirmed the engagement at court, he was still opposed to it. Although he has changed his mind since."

Kendra frowns. "No one can force the hand of the Monarch of Norsecount."

"The Sword of the First can," Derian corrects, "Now that it has resurfaced."

Kendra's expression twists wryly, "The news and gossip of the court has been rather bizarre of late. Is the truth any less so?"

Derian and I both shake our heads.

"So you're to be married very soon, I hear... the thirtieth of this month, correct?"

"Yes." Derian nods.

"Yet it is still to be a formal, state wedding, is it not?"

Derian chuckles. "Florence was given fourteen days to have everything ready. So far she's done amazingly well."

"But why the hurry?" Kendra frowns, "You must be aware of the speculation surrounding it all."

"The Sword and its wielder want Father off the throne and he had little room for negotiation. Currently he has until I have an heir, but tolerance for delays is almost nonexistent."

Kendra's frown deepens. "That seems to me rather an unreasonable expectation. The hand of nature is less easily forced than that of the Monarch of Norsecount."

"It's said one of the Second Shield can do it," Derian responds, "Few would question such and fewer object."

"What of your lady?" Kendra turns to me.

"I don't object. I also grew up with a different understanding of marriage than exists among the nobility here."

Kendra nods and a smile returns to her face. "'Tis about time the court here had a proper lady again." Then she glances at the clock, "I do hope you'll stay to lunch."

"Of course," Derian responds, "Thank you."

It's mid-afternoon by the time we leave Kendra's and late afternoon before we reach the passageway. But even with the palace kitchens busy with dinner preparations, we manage not to encounter anyone until we reach the sitting room in the old south tower. There we find Laine and Sefu waiting for us.

"His majesty was looking for you," Laine informs us immediately, "An' I think he's a little pissed."

Derian sighs. "Then I'd better change and see what he wants." He turns to me, "Will I see you later?"

I nod and accept a kiss. Then he leaves and I head upstairs to change before dinner. Sefu and Laine accompany me.

"So where'd you go?" Laine asks once we reach our dressing room.

"Into Monarch's Town," I start by removing the flower from my hair and setting it on the dressing table, "The lady he wanted me to meet used to be his mother's ladies maid."

Laine nods to herself. "I'm not sure his majesty wasn't looking for you as well."

I shrug it off. "Easier to leave the explaining to Derian."

Laine chuckles. "You mean 'cause it was his idea anyway? Oh, just to warn you, Father's none too happy about us being late to breakfast."

"As in don't do it again?" I guess.

Laine nods. "At least we only have to worry about it two more days."

I give her an irritated look. Laine knows I'm trying not to think about my rapidly approaching wedding.

29-10-48-06-04SM

I'm passing through the sitting room when the telephone rings so I change direction to answer it.

"Hello?"

"Good morning, Nerita," It's Natalia on the other end, "You wanted information on the group currently with Experiment Redemption calling themselves Black Oak Court?"

"It's a group of eight girls from the Old Quarter of South City under Nathania Leyshon, right?"

"And what would you do with the information?"

"Call it what you will, but I like knowing how my people 're doing."

"I see," Natalia sounds amused, "Are you busy this afternoon?"

"Not especially... or at least not until four."

"Then I can arrange for you to get the information direct... so long as you don't mind dealing with Becky."

"Whatever it takes."

"Then you'll receive a message once everything is arranged."

"Thank you." I hang up the telephone, well aware of the look Laine is giving me.

"How'd you find out about that?"

"Cattie."

"And what are you planning to do with that information?"

"Depends a little on what I get," I shrug, "I'll have to wait and see."

Immediately after lunch, Carl comes looking for me.

"Lady Nerita, a vehicle just arrived and the driver has instructions to take you and whomever you wish to the Pleasure Society embassy."

"It'll just be me and Sefu," I ignore the look Laine gives me, "I'll need a minute to get ready."

"Yes, my lady."

I head upstairs to get a jacket and change shoes. Laine follows me, clearly annoyed.

"It this's Black Oak Court business, you should take me at least, if not Cattie."

"Not this time."

"But you don't know what you're walking into, let alone what you'll actually get."

"I know," I quickly find the jacket and shoes I want, "You're still not coming. Besides, I thought you had plans."

Laine groans. "And you complain about me getting myself in trouble."

"I can look after myself, remember? I'm only going as far as the Society embassy and I should be back long before four."

Laine doesn't say anything more as I finish getting ready to go. Back down in the sitting room, Carl is waiting to escort me and Sefu to the main entrance of the palace.

We arrive at the doors only to be intercepted by Derian, who doesn't look happy. I signal to Carl that he's dismissed and he slips away gratefully.

"Where are you going?" Derian's eyes meet and hold mine.

"Not far and not for long. I asked Natalia for some information and I have to go to the Society embassy to get it."

"Unescorted?"

I have a feeling I just lost this argument.

"This's my private business."

"Nerita."

"Didn't you say you have work this afternoon?"

"Nothing urgent."

I sigh. "Fine. I need to go if I'm gonna be back in time."

Derian moves aside long enough to let me and Sefu past. Then he follows us to the waiting vehicle.

It's a long, low vehicle bearing the crest of the Pleasure Society chancellors and the driver is in the uniform of the Chancellor's Messenger Service. He holds the door so the three of us can get in before going around to his own seat.

The drive to the embassy isn't long and the gates swing open as the vehicle approaches. When we pull up to the foot of the main steps, another of the Chancellor's messengers appears to let us out.

"Lady Nerita Chassaven?" She waits for me to nod, "Natalia Burren requested us to set up a televideo conference with Experiment Redemption's Lake Prince location for you. This way, please."

The three of us follow her inside the embassy, to a conference room with windows facing the back gardens. One of the end walls of the room is a giant screen.

"If you would please sit here," The messenger pulls out a chair for me, "Lake Prince is standing by."

"Thank you," I sit and Sefu stretches out behind me, "How much of the room does the camera pick up?"

"Only this end of the table." The messenger indicates where I'm sitting. Then she leaves the room, closing the door. Derian seats himself at the far end of the table from me.

A moment later, the screen turns on and I can see Becky Riverson seated in a similar conference room.

Becky is another member of Sedya's Second Shield as well as Natalia's personal attendant... when Natalia doesn't have her doing other jobs. As far as I know, they're unrelated, but they could pass for twins. However, unlike Natalia, Becky tends to wear jeans, t-shirts, and a denim jacket of indeterminate age. They don't sound much alike either.

"Hey, Nerita," Becky's voice sounds surprisingly near and clear, "I'd like you to meet Doctor Deborah Huntindom, Gerald's sister an' head of our Lake Prince location."

The woman who appears on the screen beside Becky looks enough like Doctor Gerald Huntindom, who's in charge of Camp Streton, that I'd've guessed they're related without Becky saying anything. I nod politely and wait for one of them to continue.

"One thing," Deborah doesn't look entirely happy, "What exactly is Black Oak Court? This all seems very strange."

I chuckle. "Obviously your people in South City didn't dig deep enough. Anyway, I've been over that with Natalia."

"So she said." Becky isn't happy either.

"Of all the girls of Black Oak Court, I've accounted for all but the eight currently with Experiment Redemption and I'd like to know where they're at."

Becky and Deborah exchange glances, then Deborah sighs.

"Initial testing allowed them to enter the advanced track. They'll graduate in six weeks."

Becky grimaces. "If they were older maybe Natalia could arrange marriages for them, like she did for the original group..."

"Even Nathania 's a bit young for that..." I catch Derian's questioning look and shake my head, "Anyway, I just want to know how they're doing right now. Anything else can wait until after tomorrow."

Deborah frowns, but Becky nods to herself.

"We do have six weeks yet," Becky observes, "But, if you want, you could talk to any or all of them now."

"Please," I nod, "Just one at a time."

Becky and Deborah leave the screen. Derian looks at me and opens his mouth to speak.

I shake my head. "We'll talk after."

He nods.

A moment later, Nathania appears, looking nervous and takes the chair Becky had vacated. Not until she is settled does she look up at the camera.

"Nerita!"

I grin. "What'd they tell you?"

"Just there was someone who wanted to talk to each of us," Nathania takes a deep, shaky breath, "Where are you? We've never heard anything..."

"You didn't ask either."

Nathania's guilty expression confirms my guess.

"I'm in Monarch's Town, Norsecount... so's Cattie."

"Oh, wow! Seriously?"

I nod. "We only actually graduated at the end of September, but it's been quite the month. As for Cattie, President Gayre sent John Simeon as ambassador to Norsecount and he brought her as part of his staff."

"So only Mellie's left in South City?"

"According to Cattie, she and Ross just had a baby girl."

"Ross 'll be happy then. He wanted a girl the first time around."

"Anyway," I don't give her a chance to ask another question, "Cattie filled me in on everything she knows about. So how've you been doing?"

Nathania slumps in her seat. "How'd you an' Cattie do it? Everyone 's agreed we want to graduate an' get out of Arawn... but..."

"I almost couldn't get that. They said you've only got six weeks left."

"But they don't know what to do with us after," Nathania is nearly in tears, "Cattie relaxed some of the rules a little, but to get them to stick to that even..."

"I intend to talk to all of them," I wish I was in the same room as Nathania instead of a continent away, "I need you to hang in there 'til graduation. Don't worry about anything after that."

Nathania swallows. "Can you actually do anything?"

"I don't know yet. I probably won't until after tomorrow."

"What's tomorrow?" Nathania frowns warily.

"My wedding."

"Wha...? Nerita!"

I chuckle. "You heard me. And if you didn't hear about the engagement, you haven't been paying enough attention to things. Anyway, one of the rules that got relaxed wouldn't happen to be the one about visible piercings?"

Nathania's expression twists wryly. "She wanted to get her nose pierced. I don't know why... it's barely even visible."

I nod to myself. "Just do me a favour and pass on the news. I want reports, not to repeat myself over and over."

"I will. Oh, did Cattie say what Mellie an' Ross named their daughter?"

"Milicent Nerita."

"Thanks."

"You take care of yourself."

Nathania nods. Then she gets up and it takes a couple minutes for Natika to appear. I study her as she sits.

Natika has always had dark colouring, even when we lived in the city where no one sees the sun. Now her skin is darker than ever, causing the piercings in her nose and eyebrow to stand out. Her thick, curly, black hair just brushes the tops of her shoulders.

"It figures," I ignore her glare, "You always were a pain in the ass."

"Ain't your problem." Natika crosses her arms over her chest.

"The only way it wouldn't be my problem 's if you'd stayed with Drek."

Natika's expression turns stony, confirming my guess at her reason for remaining part of Black Oak Court.

"But since that obviously didn't work out and there's a chance you could be headed my way, I suggest you straighten up."

"Fuckin' stupid rules..." The words are just barely audible over the connection.

"Unless you're planning to stay in Arawn or find a way to the other continent, you better get it straight in your head that those aren't just my rules. You're taking etiquette, aren't you?"

"Yeah... fuckin' bullshit."

I shake my head. "Two years ago I gave you a choice of going or staying... and I left Cattie in my place to look after anyone who stayed. Don't blame me for what you chose to do."

Natika doesn't say anything for a couple minutes while she struggles with what I've said. Finally, she relaxes her arms and meets my eyes.

"Would they really send us to you?"

"They don't know what else to do with you."

"What'd they do with you guys?" Natika frowns.

"Arranged marriages for everyone except Laine."

Natika shudders. "Why'd you even agree to that? How'd you get the others to agree?"

I shrug evasively. "You're too young for that, but no one knows exactly what'll happen yet."

"I guess."

"Just do everyone a favour and cut Nathania some slack 'til you're finished there."

Natika grimaces, but nods.

"And stay out of trouble."

"Yes, Nerita."

Natika is quickly replaced by Vlaria, who also has hair that just reaches her shoulders. But it's copper and I seem to recall her being blonde. Then she pulls it off, revealing golden fuzz.

"Was that deliberate or someone's idea of a prank?"

Vlaria scowls. "Not really either. I guess it'd be a little over a year ago now... they changed an ingredient in the protein paste an' some people had really bad reactions to it. I got sick an' lost all my hair... an' I mean everywhere."

"Ouch." I can see Derian swallow hard.

"Yeah, well, it was hard on Cattie too 'cause she didn't want me sick all the time, but it's so hard to find enough of anything else to eat. I don't blame her for sending me away."

I nod.

"Anyway, when we got here they said they could help, but the treatments 'd take time to work. An' in the meantime, if I wanted a wig, it'd be easier to look after a short one."

"Fair enough. How're you doing other than that?"

"I've been okay. I'll be glad to get outta here though."

"I'm told you've got six weeks left. You just need to hang in there."

"Thanks, Nerita." Vlaria smiles appreciatively. She pulls the wig into place before leaving the screen.

Winifred appears next, looking almost exactly as I remember.

"Hey, Nerita," She studies me curiously, "Are you really in Norsecount?"

"For a month now."

"What's it like?"

"It's different."

Winifred looks annoyed at the evasion. "Where're you actually living?"

"At court."

"You've got to be kidding... 'cept you don't mess with people's heads," Winifred swallows hard, "Not on shit like that."

I chuckle. "How've you been doing?"

"I'm fine. I don't miss the city an' Experiment Redemption 's interesting," She shrugs, "But what about the others that left with you?"

"They're all just fine."

"You're not gonna say anythin' more, are you?"

"Not today. I want to know where you're at."

"How'd you even get to do this?"

"The head of Cemen Group 's an interesting lady."

Winifred grimaces frustratedly. "You're same as ever."

"You'll find out more sooner or later. Anyway, take care of yourself."

Winifred nods. After she leaves the screen, Jasmina takes the chair. She also looks like I remember: Green hair, very bright blue eyes, silvery skin, slightly pointed ears.

"In all their testing, did they figure out what's with your hair?"

Jasmina grimaces. "Yeah. They asked this blue haired woman called Channa to sit in on my first physical."

"I've met Channa. What'd she say?"

"I'm not really human."

"That's been obvious all along. What'd Channa say?"

"I'm more Sedyr, if you've heard of that, than human, but some of the Sedyr genes 're mutated like she'd never seen before."

"That explains a lot. How've you been doing?"

"Mostly okay. I won't miss this place once we finally get to leave."

"That'll be in six weeks... or so I'm told. Hang in there."

Jasmina nods. "Thanks, Nerita."

Next is Tiana, who looks more like Rowena than ever.

"Where's Aunt Rowena?"

"She and Nadine 're both fine. They're here in Norsecount and, depending how things go, you might be able to see them before the new year."

Tiana brightens at that, "Why won't you just say what's going on?"

"You'll find out all in good time."

Tiana makes a face, "We've still got a bunch more tests, don't we?"

"They need results to compare to when you first came. Unless you've been really having trouble with something, don't worry about that. They're not expecting model citizens."

"Not if they let you an' Andrina graduate," Tiana sighs, "You'll tell Aunt Rowena you saw me, won't you?"

I nod. "She'll want to know how you're doing."

"I'm okay," Tiana shrugs, "Mostly. Cattie told you about Father, didn't she?"

"She only told me he died. I don't know how much more than that she told Rowena."

Tiana nods. "Thanks, Nerita."

"You take care."

After Tiana leaves the screen I can hear all too familiar giggling. Then Monica and Allison perch on the edges of the chair.

"What part of one at a time did you two miss?"

"Nice to see you too, Nerita."

"How come you're still a spoilsport?"

Suddenly I'm feeling the beginnings of a headache.

"Nerita, aren't you happy to see us?"

"I specified one at a time for a reason. Obviously you're doing just fine."

"You're as mean as ever."

I fail to suppress a sigh. "Do me a favour and tell Becky I'd like a word with her."

"Okay." They chime in unison. Then they go and Becky reclaims the chair.

"The twin act 's a bit much?" Becky looks entirely too sympathetic.

"Let's put it this way: I gave up trying to tell them apart years ago. What's worse 's they don't seem to care."

Becky nods. "But that's not what's bothering you."

"Part of it's Tiana, part of it's Nathania..." I sigh.

"You do realize Natalia likely has her own ideas on the matter."

"When doesn't she?"

Becky chuckles. "It seems to me you've got a fair bit to do yet today. You should go. I'll see you tomorrow."

I nod. "Thank you."

The screen goes dark. Then the conference room door opens and the messenger enters.

"The vehicle is waiting to take you back to the palace. This way please."

Sefu yawns and stretches while Derian and I get to our feet. We follow the messenger back through the embassy and get into the vehicle. Not until we're settled does Derian speak.

"Natalia 's going to drop this one in your lap, you know."

"She can't do it without his majesty's approval."

Derian nods to himself. "I can't see Father refusing, but they would be your responsibility."

"They're that regardless."

Derian studies me carefully for a moment, but doesn't say anything more.

We arrive at the palace to find Nerissa hanging around the main doors.

"Where were you?" The girl is mainly addressing me, "Lady Irina said I could have this afternoon off, but all Lady Laine would say is you'd gone out."

"Your highness," I guide her inside, "There are times when my business is just that."

"Only to a point." Derian observes as a page approaches us.

"My lady," The page bows his head to me, "His majesty wishes to see you in his study as soon as possible."

"Thank you."

The page bows and vanishes.

Nerissa frowns in confusion. "What...?"

"I think I know," I have to shake my head, "Better to deal with it now though."

Derian chuckles dryly, but doesn't say anything. He and Nerissa accompany me and Sefu as far as the door of the Monarch's study. They leave as I knock.

"Come in!"

I let myself and Sefu in and find Monarch Reginald seated at his cluttered desk.

"Your majesty wished to see me?"

"Yes," He looks up, "Please close the door and be seated."

I do that quickly and wait for him to continue.

"Natalia's being her usual officious self..."

"I only asked her for information."

"That can sometimes be dangerous," The Monarch observes dryly, "She only told me you may need some assistance with a problem."

"Natalia isn't entirely uninvolved in this one."

"If you would start at the beginning please."

"When I left South City, I left Cattie Varlok my work and my family's house. She continued things from where I left off and eventually the group got big enough for Experiment Redemption to issue another invitation. But, once again, they're not sure what to do with the group after graduation."

Monarch Reginald frowns. "How many are there and how old?"

"Eight... all girls between fifteen and eighteen. And all born in the Old Quarter."

"I see," The Monarch nods to himself, "How long until this has to be dealt with?"

"They graduate in six weeks."

He nods again. "Then I've only one more immediate concern on the matter. How many of these eight are underage?"

"Two."

"Is there no one with closer claim to guardianship of those two?"

"Natika Gadhra was left in my care by her mother, who had also been part of the group. To the best of my knowledge, they had no other family."

"That would require her return to your care," The Monarch observes, "And the other?"

"Tiana Halth is niece to Rowena Halth Pelmont and Nadine Halth Rossa. Of those two, I believe Teddy would have left custody to Rowena. Regardless, were Tiana brought here, I would ask that Pelmonts take her."

Monarch Reginald nods to himself. "We will speak more on this matter later. You'd best go prepare for a very busy evening."

"Yes, your majesty."

Four o'clock is the rehearsal for the wedding ceremony, which is followed by a dinner for the participants and select others. It's eight thirty and I'm exhausted by the time that's all over. But I know Laine has been plotting something, although I'm not sure what or with whom. And I also remember what was pulled on Angelita the night before her wedding. Still, I can't help being relieved to accompany Laine up into the old south tower. I should've known better.

We reach the top floor to find our sitting room packed. All the girls of Black Oak Court currently in Norsecount are present, along with Carina, Angelita, and Xylia.

Laine chuckles at my expression. "You were expecting anything else?"

I just shake my head.

"Come sit." Cattie gestures to the chair next to her with the envelope in her hand. I cross the room to do that and, once I'm settled, Sefu stretches out at my feet.

"This arrived at the embassy for you." Cattie hands me the envelope.

I open it to find a piece of paper folded around a picture. The paper is a short note of congratulations from Mellie. The picture is of her, Ross, and their children. I pass the picture to Cattie and it circulates from there.

"Nerita," Laine is now sitting as close to my chair as she can get, "You never did say what Natalia had for you earlier."

"She set up a televideo conference with Becky at Lake Prince and I got to talk to each of the girls there."

"Nice," Cattie grins, "How're they doing?"

"They're finished there in six weeks."

"And then what?" Rowena queries, "Is Natalia sending them here?"

"If his majesty gives his approval. However, when I spoke to him about it briefly, I was reminded that the Canon and the Society Treaty tie everyone's hands on some of it."

Angelita frowns. "How so?"

"Two of the girls, Natika and Tiana, are underage."

"And legally have to be sent to whoever has closest claim to guardianship." Angelita nods to herself.

"Tiana would have to come to me then," Rowena frowns slightly, "Yet..."

"Do you really think Lord Pelmont would turn away your niece?"

Rowena's expression twists wryly. "I guess not. That leaves you stuck with Natika."

"More likely all seven," I shrug it off and turn to Cattie, "You forgot to tell me a few things."

Cattie flushes and won't meet my eyes.

Rowena raises an eyebrow. "Like?"

"About Vlaria, who's currently a redhead."

Cattie winces. "Sorry."

Haylie frowns. "Wasn't Vlaria blonde?"

I nod. "And will be again, since FTK's people were able to reverse the effects of her reaction to that bad batch of protein paste. Which, I gather from other sources, was a worse problem than usual."

Cattie nods grimly.

Haylie swallows hard. "Vlaria lost her hair?"

"Yeah," Cattie nods again, "All of it and it wasn't coming back on its own."

"It is now," I assure them, "All of them seem to be doing pretty well. Some better than they think."

"Did they figure out what's with Jasmina?" Laine queries.

"They asked Channa, who said she's more Sedyr than human, but something 's mutated the Sedyr."

Laine winces. "That explains a whole lot."

Ilaria, who's clearly been doing some mental math, frowns. "Who all 'd you take on?"

Cattie scowls. "Elspeth Galacia died an' no one wanted the twins."

Andrina raises an eyebrow. "You mean no one's killed them?"

I sigh tiredly. "Not yet anyway."

Ilaria shakes her head. "At least the others could eventually be married off. But no guy in his right mind would touch either of those two."

I shrug. "We'll see what happens. Nothing 's settled for certain yet."

"And possibly won't be 'til after tomorrow." Laine adds.

"Nerita," Nadine studies me curiously, "Are you getting any kind of honeymoon?"

"Yeah, although we won't leave until the second."

"Do you know where?" Cattie queries.

"Away from Monarch's Town."

"No shit." Nadine rolls her eyes.

"You know," Amalia looks amused, "You and Laine 're actually gonna have to figure out who owns what."

Laine shakes her head. "We already know that. The pain in the ass 's gonna be sorting out what gets moved, what gets packed, and what just stays."

"You are comin' out to Seeri Meadow then?" Angelita queries.

Laine nods. "Prob'ly the biggest thing 's gonna be moving my horse."

Angelita nods to herself.

"His grace is remaining here, is he not?" Carina is understandably concerned.

"I doubt he'll ever leave," Laine responds, "I never intended to stay."

Rowena turns to me, "Does that mean you'll be assigned an attendant?"

"Natalia 's promised me a graduate of Experiment Redemption," I grimace, "Problem is, she doesn't finish for a couple months yet, but his majesty 's having trouble finding anyone suitable."

"There was another suggestion made." Laine reminds me.

I sigh. "I can't see how that would work out, even temporarily."

"What's the suggestion?" Angelita enquires.

"A temporary revival of the Imperial tradition." Laine replies.

"I doubt it'd be that bad," Rowena observes, "Provided you're allowed to pick and choose your ladies."

"His majesty doesn't have a problem with that. I'm just not sure who'd be willing and able to do it."

Rowena makes a face. "You really think I'm gonna have anything better to do this winter? We're here 'til April, at least."

"I may be here longer than that," Haylie adds, "Lady Tremauld 's decided, for a variety of reasons, that the family needs representation at court and since Raymond and I have the least to do at home..."

Lillian frowns. "I thought Lady Tremauld liked you."

"She does. But Karigan and Sophronia 've decided I make them look bad somehow," Haylie scowls, "As if they needed help with that."

Amalia grimaces. "Karigan 's one of Lord and Lady Covak's daughters, isn't she?"

Haylie nods.

I shake my head. "You haven't heard Lady Covak on the subject of all her children, even the unmarried son."

"Is that a little like Lady Bowerstone?" Lillian queries.

"Probably," I grimace, "Along with most of the older middle nobility."

"And the upper nobility?" Angelita queries.

I shrug. "Most of them don't care to talk to me."

Angelita nods to herself.

30-10-48-06-04SM

Last night ended up being a very late night. Fortunately things aren't too rushed this morning. Nerissa and I take Sefu out for his exercise so he'll sit quietly through the wedding. Laine is busy setting up transportation for her mare, since she leaves for Seeri Meadow with Angelita tomorrow.

It's after an early lunch, which I'm too nervous to eat much of, that things get really crazy. Carina comes up to join me and Laine in preparing, bringing everything she needs. Then there's the stylist hired especially to do our hair today and her cart full of stuff.

Laine and I decided the only jewelry we'd wear today is earrings, but she'd told me not to pick any out. Now, she gives me a small box, which I open to find a pair of earrings wrought of faerie silver and set with white stones that sparkle every colour of the rainbow.

"Wow," I look up at Laine, "These're beautiful."

She grins. "And unique."

I nod. "Thanks."

My shoes, veil, and everything else the designer thought I'd need with my gown were delivered a couple days ago. The shoes are simple and white, although high heeled. The veil is layers of lace attached to a delicate white gold tiara.

The stylist does up my hair first, with the veil and a bit of ivy. And endless comments on the thickness of my hair. Laine's hair is also done up with ivy. Carina, however, has hers styled around a silver and sapphire tiara.

Laine helps me dress, which seem to take longer than it should. Maybe it's just my nerves. Then Laine gets herself ready. The stylist leaves once she's finished with Carina, leaving us to finish dressing and sort out our flowers.

Laine's bouquet is two blue iris and two white lilies surrounded by ivy leaves in an elaborate holder. Mine is far bigger and more colourful and rests along my arm. Carina, as part of the Monarch's family, has a matching corsage, which Laine carefully pins in place.

With all that, we're only just ready when Duke Malin comes looking for us. He's wearing a brand new suit with an iris pinned to his jacket.

"I hope you are ready, else we'll be late."

I take a deep breath. "Let's just go."

The Duke offers me his arm, which I gratefully accept. Between my shoes and my skirt, I'm really uncertain of stairs right now. Having one arm full of flowers doesn't help.

Carl, dressed in his formal uniform, is waiting in the sitting room to escort us to a room near the Empire Chapel, which's used almost strictly for weddings within the Monarch's family. Carl leaves us in the waiting room and goes to claim a place in the servants' gallery. I carefully arrange my skirt so I can sit for now. Sefu, who's been very subdued since lunch, curls up at my feet.

There's a tap on the door. Duke Malin opens it and lets several people into the room.

Nerissa enters with Lady Irina, attracting Sefu's attention.

"Lady Nerita," Lady Irina looks slightly disapproving, "How long will Nerissa be required to watch Sefu?"

"Until the end of the reception."

Nerissa grins, but Lady Irina frowns. She hasn't been nearly so warm towards me since we disagreed about High Lady Ayson.

"Your highness," Lady Irina turns to Carina, "His majesty is waiting for you."

Carina nods and leaves the room with Lady Irina, Nerissa, and Sefu. I turn my attention to the others.

John Simeon studies me with a fond smile, but doesn't try to say anything. Cattie, clearly less than comfortable in her formal gown and high heels, looks amazed.

"How can you deal with that?"

I chuckle. "There are certain advantages to having graduated from Experiment Redemption."

"Indeed," President Gayre rubs his tiger's head, "And some very interesting things have come of it. But time is running short so I'd like to congratulate you on your marriage and wish you the best in the future."

"Thank you, sir."

President Gayre leaves the room with John Simeon and Cattie. However, General Verdas remains with Channa, Becky, and Natalia.

Natalia studies me for a moment, her expression hard to read, "So much more has already come of Experiment Redemption than we could have guessed," She smiles wryly, "I never thought I'd see the day Rodq Lendar's abilities would become so limited... yet another sign of rapidly changing times," She sighs, "All of Sedya's Second Shield wish you only the best. But I think you'll see and hear very little of us in the future."

I nod. "Thank you... for everything."

Natalia chuckles. "I only begrudge resources when they're wasted."

I nod again.

"I believe someone else wants a word with you," Natalia tells me, "We'll see you later."

She, Becky, Channa, and General Verdas leave the room.

Seconds later, Tory, Nikki, and Angelita enter.

"Nervous yet?" Angelita queries dryly.

I shoot her a withering glare.

Tory shakes her head. "How've you been doin'?"

"Fine so far."

Tory nods and catches her sister's eye. Nikki comes over to rest a hand on my shoulder. She closes her eyes briefly, then shakes her head.

"I want to see you in the morning."

"That's fine." Although apparently I'm not pregnant yet.

"It's nearly time," Tory grimaces, "So we'll see you later."

I nod as the three of them leave.

Duke Malin goes over to look into the corridor. "The dignitaries are gathered now."

That means it really is almost time.

According to the programme I saw at the rehearsal yesterday, two o'clock is actually the seating of the dignitaries present. First will be Monarch Reginald with Carina, Nerissa, and Sefu. Then, because I'm from Arawn, the second group is President Gayre, John Simeon, and Cattie. Following them should be the Monarch of Ouestlun and his ambassador and the Monarch of Midkingsen and his ambassador. Then Natalia and Dolan to represent the dying Pleasure Society Chancellor. And, finally, the West Continent President. That all of the above are even present says a lot about what can be accomplished in fourteen days.

Once the last dignitary is seated, Derian and Marcellus will take their places and then we have to be ready to go.

"The West President just entered." Duke Malin reports.

Laine helps me to my feet and glances over me. "You really do look like a princess."

"Thanks." I take a deep breath.

Laine enters the corridor first and I take the Duke's arm before following.

There's a page waiting at the chapel door, who signals for us to wait. The Empire Chapel is even bigger than the throne room and it takes time for the West Continent President to reach his seat. Not that I can actually see anything right now.

Finally, the page signals to Laine to enter. For as cool and collected as she looks, her bouquet is trembling. Duke Malin and

I move to the doorway in time to see her take her place opposite Marcellus.

Now it's our turn and I think I'd be in trouble if I didn't have the Duke's arm for support. The gigantic chapel is full of standing guests along with the galleries above. It's not so bad if I keep my eyes on Derian though.

The dress uniform of the Norsecount Militia is very different from the military uniforms I'm used to. It's far more decorative and Derian looks really good in it. Although still not as good as when he's only wearing old jeans. He does look a little nervous right now though.

The walk down the aisle feels twice as long as it really is. When we do reach the end, Duke Malin places my hand in Derian's. The Duke remains standing at the end of the aisle as Derian guides me onto the dais to stand in front of the official.

The wedding ceremony used by the east continent monarch's families is the longest used anywhere in the world. Just the opening speech is five minutes long.

Eventually, the official moves on, "Who, on this day, giveth this lady to be wed?"

"On behalf of those unable to be present, I do." Duke Malin's words are accompanied by a warm, gentle breeze. That's a little weird in a room where the windows don't open and all the doors are closed. From the corner of my eye, I can see John Simeon and President Gayre nodding approvingly.

The official doesn't seem to notice anything and goes into his next, even longer, speech. My eyes meet Derian's and we almost lose track of what's being said. Still we're not caught completely off guard when the official gets to the part about objections and impediments to the marriage. No one speaks when offered the chance so the official continues with his longest speech of the ceremony.

I think everyone present is thoroughly bored long before the end of this one. Although I'm guessing, from the way Derian's eyes eventually glaze over, it's worse for those who've heard it before. Still, I manage to pay enough attention to catch when the official begins to wind down. I squeeze Derian's hand just enough to recall his attention.

We get into vows next, which, being written specifically for the crown prince and monarch, are longer and more involved than usual. Given what I've heard of Derian's second wife, I honestly don't know how she managed not to choke on this stuff. I bet she didn't even try to meet Derian's eyes. I do because I mean every word and I want him to see that.

Then I have to pass my bouquet to Laine so Derian and I can exchange rings, which's the first I've seen of them. Both are beautiful and are set with tiny stones that match his mother's ring. Once that's done, Derian is allowed to kiss me. It's not a really long kiss, but it leaves both of us breathless.

After that, there's the register to sign. This isn't the average book used for most marriages. This's a massive, ancient tome containing records of the marriages of the monarchs and princes of Norsecount for centuries. Each page is a separate record. Fortunately, we're on a left hand page so the previous entry isn't visible. Derian signs first, then me. Marcellus is next, followed by Laine and, finally, the official. Once all of us have returned to our places, the benediction takes another five minutes.

"With great honour, I give you Crown Prince Derian Regan and Crown Princess Nerita Amy of the Monarchy of Norsecount."

As I take Derian's arm, I can feel the warm, gentle breeze again.

We start up the aisle with Marcellus and Laine not far behind. Out in the corridor, we form a receiving line to accept congratulations as the chapel empties.

Monarch Reginald comes out first, looking happier than I've ever seen him. He speaks quietly with first Marcellus, then Laine, before turning to me and Derian.

"I trust you two will be somewhat better behaved after this."

Derian and I exchange amused glances.

"How about if we behave as a married couple should?" I query.

The Monarch chuckles. "That I can accept." He kisses my cheek and briefly clasps Derian's hand before moving on.

Immediately behind him are Carina, Nerissa, and Sefu.

"How's he been?" I ask Nerissa.

"He's fine," Nerissa is grinning broadly, "I just can't believe you're really married now."

Derian and I laugh. Then each of us accepts a hug before Nerissa and Sefu follow the Monarch.

"Do you think she'll really grow up for time in Ouestlun with Lady Irina?" Carina shakes her head.

"I certainly hope so." Derian sighs.

I shrug it off. "Let Lady Irina worry about her, since I believe they leave tomorrow."

Carina nods, her expression wry. "Why do I feel like I've got an older sister, not another younger one?"

I have to laugh. "You wouldn't want another younger sister anyhow."

Carina just shakes her head and hugs me. Then she goes after her sister.

"You always did have a way with people," John Simeon watches her go, "More so than your father, but perhaps something like what is said of his mother."

I shrug lightly. "It's Father I remember."

John Simeon smiles fondly. Then he turns and bows his head to Derian before stepping aside.

Cattie is next and she takes a deep breath as she studies me, "How I wish all the others were here..." Her expression twists wryly, "I know I shouldn't..."

I shake my head. "Sometimes I do too."

Cattie nods and takes another deep breath, "This's all so unbelievable..." She hugs me quickly, then turns an impish grin on Derian, "You better be good to her."

He chuckles. "Don't worry. I can't afford not to."

Cattie nods again and goes to join John Simeon.

"She thinks so much of you," President Gayre observes softly, "And I've met so many others who do as well. You really do have a way with people."

I smile wryly. "That only goes so far though."

He chuckles. "It's carried you to Crown Princess of Norsecount."

"And earned her a great deal of support." Derian observes.

President Gayre bows his head. "My best wishes to you both."

"Thank you, sir."

After President Gayre moves on, I'm introduced to the monarchs of Ouestlun and Midkingsen, along with their families and ambassadors. Then it's Natalia and Dolan's turn.

"On behalf of Chancellor Thomas Burren, we congratulate you and wish you the best in the future."

"Thank you." Derian looks slightly bemused.

Natalia chuckles. "The Second Shield may be waning, but I can still see some things. That this marriage will only bring good things is one of them."

Derian nods. "Thank you."

Natalia and Dolan move away and I'm introduced to the West Continent President and his family. Once the last of the dignitaries have gone, Angelita appears.

"Devin didn't come?" I query.

Angelita shakes her head. "Don't count on ever seeing him away from Seeri Meadow."

I nod to myself. "You know, you never did owe me any favours."

Angelita laughs. "Ain't hard to give up what you never wanted."

I shake my head. "It's no wonder we never got along."

She shrugs it off. "Long as you're happy with this."

After Angelita walks away there's less order to the remaining guests. Among them, I count another five members of UnderGround Club and all the girls of Black Oak Court currently in Norsecount. But there are so many others, many of whom I've never met, it makes me glad I didn't know the number of guests beforehand.

Finally, the last guest is gone and a page comes to take us for the portrait session. After that's done and over with, the four of us get a chance to rest for a short time.

"Let's see your ring," Laine examines the wedding band on my left ring finger, "Wow!" She shakes her head.

Derian chuckles. "Smyth is known as the best jeweller in Norsecount."

"How late was he on delivery this time?" Marcellus queries dryly.

"Father said the twenty-fifth. We had them the next day."

Marcellus looks amazed. "Who stood over him this time?"

Derian laughs. "He was working for a substantial bonus... namely Father's blessing on his granddaughter's marriage, which was the twenty-seventh."

Marcellus nods to himself.

Laine stretches out her neck. "That was an awfully long ceremony though."

Derian makes a face, "I'd just as soon never hear it again."

"Not even if it's for your child?" I query.

Derian considers that, "Perhaps by then I'll have forgotten just how bad it is."

"Seems to me today wasn't as bad as the last time," Marcellus observes, "And the reception should be infinitely better."

"Well," Derian looks bemused, "You're less likely to offend the family of the bride."

"I was trying to avoid offending the bride," Marcellus retorts, "It was a no win situation. Just don't count on the other speeches being any shorter."

Derian groans. "As if today hasn't been long enough already."

Eventually the page returns to escort us to the reception hall. I take Derian's arm and Laine takes Marcellus's. All the guests are standing as we enter and remain that way while we cross the room to the head table. When we reach it, Derian helps me into my chair and kisses my cheek. As he takes his seat, I set my bouquet on the table and glance over the guests. They're now seating themselves, but I catch a few disapproving looks directed our way. I also catch sight of Tory and Ford sitting with Monarch Reginald, President Gayre, John Simeon, and Duke Malin at a table just below the head table. Probably because of the Sword.

Once everyone is seated, dinner is served. It's more courses than I care to count, but not really enough to eat. Or at least not for me when I could barely eat anything at lunch. As dessert is served, I'm aware of Derian studying me concernedly.

"Are you well?" His voice is so low only I can hear him.

"It's just been too long since I ate properly." I keep my voice equally soft.

Derian nods. The next time a servant passes by, Derian has a few quiet words with him. Shortly after that, platters of fruit and appetizers appear on the head table. Hopefully that'll be enough to get me... and Laine... through the rest of the reception.

Once dessert is finished and the last of the dishes are being cleared away, Derian slides his chair closer so he can rest his arm on the back of mine. I've gotten used to him doing that. Unfortunately, the upper nobility of Norsecount haven't.

"You two ought to be ashamed of yourselves!"

Everyone in the room looks over at High Lady Vorsen, who's on her feet, looking outraged.

"You ought to know better than such inappropriate..." She's cut off by a hand across her mouth as two of the men from her table forcibly remove her from the room.

All the other guests look stunned and dead silence falls over the reception hall. Then, finally, Lady Vorsen's muffled shrieks of outrage cease. Monarch Reginald glances at Derian, who turns to me.

"Are you all right?" He keeps his voice soft.

"I'm just fine."

"You're sure?"

I turn my head so our eyes meet. "Why should I let her ruin my day?" Then a thought occurs to me and I can't help a small, mischievous smile.

"Nerita..." Laine looks wary, "What's on your mind?"

"Just a tradition from weddings in the Old Quarter."

"The speeches?" Laine's suspicion turns to amusement.

I nod.

Derian frowns, but before he can ask, I quickly explain for his ears only. When I'm finished, he also looks amused.

"Sounds good to me."

"Laine." I tilt my head towards where John Simeon is sitting.

By now the initial shock has worn off and the guests are too preoccupied with discussing the incident to notice Laine slip away from the head table. I watch as she speaks with John Simeon for a minute before returning to her seat beside me.

After that, there's some discussion at the table below ours. Then the Monarch turns to us, looking amused, and nods. Obviously he approves of the idea.

Meanwhile Marcellus is looking uncomfortable. He's supposed to be giving the toast to the bride right now, but with the confusion following Lady Vorsen's outburst, no one seems quite certain what to do. Then there's the sound of cutlery being tapped against a glass. That recalls attention to the head table and, gradually, the room falls silent. Marcellus takes a deep breath as he gets to his feet.

Two things quickly become obvious as Marcellus speaks. First, he's very good at public speaking. Enough so that Lady Vorsen is forgotten long before he's finished. Second, he's been spending a lot of time talking with his wife. He neatly avoids anything potentially offensive or embarrassing and I can see people all around the room nodding their approval as he finishes.

After the guests have drunk the toast, Monarch Reginald gives his speech as father of the groom. At the end of that, Derian and I kiss, after the tradition of the Old Quarter. Then I glance at the doors and spot a couple of the upper nobility leaving.

I was expecting Duke Malin to speak next, but it's John Simeon who gets to his feet.

"For many years it was my honour and privilege to work alongside Lucian and Klara Chassaven. I was present to witness and record their daughter's birth and I especially remember Klara's words that night... Her hopes that her daughter would not have to live her life in a continued state of war... That her future would be brighter than anyone then had reason to believe..." John Simeon takes a deep breath, "Though Lucian and Klara are many years gone, I have no doubt that they would be proud of and happy for their daughter today. I know Klara especially wanted nothing more than to see her daughter so happily married to a man who will treat her as a husband should treat his wife. Your highnesses," He turns to us, "I congratulate you on behalf of Lucian and Klara Chassaven." Then he finishes with what I recognize as the traditional blessing on marriages used in the Old Quarter.

I'm not far from tears and Derian seems to realize that. As he kisses me, he slips his arms around me and, after, allows me to rest my head on his shoulder.

More speeches follow... mostly pompous, long winded bullshit I don't care to remember. Then, finally, everyone expected to speak is through. Derian gets to his feet and helps me to mine as the light background music that's been playing the whole time changes to an old traditional wedding dance. I take Derian's arm as we cross the hall to the dance floor.

The first dance is strictly for the wedding party. Technically it's also for the parents of the bride and groom, but only the father of the groom is actually present.

Starting with the second dance, anyone can join us. Marcellus goes looking for his wife and I soon spot Laine with Rylan. Derian and I remain together for the second dance, but after that, Monarch Reginald and Duke Malin each claim a turn.

It's late and I'm exhausted when I return to my seat at the head table. Derian quickly joins me, looking concerned.

"I'm just tired." I tell him before he can ask.

"We should be able to go soon," Derian kisses my cheek, "Just wait here."

I nod and he slips away.

At the end of this dance, the light background music returns. The guests reclaim their seats and Derian, Laine, and Marcellus join me at the head table.

Monarch Reginald gets to his feet to make a relatively short speech, after which I pick up my bouquet from where it's been resting on the table. I go over to the dance floor, where all the single women in the room are gathering. I turn my back to them and throw the bouquet over my shoulder. When I turn back, I spot it in the hands of Princess Carina. She's very obviously happy about it, but I have a feeling Monarch Reginald won't be.

However, I'm too tired to worry about that tonight. Instead, I go looking for my tiger and quickly find him with Nerissa and Lady Irina.

"That was a beautiful throw," Lady Irina looks amused, "Now to see if anything comes of it."

I shrug. "I wouldn't object to seeing her married. Anyway," I turn to Nerissa, "Sefu needs to come with me now."

She nods reluctantly. "Will I get to see you tomorrow?"

"You should. Derian and I don't leave until the next day."

"You're to be gone two weeks, are you not?" Lady Irina waits for me to nod, "Do you know where?"

"Some place quiet was the suggestion. After this last month I certainly don't object."

Lady Irina chuckles. "A good night to you."

"Good night." Nerissa echoes, although addressing Sefu more than me.

"Good night." I tell them before guiding Sefu to the head table where Derian is waiting for us.

"How fast do you want to get out of here?" He slips an arm around me.

"Can we do it without anyone stopping us to talk?"

He chuckles. "This way."

I'm sure more than a few people are left wondering at our sudden disappearance, but I've never been so grateful for Derian's knowledge of the hidden doors and back corridors of the palace. Maybe some people won't be too happy about it; I'm just too tired to care.

ABOUT THE AUTHOR

A. A. 'Lexa' Cheshire lives in northern British Columbia, Canada. She is a wife and mother who enjoys to read and write fantasy and science fiction.

She can be found on facebook.com or goodreads.com by searching A. A. Cheshire. Readers are more than welcome to post reviews of this and any other works on amazon.com or goodreads.com.

More information about Mantler Publishing can be found at mantlerpublishing.com.

Made in the USA
Charleston, SC
12 January 2014